Dear Me

By Robin Alexander

DEAR ME
© 2016 BY ROBIN ALEXANDER

ISBN 13: 978-1-935216-80-3

First Printing: 2016

This Trade Paperback Is Published By
Intaglio Publications
Walker, LA USA
WWW.INTAGLIOPUB.COM

CREDITS

EXECUTIVE EDITOR: TARA YOUNG
COVER DESIGN BY: Tiger Graphics

Dedication

For Becky, who reminded me daily that I could defeat writer's block. Without her encouragement, I might've lost all hope.

Acknowledgments

As always, I humbly thank Tara and my editorial team for making me look like I know what I'm doing with all those commas because I don't.

Dear Me,

At thirty-six years old, I'm journaling for the first time ever because I want to confess things that I won't even admit to my best friend. In this book, I will hide my thoughts, desires, and mostly bitch. So here goes. I would like to fall in love again. There! I've admitted it to me. I know I actually have to date to accomplish this, but I just don't want to. It's the letdown I dread. I meet someone, I have high hopes, we go out a couple of times, and I feel absolutely nothing, not even a hint of interest. I don't know what's wrong with me, and I'm terrified to think I may be just like my mother.

Mom goes through men like potato chips. She'll go out with a guy, and the second he starts to get attached, she drops him like a hot rock. She always says it's not in her nature to be owned by anyone. She says she's incapable of falling in love, and I wonder if I inherited that from her.

She did fall once, and it was with my sperm donor. She was eighteen, and when she got pregnant, he left her. I was three when he returned. Mom took him right back into her life because she believed that he meant it when he said he wanted to settle down and have a big family. They didn't marry, but Mom got pregnant again, and this time, the donor hung around until Alana was born but left soon after. None of us ever saw him again, and I worry that I could be just like him. Maybe he thought he wanted to be in love and have the house with the white picket fence and the family. Once he had it all, though, he realized he'd been wrong.

1

I've been in love only once. It happened in my first year of college. Lily swept in and stole my heart, then broke it six months later. I wonder if it had lasted longer if I would've grown uninterested like I've done with every woman since her. I still remember that drunken crazy feeling whenever I was around Lily. I was completely consumed with her. I needed her more than food or oxygen. I didn't care what we did or where we went as long as I was with her. I've never felt that since, even though I've tried to make myself feel it. I've managed to fool myself for a while when a relationship is new, but the day comes so fast when I wake up and realize I'm hollow inside.

My last attempt lasted two years. The hollow feeling came one week after I started seeing Michelle, but I told myself that I could work through it, the feelings would come. I wanted a relationship, so I told myself this was how adult love is. Thrills and all-encompassing feelings are only reserved for the young. In the end, Michelle grew to hate me, and I hated myself.

But here I am again, wanting. I wanna be in love.

Me

Chapter One

"Oh, my God, look at that house," Allison Holt said. "It just keeps growing bigger and bigger the closer we get. I ask you, who needs a home this big?"

Alexis slowed her truck when she noticed that someone was actually directing the drivers where to park. "It's a status symbol, Mom."

"I already feel underdressed." Allison clutched her brow. "I should've worn my lavender sheath dress and my pearls."

"I told you, didn't I? It's always better to overdress than under," Elise said and sighed loudly.

"Alana said it's an ultra-casual gathering." Alexis glanced at her mother's linen pantsuit. "If anything, you're overdressed." She glanced into the rearview mirror at her grandmother. "You look great too, Grammy."

Elise had on a nice pair of tan slacks, a white button-down shirt, and red cardigan thrown over her shoulders. Alexis had taken ultra-casual to heart. She was sporting a pair of khaki pants, a green sleeveless button-down shirt, and loafers. Though she wouldn't admit it aloud, she was somewhat intimidated by the looks of the Kirkland home, as well, and regretted her choice of clothing.

Alexis parked her truck where she was directed but didn't kill the engine. "How about I just drop y'all off and you call me when you're ready to go home?"

"Out of the question, Alexis, you're suffering with us," Elise said. "I'm sure there will be delicious food. We can at least enjoy that."

As the Holt women got out of the truck, a tram cart pulled up beside them, and the driver said, "Ladies, climb aboard, and I'll save you a few steps. No tipping allowed, and please keep your hands and feet inside the ride, and remain seated until we come to a complete stop."

All three women squeezed onto one seat as more people rushed to catch the cart. Elise was sandwiched between Alexis and Allison and whispered, "I can't imagine how much they shelled out on this shindig. I hope they don't send us a bill when Alana dumps Jason at the altar. How many times has she been engaged?"

Alexis thought for a moment. "Five?"

"Four," Allison said softly. "But she did actually marry Ben."

The driver took them across the sprawling front lawn. A mild spring breeze mussed Alexis's auburn hair as she breathed in the scent of flowers in bloom. It was a perfect day, not a cloud in the sky, and Alexis wished she was anywhere but the engagement party.

Elise released a tiny whimper when the cart rounded the back of the house and they saw the large crowd. "Good God," she whispered. "Are all these people related to Jason? How on earth did they find time to make all the money they obviously have if they've been so busy procreating?"

Alexis got out of the cart first and held out her arm for Elise to take. Elise smiled as she took it and said, "Sweetie, you look like someone just gave you an ice water enema."

"Oh, good, that means I look better than I feel."

Alana's fiancé, Jason, spotted them first, and with Alana in tow, he rushed over to greet his future in-laws. "Now we can party," he said and kissed each of the Holt women on the cheek. "I can't wait to introduce y'all to everyone."

"Honey, that's gonna take all day," Allison said, wide-eyed as she looked around at all the people milling around.

Jason grimaced. "Yes. When Mom told me she was going to invite just a handful of guests, I knew we were in trouble."

Alana hugged Alexis and whispered against her ear, "I know this is your version of hell, but I'm so glad you're here."

4

"I thought this was supposed to be ultra-casual," Alexis said and held on to Alana as she began to pull away from the embrace. "I'm gonna kill you slow." "You look fine." Alana grunted. "You're squeezing my guts out."

Alexis released her sister, silently cursing her own stupidity. When her mother had invited Jason's parents over for dinner one night, they'd arrived at the informal gathering dressed as though they were dining at the Ritz. She should've known that the Kirklands' idea of casual was vastly different from hers.

Audrey Kirkland spotted them and came rushing over. Her thick jaw-length blond mane looked like a helmet and didn't budge when a strong breeze swept over her. Her lipstick and nails matched her pink sleeveless dress that accented her tall slender frame. She doled out air kisses to everyone, then looked them over with one brow slightly raised.

"You all look so lovely," Audrey said dryly as her gaze settled on Alexis. "You have to meet Jason's cousin Stacy, she's a lesbian too. She and her girlfriend are around here somewhere, and as soon as I spot them, I'll make introductions. Come, come."

Alexis found herself being dragged into a group of people, and Audrey uttered what she would repeat endlessly throughout the day. "Everyone, this is Alana's family, Allison, her mother, Elise, her grandmother, and Alexis, her sister, who's a lesbian. Has anyone seen Stacy?"

"Why don't you slow down?" Stacy asked Janey, who grabbed two glasses of champagne when a server presented them with a tray.

"Your family has no respect for our relationship," Janey snapped. "They keep coming up to you asking if you've met Alexis the lesbian yet. They act like I'm not even here. It's rude of them to try to hook you up with someone else right in front of me. Did you have to tell everyone we're on a break?"

"Lower your voice," Stacy said and looked around. "I didn't tell anyone anything."

5

"We were supposed to spend this weekend working on us, instead we're at this stupid party."

Janey had found Stacy's last nerve, and she was steadily driving a stake through it. Stacy didn't want to make a spectacle, but her patience was waning. She chose her words carefully. "You wanted to come, you told me that. Jason wants me to meet Alana's family, and I can't leave until I do. Let's go find them and get it over with."

"Well, I don't want to meet them, and you told me we weren't going to stay here long, but you've been chatting everyone up." Janey gulped down a glass of the champagne and handed the empty flute to Stacy. "Don't look at me like that. It's hot, and I have to drink something to keep me cool."

"Ice water maybe?" Stacy regretted the remark when Janey glared at her.

Janey swayed slightly. "This is why I needed a break—the harping. You treat me like a drunk, and I am not a drinking problem."

"You want to try that sentence again?"

"You know exactly what I meant!" Janey retorted loudly.

Stacy moved close to Janey and whispered, "Vicky is about to leave because one of her kids isn't feeling well. I can ask her to drop you by our place. It's on her way."

"I don't want to go home with your sister," Janey snapped. "Are you trying to get rid of me, so you can talk to Alexis the lesbian?"

Stacy chewed her lip and looked around, hoping no one was paying them any mind. Her neck and jaw ached from the tension building there. She deeply regretted agreeing to spend time with Janey that weekend; there was nothing left to work on. She'd known for a while their relationship was history. Stacy's tense gaze landed on a group of women speaking with her mother, and every muscle in her body became rigid, and she was glued to the spot where she stood.

They all had the same dark red hair as Alana, except for an older, small portly woman who had obviously dyed her pixie cut light red. Though they had never met, Stacy knew exactly who Alexis was. When Jason first met Alana, he told Stacy to go to the Holt's Garden Center website and check out the gardening videos. Alana was in one of them assisting in the planting of a tree. Stacy watched the video, and after she caught sight of Alexis, she watched the rest of them—repeatedly.

Janey was steadily bitching about a wasted weekend, as Stacy's mother, Theresa, suddenly turned and caught Stacy's eye. She pointed directly at Stacy, and Alexis headed her way. Tall and thin, brown-eyed, fair-skinned with a head full of dark red hair, Alexis was much better looking in person. Stacy's mouth went dry as Alexis drew nearer. She'd developed a crush on a woman she only knew in videos about killing aphids and how to plant and fertilize fruit trees.

Stacy had hoped to meet Alexis when Janey wasn't around. She feared her secret interest in Alexis might show, and Janey would home in on it in a heartbeat. The explosion would be legendary, so Stacy stiffened even more when Alexis spoke the wrong words at the wrong time. "Hi, I'm Alexis the lesbian, everybody's been telling me I need to meet y'all."

"I'm...um...I'm—"

"Stacy," Janey said and rolled her eyes. She moved so close to Stacy their hips touched. "I'm Janey Simoneaux, her girlfriend that no one seems to realize exists."

"Nice to meet you both." Alexis extended her hand and almost withdrew it before Janey released a loud sigh and begrudgingly shook it.

"Stacy and I were just talking about how she was dying to meet you," Janey said with a sneer as her gaze swept over Alexis. "Did you just leave your job and not have time to change?"

Alexis narrowed her eyes. "Excuse me?"

"No, excuse us." Stacy found her feet then and took Janey by the arm. "It was a pleasure meeting you, Alexis. We have to go now," she said and led Janey away.

"Are we done here yet?" Alexis asked when she rejoined her mother and grandmother.

Allison kept her voice low and a smile on her face. "Don't be rude, we haven't even been here an hour."

Alexis leaned in close to her grandmother and whispered, "If you love me, pretend to fall so I can carry you out of here."

"Oh, my stunt fall days are over. If I go down, it's for real. Fling yourself into the holly bushes," Elise said with a smile. "I'll be sure to scream right after I have two more glasses of champagne."

Alana made her way over to them and asked, "Are y'all having fun?"

Alexis's mouth flew open and a sarcastic retort was perched on her tongue, but her grandmother's glare kept it from being launched. "Great time," she said instead.

"Lex, Stacy is over there next to Jason. Let me introduce y'all." Alana took Alexis's arm.

Alexis planted her feet firmly and didn't budge when Alana gave her a tug. "We've already met. I spoke to her and Jackal earlier."

"Isn't she sweet?" Alana gushed. "I just adore her. She's so pretty, I'd kill to have her skin," Alana said, then covered her mouth with her hand. "That sounded really bad. Anyway, she had me put her hair up. Her girlfriend doesn't like it, but I think it's adorable. Don't you think she's gorgeous?"

Alexis spotted Stacy standing beside Jason. She was pretty; her green eyes were stunning against her olive skin. The teal sheath dress she wore showed off her lithe figure and long toned legs. "Yeah, she's a doll," Alexis said, trying to keep the seething anger out of her tone. Stacy and Janey had just looked at her like a mangy stray dog that had wandered into the party, and Alexis despised them both within seconds of meeting them.

"They look more like siblings than cousins, don't you think?" Alana asked as she waved at Jason.

"Sure," Alexis replied drolly. "Is Stacy's hair as long as Jason's?"

Alana shook her head with her gaze fixed on her fiancé. "Hers is darker and longer. Jason looks just like Thor, except he's a little smaller…and he doesn't have the big arms or the stomach that looks like a washboard or the—"

"Hammer?" Alexis interjected with a smirk.

8

Alana threw a hand on her hip. "He has pretty green eyes, a beautiful face, and nice teeth."

Alexis grabbed a champagne flute from a tray as a server walked by with it and noticed Jason was leading Stacy in her direction. Alexis turned and made her way through the crowd unwilling to be humiliated again.

Chapter Two

"I need your help today," Stacy said when Jason answered his phone.

Jason opened one eye and stared at the numbers on his alarm clock. It wasn't even six a.m., and it was Sunday. "What're you doing up at this hour?"

"I haven't been to sleep, I've been packing. I need you to help me take my things over to the cottage."

"Wait, wait," Jason said quietly as he got up gently so as not to disturb Alana. He walked out of the bedroom and closed the door softly behind him. "What's going on?"

"Janey and I are done. We both thought that the break might make us feel differently. You know, the absence makes you miss someone and think about all the reasons you love them. We didn't miss each other, and I enjoyed the peace while she stayed with her sister. I have to get out of this apartment. Her name is on the lease."

"I'll certainly help you, but don't go to the cottage. You'll basically be moving back in with your parents if you do that. We have plenty of room, you're staying with us. At least now I'll be able to see you."

"I wasn't avoiding you, I hope you know that. I didn't feel very social while I was sorting things out, and before the break, I couldn't bring Janey around Alana. One minute, she would be perfectly fine and the next mean and insulting." Stacy lowered her voice. "I think she's possessed."

"She's something," Jason said with a laugh. "I'm sorry if you're sad, but I'm happy to get you back."

"Your offer is really sweet, but shouldn't you talk to Alana about this first? She may not want me in her house."

"She's all about family, that's one of the things I love about her. We won't take no for an answer. I'm gonna wake her up, and after we get dressed, we'll be right over. Where's Janey, and does she know what you're doing?" Jason yawned and said, "I have one question, may I be rude to Janey?"

"I'd say yes, but she won't be here. She's at her sister's, and I have until noon to get out."

"I'm going to put on some clothes, wake up Tim next door, and borrow his truck. Alana and I'll be there soon. We'll pick up breakfast on the way. Everything's going to be okay."

"Are you sure you don't want to unpack some of these?" Alana asked Stacy as they stuffed another box into what Jason considered his home office. The other spare room was filled with her furniture.

"No, I'm not going to stay long, but thanks. I have my clothes and my toiletries, that's all I need for now. I'll do my best not to make an interruption in your lives. I'll be scarce, I promise."

Alana surprised Stacy with a tight hug. "No, don't do that. I'm looking forward to spending time with you. I'm so glad you're here, and Jason is too. He told me on the way to your apartment this morning that he has really missed you. You're more than a cousin to him, you're one of his closest friends." Alana pulled away and gazed at her. "You know what makes me feel better? A mani-pedi. Nothing is more healing than breathing in the chemicals in a nail salon. There's a new one down the street. Would you like to go after lunch?"

"Oh...thank you, but I don't like people touching my feet, and I'm really not a manicure kind of girl," Stacy said with a weak smile.

Alana laughed. "You sound just like Alexis. She says all the time that she has clippers and nail files, and she doesn't need anyone to operate them for her. She hisses like a cat at nail polish."

11

"I made lunch," Jason said as he appeared in the doorway.
"Well, I ordered pizza."

"Chase, we need more fruit trees on the lot," Alexis said over the radio.

"What kind?" he asked.

"All of them," Alexis responded with a smile as she walked past the checkout line that wound through the store. "Julie, we need more cashiers to the front." Alexis walked over to one of the counters and signed into the computer. When she looked up, she noticed that customers had already lined up at her register before she had a chance to announce she was open.

Spring brought rebirth not only to nature, but also to Alexis's business accounts. January and February were notoriously low months for her garden center, and Alexis had to budget carefully all year to cover them. April, however, was the best. Warm weather had set in, and people were ready to plant flowers and vegetables, and they came in droves.

Julie joined Alexis at the register and quickly took Alexis's place between customers. Alexis thanked her and headed outside to what she called the showroom—acres of greenhouses and in the middle, rows of every variety of tree and shrub that grew in south Louisiana. Alexis wanted to run through it all skipping and singing, and at night, when no one was around, she did.

"Excuse me, I'm looking for purple fountain grass."

Alexis turned to the familiar voice and grinned. "Grammy, what're you doing here?"

"I'm really looking for the grass. I think it would be pretty in the corner of the front flowerbed."

"I would've brought it to you," Alexis said. "You didn't have to come out here."

"Yes, I did. Your mother has a paramour visiting, and I couldn't stand to hear any more of her fake laughter. I give that poor fellow maybe a week before she dumps him." Elise frowned. "And he's as sweet as he can be. It's like watching a lamb go into a lion's den."

"If you stick around here, I'll put you to work," Alexis said jokingly.

"Please do. Give me a smock, and I'll stand out here and give planting advice." Elise wagged a finger. "You should really let me do that. Not everyone who comes in here knows how to properly plant things. I could do little gardening classes. I taught you, remember?"

"I'd set you up a booth in a heartbeat if I thought you were serious."

"I am. All I'd need is one of those patio tables with the umbrella, a chair, a fan, a cooler with cold drinks, quick access to the bathroom, and I'm all set."

"That's all, huh?" Alexis mulled the idea. "Are you really serious?"

"I know I just said I was...didn't I?" Elise asked. "Sometimes, I think I've said something, but your mother says otherwise. I really think she ignores me, though."

"Do you want to try this today?"

Elise looked like a child when she grinned and nodded. "Yes."

Alexis looked around and pulled her radio from her belt. "Chase, would you get one of the umbrella tables and set it up...by the entryway greenhouse, please?"

Chase was quick to reply. "On it, Lex. Any particular color?"

"Red," Elise said excitedly.

Alexis keyed the mic with a smile. "Red, please." She gazed at the sweat beading on her grandmother's forehead. "Grammy, you have to be honest and tell me when you get tired. It's hot out here, and I don't want you getting heat stroke."

"I'll be just fine, it's breezy. The spot you picked for me, is it close to the bathroom?"

All of Elise's requests were met. She had a shady spot, a fan, the cooler, and a chair, and she was sporting a smock with the Holt's Garden Center logo. Alexis had even made her a sign that read *Elise's Gardening Tips and Advice*, but she hadn't attached it to the table before Elise had drawn a few people over. Alexis stood back and watched her grandmother work her magic.

13

"Now I love verbena. It comes in a variety of colors, it's hardy, and blooms all summer long. Mine at home even had a few blooms on it during the winter. It's very showy, you can put it in a planter and let it cascade, or you can put it in a flowerbed, and it makes a beautiful ground cover," Elise said as she took a young verbena plant from its container. "You gently pinch the root ball, place it in soil that is well drained, mind you, they don't like to sit in mud. Dig a little hole with your hand or spade deep enough for the root ball to fit but not so that the plant is buried up to the foliage." Elise demonstrated. "Then you press the soil tightly around it to get rid of air pockets, and you water."

Alexis was taken back to her childhood when she used to kneel in the dirt at Elise's side. They planted flowers, vegetables, and just about everything else that went into the dirt, including Chirpy, her parakeet, when he died. Currently, he was enjoying eternal rest beneath the rose garden behind Alexis's childhood home where her mother and grandmother still lived.

"Oh, my, I know how that is. I no sooner get out into the yard than I have to go back inside to the bathroom. Lord, help me if I ate anything spicy the night before because that's an urgency of a different kind." Elise laughed. "I've wilted a few roses."

Alexis's smile fell from her face, and she turned and walked away.

"Jason and I want to have you over for dinner."

Alexis cradled her phone against her shoulder as she pulled off her boots. "I hope you don't mean tonight. I had a really long day at the nursery. You know how weekends are."

"You say that every time I invite you, regardless of what day it is. Mom says you haven't been to her place in weeks."

"Because I'm very busy. I did take off Saturday to be at your party. You just saw me, remember?" Alexis said with a sigh as she stepped inside her house.

"Well, I'm not talking about tonight, but I do want you to come on Wednesday. I'm at the store right now getting groceries, and I think I'm gonna make lasagna. That's your favorite."

Alexis opened her refrigerator and eyed a slice of lemon doberge cake. She really wanted to have that for dinner but grabbed a premade salad instead. "What's the occasion?"

Stacy broke up with her girlfriend, and she's staying with us for a little while. She's kinda in the dumps, and I thought she might like to talk to someone she can relate to."

Alexis dropped the salad on the counter "Hey, Dr. Philomena, don't volunteer me to *relate* to anyone, especially not her. I'm sure she's got some snobby friends with boney little shoulders she can lean on. I don't appreciate you throwing out the food lure to reel me into being some…something I don't want to be."

"Whoa! If you're all bent because you think I'm trying to fix you up with her, you can back up right now. That's not what she needs, and what do you mean snobby? Stacy is a sweetheart."

"To you, maybe. When I met her at the party, she looked at me like I was a stray dog that wandered in, and she couldn't get away from me fast enough. I'm obviously not her kind of people, and I can guarantee you she would not be happy if I showed up Wednesday. Like I said, if she needs a buddy, call up one of her snooty friends."

"You're being mean!"

"You sound just like you did when you were four. Are you gonna tell Mommy?" Alexis asked, her tone dripping with sarcasm.

"No, I'm gonna hang up on your face."

Alana did just that. Alexis tossed her phone on the counter. She grabbed a fork, a bottle of water and her salad, and took it to her living room where she sat in front of the TV.

She liked Jason, he was a really nice guy, but Alexis didn't think he'd be around long, and she didn't want to get attached. Jason and Alana had only been dating two months when he'd popped the question, then Alana moved in with him. Alexis was stunned that four months later they were still together, but they hadn't set a date for the wedding. She was pretty certain that any day Alana would make her usual statement, "Well, it just didn't work out."

15

Alana did have a talent for finding genuinely nice guys, and Alexis saw them all like the bugs drawn helplessly to a zapper light. Alana was beautiful, but she packed one hell of an electrical charge. Some of her exes were burned to a crisp before they even knew what happened to them. Alexis couldn't be around Jason because she wanted to grab him by the shoulders and yell, "Run, fool, she's gonna light you up and not in a good way."

Alexis groaned when her phone rang again, and she regretted that she didn't bother to bring it into the living room with her. She set her salad aside and went into the kitchen. *Mom* was on the display.

"Let me guess why you're calling," Alexis said when she answered. "Alana complained to you that I was being mean."

"No, actually, I was calling to say that whatever you did to Momma knocked her out. She ate dinner, had her bath, and went to bed. Could you do it again tomorrow? I haven't had this much peace and quiet in ages. Since you ratted on yourself, why're you being mean to your sister?"

"I wasn't. She accused me of it because I wouldn't go along with her dinner plans on Wednesday." Alexis returned to what was left of her salad. "Jason's cousin Stacy is staying with them because she broke up with her girlfriend. Alana was trying to call in the clown to cheer her up, and I'm fresh out of red rubber noses."

"Why do you think Stacy is a snob?"

"Aha! I never mentioned that to you, so you did talk to Alana."

"She called me in a tizzy right after she hung up on you. I know you don't believe it, but I think she really does love Jason. Stacy is important to him, so that means she's important to Alana. She wants us all to be one big happy family, so go have dinner with your sister."

"I am not, Mom. Stacy is a snob, and I'm not gonna give her another chance to look down her nose at me. Furthermore, Alana's lasagna is horrible. If you like Jason so much, then you need to tell Alana the truth about her cooking. See, this is the problem with our 'sweet little lies' as you call them. You don't

16

want to hurt anyone's feelings, but these deceptions always come back to bite us in the ass. A fine example of that was when you told Grammy her hair looked great the time she dyed it pink, then her quilting club friends made fun of her and hurt her feelings. You told Grandpa he looked great in that stupid plaid suit, and he requested we bury him in it. Everyone who viewed his body at the wake said the suit distorted their vision. There was a bunch of old people walking into walls. The last time I ate Alana's lasagna, I chipped a tooth because she cooked it into a brick, and you wouldn't let me tell her. Jason could die eating that stuff. A pasta shard could cut his throat."

"Well, I'll tell you the truth about this, you are overly dramatic. I want you to think back to when you were with Michelle. Alana bent over backward to make that woman feel like a part of our family. She always remembered Michelle's birthday. Alana would invite her places when you were too busy, and may I remind you when your working too much became a problem between y'all, Alana did her best to smooth it over. She had your back, now it's time you cover hers."

"You can play the guilt card so masterfully," Alexis said in awe.

"That's because your grandmother holds a doctorate in that subject."

Chapter Three

Stacy worked late Monday and Tuesday night, or at least that was what she told Jason she was doing. When everyone went home and the office quieted, she sat at her desk staring out the window soul searching. She was convinced she was losing her mind, or at the very least emotionally unstable.

Throughout the workday, she promised herself she would not click the saved link to Holt's Garden Center, but when everyone left, her fingers betrayed her, and she watched videos about aphids, fertilizer, and how to plan and plant a flowerbed. Stacy didn't possess a green thumb, and what little she knew about gardening, she'd learned from watching Alexis.

Stacy began to dissect her fascination with Alexis and had decided though she found Alexis incredibly attractive, she was a distraction from a very unhappy existence with Janey. Everything Stacy wanted Janey to be, she poured into an imaginary version of Alexis that lived only in her head. At times, the fantasies she had about Alexis were so vivid and sexually charged she felt as though she'd been unfaithful to Janey.

She glanced at her watch and released a heavy breath. She was about to face her fantasy in the flesh again that evening, and she wasn't exactly thrilled. She was embarrassed by what Janey had said to Alexis and that she failed to apologize to Alexis that day. Stacy had been so stunned by Janey's remarks and Alexis's presence that her brain seemed to stall out on her. By the time she was thinking clearly, she asked Jason to introduce her to Alana's mother and grandmother, in hopes of having a moment

18

to speak to Alexis again. Alexis walked away before she had a chance.

On Wednesday night, Alexis stood at Alana and Jason's door with a Boston fern tucked in the crook of her arm. She raised her hand to knock but couldn't bring herself to actually do it. She thought for a moment about leaving the plant on the doorstep with a note attached saying she'd been abducted by aliens, but they promised to have her back the next morning before the nursery opened. Alexis was grinning at the absurd notion when the door opened, and she came face to face with Stacy.

Stacy gazed at Alexis standing there with her fist in the air sporting a maniacal smile. "Um...hi."

"Hello," Alexis said coolly and slowly lowered her hand. Stacy stood there gazing at her with those light green eyes, her hair down and hanging partially over one of them, lips slightly parted as though she wanted to say something. Alexis noticed the tiny cleft in Stacy's chin and the light freckles on her cheeks. "Am I allowed in the house?"

"Oh! I was just going to get something from my car...you surprised me." Stacy opened the door wider and allowed Alexis in. "They're in the kitchen."

"Thanks," Alexis replied dully and walked past Stacy, who still stood there staring at her.

Alana met Alexis in the living room and threw her arms around her as though she hadn't seen her in years. "Oh, I'm so glad you came!" Alana said and kissed her cheek twice. "You didn't have to bring a plant."

"I left work too late to pick up a bottle of wine, and plants last longer...well, it might if you actually water it," Alexis said with a smile when Jason joined them and gave her a hug too. "Dinner smells...is it burning?"

"Oh!" Alana whirled around and ran into the kitchen.

Jason watched as Alexis chose a spot for the fern and asked, "Would you like a glass of wine?"

"Yes, I would." Alexis followed him into the kitchen. "Big girl glass, please."

19

"How was your day?" Alana asked as she frantically searched for hot pads.

Alexis watched Jason open the wine and said, "It was busy, even for a weekday. That makes me very happy."

"What else have you been up to besides work? Regale me with something exciting." Jason handed Alexis a glass.

"I…uh…went grocery shopping, and I washed my cats. That was a lot of fun. They shed really bad this time of year, so I give them a good scrub-down, and I'm happy to say I didn't have to go to the hospital afterward. What've y'all been up to?"

"We've been playing badminton," Alana said as she took the lasagna from the oven. "Jason put up a net in the backyard, and we play after dinner for exercise. It takes me back to when we were little and Grandpa would make homemade ice cream, and you and I would play doubles with Mom and Grandma."

"We should play tonight," Jason said excitedly. "There's four of us, it'll be a blast."

Alexis's eyes flew open wide. "No, it'll be a boatload of pop knots just like when we were kids. Mom's backhand was lethal."

"That's because we were short then, and our heads got in the way," Alana said with a laugh.

Stacy walked into the room and avoided eye contact with Alexis. "The table is set. Are you ready for me to put out the salad?"

"Yes, please," Alana said with a nod. "I think we're ready to eat."

Alexis ate her salad slowly and watched as Jason and Stacy had their first bites of Alana's lasagna. Jason's right eyebrow twitched, but he kept on chewing with a pleasant expression on his face. Stacy lucked out and had one of the inner pieces but chewed for what seemed like five minutes before she dared to swallow.

Alana all the while was going on about her and Alexis's childhood and how they would play badminton until late in the evening on summer nights. "You know, you don't realize how special something is until it's gone. When I was little, our backyard seemed so huge, and it was such a magical place.

20

Grandpa would tell us about the constellations, and he'd help us catch fireflies. We called them lightning bugs then. Grammy would grill burgers, and the meat was a tight ball she'd put between two regular slices of bread. The mustard and ketchup would seep through, and we'd be covered in it. I would always be excited because they'd let us stay up late, and we didn't have to go to school the next day."

"For me and Stacy, it was basketball." Jason gazed at Stacy with a smile. "She always beat me because she was a head taller until I got into my teens. We'd stay on the court from sunup to sundown in the summers. Both of us were tanned, with pink knees and elbows because they were scraped up all the time. Remember that?"

"Fondly," Stacy answered with a faint smile. She didn't know which was worse—the lasagna or the contempt she saw in Alexis's gaze whenever she looked at her.

The conversation lagged after that, and Alana brought up the nursery. "Alexis owns Holt's Garden Center, Stacy. Have you heard of it?"

"Jason told me about it."

Alana pointed her fork at Alexis. "Lex, tell her about the nursery."

Alexis gazed at Stacy, eyes dull. "We sell plants and trees and bushes."

Jason laughed. "She's being modest. Holt's is the largest garden center in south Louisiana. She has everything from fountains to…"

"Manure," Alexis added when Jason stalled.

"That sounds delightful," Stacy said before she took another bite of lasagna and started the process of laborious chewing again.

"Stacy works at Simon and Gutierrez, it's a corporate property management company. She heads the marketing team there," Jason said.

Alexis nodded. "That also sounds delightful."

Conversation lulled again, and Jason spoke up suddenly. "Do y'all think my hair looks unprofessional?"

21

"Why? Has someone in your office said something about it?" Stacy asked.

"No, but Mom keeps complaining about it," Jason replied as he went at the lasagna with a steak knife.

Alana gazed at him all dreamy-eyed. "I think you look like Brad Pitt in *Legends of the Fall*. It's so sexy. I don't want you to cut it—unless you want to, but I don't want you to."

"She's the only hairdresser who has ever talked me out of cutting my hair," Jason said with a laugh. "I walked into the salon where she works that first day we met with the intention of getting a buzz cut, and she refused."

Alana smiled demurely. "I waxed his knuckles instead, and I wrote my phone number on his palm. Stacy's gonna let me cut her hair. She wants it to rest on her shoulders."

"I want to do something different, but I'm not brave enough to cut it short." Stacy gazed at Alexis's hair. It was short, but long on top, and she wore it in a tousled carefree style. "I like yours, Alexis."

Alexis flashed a smile that held no warmth.

"I used to wear my hair like that too, and everybody thought Alexis and I were twins." Alana groaned. "But oh, my God, it's so hard to let that style grow out. My hair would get into those awkward stages, and I'd have one of the stylists I work with trim it. I think it took a year for it to even become shoulder length—Stacy, you're not eating. Is everything okay?"

"Sure…um…I'm just a slow eater." Stacy took a bite and smiled.

Alexis grinned as she listened to Stacy chew the brick that was Alana's lasagna.

Chapter Four

"Me and Jason against you and Stacy." Alana handed Alexis a badminton racket and grinned.

"Yay," Alexis said without even a smidgeon of enthusiasm.

"Do you want to serve?" Stacy asked Alexis when Jason and Alana moved to the other side of the net.

"Serve you what? There's no staff here to take care of your every whim, princess," Alexis said lowly so the others wouldn't hear.

Stacy recoiled at the remark, then her temper flared. "You know what I was asking," she replied coolly.

"You can serve. Here's the birdie," Alexis replied and handed it to her on her middle finger.

"Shuttlecock," Stacy corrected.

"Butthole...cock." Alexis shrugged when Stacy glared at her. "That's what we used to call them."

"Uh-huh," Stacy said as she prepared to serve.

The birdie sailed over the net, and volley began. This went on for a few minutes, then Alexis heard a hard thwack behind her, and the birdie stung her on the back of the thigh. She turned and looked at Stacy with fire in her eyes.

"My bad," Stacy said nonchalantly.

Alexis picked up the birdie and tossed it to Alana, who handed it to Jason to serve. The birdie sailed just over the top of the net. Alexis dove for it and missed with her swing. Alana hopped around swinging her racket and yelled, "Baby, that was awesome."

Alexis picked up the birdie and hit it toward Jason. He served again. Stacy returned and nailed Alexis in the back of the head. "I'm so sorry," Stacy said with an acerbic smile. "I'm having a hard time getting my shuttlecock up for you."

"Good one," Alexis said and hit the birdie to Jason.

He sent the birdie toward Stacy again, and this time when she hit it at Alexis, Alexis was ready. She turned and hit it back at Stacy, who was quick and managed to hit it, as well. An intense volley began, and Alana said, "Uh, hey, y'all are supposed to be hitting it to us."

Jason watched in fascination. "I think they're trying to kill the birdie."

Alexis finally missed and snatched it off the ground. "We were just warming up."

"Yeah, I'm good and hot now," Stacy added between clenched teeth.

The birdie was hit to Jason, who served again, and Alexis popped it just over the net. Alana swung at it and missed. "My serve," Alexis said as she whirled around, then lowered her voice as she passed Stacy. "You're about to find out why we call them butthole cocks."

Stacy held her racket out like a sword. "How about I just waffle your ass now?"

Alexis struck a fencing pose, or at least she thought she did. "On guard, biatch."

"Are they serious?" Jason asked.

Alana rushed under the net and stepped between the two staring daggers at each other. "Hey, we want to be able to use these rackets again. Maybe we should take a break since y'all kind of murdered the birdie." Alana laughed. "It's missing two plastic feathers. How about some wine?"

"I think I'll call it a night," Stacy said as she lowered her racket. "Dinner was great, thank you." Jason handed his racket to Alana and followed Stacy inside. Alana and Alexis watched them go in silence.

Alana turned and gazed at Alexis. "What...what the hell?"

"She hit me with the bird on purpose."

24

"I'll grant you that," Alana said with a nod. "But what did you say to her that made her want to do that?"

"I...might've called her a name. I think it was butthole cock, but that was after she called me a shuttlecock." Alexis threw a hand on her hip. "She acted like she was saying it to correct me when I called the birdie a birdie, but I knew she meant I was a cock, and so butthole cock came out of my mouth."

"When I was ten and you were twelve, that explanation would've made sense to me, but coming from a thirty-six-year-old grown-ass woman, it sounds really stupid."

"Shuttlecock." Alexis pointed at Alana when her nostrils flared. "See, you don't like being called that, either."

"Let's talk," Jason said as he followed Stacy into her room.

"I'm sorry I ruined your night."

"You didn't. Watching you and Lex was more entertaining than a hockey game. I kept waiting to see who was gonna get pucked up." Jason grinned when Stacy shot him a look. "What's going on?"

"I need to get my head straight, Jason. I'm not right. It's not safe for me to be around people right now. I'm a butthole cock."

"Well...that's understandable, you've been through a lot lately. Alana thought it might cheer you up to have Alexis over." Jason scratched the back of his neck and frowned. "She's usually a lot of fun, though tonight she seemed to have a burr in her ass too."

Stacy was sweaty and took a seat on the floor rather than the bed. "That's my fault. I made a horrible first impression on her, I'm sure. Janey and I were arguing at your engagement party. She was pissed off because everyone was telling us we needed to meet Alexis the lesbian."

Jason groaned and joined Stacy on the floor. "Nobody but me liked it when you came out, but when Mom found out that Alexis was a lesbian, she couldn't stop talking about it. She treated Lex like an exotic pet at that party." He waved a hand for Stacy to continue. "Sorry to interrupt."

"Alexis walked up to us at that moment, and I froze. Janey was horribly rude, but I knew if I apologized to Alexis for her

25

behavior, Janey would've lost her mind. I whisked her away and left Alexis standing there."

"Well, that can be easily explained. I think Alexis would understand, but I don't think tonight is the best time for you two to have that chat." Jason gazed at Stacy and asked, "Now that you're really away from Janey, are you…missing her a little?"

"No." Stacy sighed. "I miss the way it was during our first couple of years, but this last one was a nightmare. I don't know what happened to us, but suddenly, we couldn't agree on anything. We both just seemed to change overnight. We took a couple of breaks that lasted about a week, and we got back together. We talked everything out, then the very next day, we were arguing about something else. This last break was a little over a month, and during that time, I realized I was much happier without her. I think I really began to accept it was over when I got interested in someone else."

Jason's brow shot up. "Y'all were seeing other people during the breaks?"

"No, and I wasn't technically unfaithful. The woman I kinda crushed on had no clue, but it made me realize that I had lost everything I once felt for Janey. The night after the party, we fought for hours, and we both finally broke and came to terms with what we had to do."

"Is she okay?" Alana asked when Jason joined her in the kitchen.

"Yeah, she's fine. She's in the shower. How's Lex?"

Alana shook her head. "She's got a chip on her shoulder, and she won't tell me why."

"I will." Jason told Alana everything Stacy had told him about what happened at the engagement party.

Alana listened intently while she poured them both a glass of wine. When Jason finished, she said, "That explains a lot. Lex does not like to be looked down upon. There was a clique of kids at school who used to torment her. One of them found out our parents never married, and they liked to call her the bastard. We didn't have a lot of money, either, so we never wore what was in

26

style. They dogged her about that too. Some scars don't heal even with time."

"Would you explain Stacy's side to Alexis?"

"Of course, but it's gonna be a while before I can do that. I love my sister, but she can be a hardheaded shuttlecock when she wants to be."

Dear Me,
I made a jackass out of myself tonight. I couldn't stop it. The second I saw Stacy, I sprouted big donkey ears and a tail. I don't know why she gets under my skin. Why should I care what she thinks of me? She'll be gone right along with Jason when Alana gets bored.

Alana's lasagna was terrible. No one noticed that I was slipping the harder pieces of it into my salad bowl and hiding them under the lettuce. It's a good thing they don't have a dog because if it was to eat the scraps, it would surely die. Jason and Stacy are gonna be shitting pasta shards. I feel sorry for Jason, not so much for Stacy.

I'll have to patch things up with Alana, so this may not be the right time to tell her that her cooking is lethal. She was pissed when I left her house. I'm sure she'll tell Mom and Grammy I was a jerk. Jason was probably mad at me too. I feel a little bad about that.

Me

Chapter Five

In the cool of the morning, Alexis watered the plants in one of her greenhouses before the nursery opened. Her staff knew not to bother her then. It was her quiet time.

"Excuse me, do have any cannabis plants?"

Alexis turned to face her best friend with a scowl. Jaime Harris's short blond hair was full of cowlicks, and her bangs stood at attention on her forehead. Her brown eyes were full of mischief as she gazed up at Alexis, who stood head and shoulders taller than she was. What she lacked in height, Jaime made up for in brawn. Her muscles looked as though they had muscles.

"Bad day already? You want a hug? Want me to take you to my bosom, baby girl?" Jaime cooed.

"Don't make me water you."

Jaime followed Alexis as she moved down the row of plants. "Be sweet to your buddy. I came to see if you'd like to have breakfast. I'm about to go back out on the rig, so I can dole out Band-Aids, cough medicine, and laxatives."

"You're going back already?" Alexis asked with a frown. "You just got home a few weeks ago. We haven't even had a chance to hang out yet."

"Another medic quit, and they're scrambling to cover his shift. Who or what put a wrinkle in your undies?"

"This totally sucks. We were gonna go to that new movie theater where they bring you real food while you lie like a sloth in a recliner."

Jaime smiled. "You could do that with a date. Rachel's been trying to fix you up for months, and you come up with a million excuses why you can't meet her friends."

"Exactly, they're her friends. If it doesn't work out, it's gonna be awkward. Tell your love I appreciate her thinking of me."

"That's a lame excuse, Lex. You're becoming a loner. You don't hang out with anyone else but me, and I'm on the rig half the time. Tell me you haven't started dressing your cats in little suits and posting their pictures on the—hey!" Jaime yelled when Alexis sprayed her shoes with the hose.

"I dressed Sprout one time as Casper for Halloween. I didn't even buy the costume. One of the girls here gave it to me. You have to admit, he was fucking adorable."

"Yeah," Jaime conceded with a laugh. "He really was, then he ripped you to shreds. Back to finding a girl—"

"Why do you always have to rag me about this?"

Jaime put her hands up in surrender. "I won't bring it up again if you agree to go eat with me."

"Fine, but you're treating, and I want to go to that hole-in-the-wall place that makes the pancakes with the crunchy edges," Alexis said, sounding like a child.

Jaime grinned. "Deal, and I'll even request a kids' menu and crayons so you can color. Hey!" she yelled when Alexis shot her shoes again.

Jaime ate her breakfast and listened to Alexis's account of what happened at the engagement party, then at dinner at Alana and Jason's place. To Alexis's chagrin, Jaime laughed. "What is so funny?" Alexis asked with a frown.

"It's funny—oh, come on, you can't laugh at that? Two grown women about to throw down with badminton rackets over something silly. You don't see the humor in that?"

"Look at my face. I'm pissed," Alexis snapped. "No, I don't think it's funny."

Jaime shrugged. "I don't understand. What am I missing? You don't like Jason's cousin, okay, but why are you so bent out of shape?"

"I wasn't born into a rich family. I've had to work myself silly all my life, so what right does she have to look at me like I'm a piece of trash?"

"She can look at you any way she wants, that's her right, and you have the right not to give a shit. Shallow, insecure people need to look down on someone to feel good about themselves, so really, you should be feeling sorry for her, not for yourself." Jaime pointed at Alexis's pancake. "You gonna eat that?"

"No, you can have it, but if you get near the bacon, I'll have to cut you." Alexis slid her plate over to Jaime's. "I hear what you're saying, and any other time, I would agree, but with one dismissive glance, that woman put a serious burr under my skin."

"You don't even know her, why should you care?"

"That's what I keep asking myself," Alexis replied distractedly.

"Is she good-looking?"

"Very," Alexis admitted grudgingly.

"You were attracted to her?"

Alexis didn't immediately answer. "I was...um...maybe a little when I first saw her, but I knew she had a girlfriend."

"It's like you got rejected twice," Jaime said matter-of-factly. "You found her attractive, and she didn't want to have anything to do with you."

Alexis's brow furrowed. "What's with the whole psych analysis thing?"

"I work on a rig with a bunch of men who think I'm their momma. I guess since I'm a woman, they want my perspective on things regarding their wives and girlfriends, so I pay more attention to human nature. We need to talk about something else," Jaime said and wiped her mouth. "You remember Abby Stassi?"

"Yeah, I haven't seen her in ages."

"Right, and do you remember why we stopped hanging out with her?" Jaime asked.

Alexis nodded. "She morphed into a royal bitch."

31

"It didn't happen overnight. She was great until she got the promotion at work, and the job was a lot more than she bargained for. It was stressful, and she gradually turned really negative." Jaime's brow furrowed as she said, "Every conversation with her was about something or someone she was fighting with. I finally had to tell her that her personality had turned into something very caustic. I did it with good intentions because I don't think she realized what was happening to her, but she told me to fuck off and hasn't spoken to me since. So, Lex, please don't do the same thing."

Alexis was slow on the uptake and stared at Jaime uncomprehendingly. "What do you...what?"

"The same thing is happening to you," Jaime said gently. "You've gotten into a bad habit of bitching about everything. You used to roll with the punches, now you resist all change, good or bad. When we talk, you're either having a problem with an employee or a customer—you're even fighting with your cats. The last time we talked on the phone, you chewed Sprout out for coughing up a hairball."

"He did it in my shoe. I've got hardwood floors and tile throughout the house, but where does he decide to puke? My shoes or the rugs. You put your foot in a shoe that has a gooey ball of fur and tell me if that doesn't piss you off."

Jaime held up a hand. "That's just one example. You're becoming a grumpy old woman, and you're not even forty. What is going on with you?"

"Do you know why old people are grumpy? Let me tell you. They've grown up and realized that the Easter Bunny and Santa Claus don't exist, and neither does the love we read about in fairytales. Life is about working your ass off, and when you have a really good sales month and dare to do a happy dance, the IRS cuts in and stomps your toes off." Alexis threw up her hands. "Simple joys in life like a white bread sandwich are dangerous because it isn't bread anymore. I put a loaf in the pantry and forgot about it for three weeks, it didn't mold!"

"I'm just gonna put it out there. I think you're depressed."

Alexis's eyes flew open wide. "I'm not sad, I'm pissed off!"

32

"It could...be the same thing. I think you've gotten yourself into a destructive cycle. Your house is right behind your business, you never escape it. You need some variety in your life, you need to make changes. Call Rachel, go out with some of her friends. When I get off my hitch on the rig, we'll go on some double dates. You don't have to marry any of these women, just get back into experiencing life. There's so much more to it than working and paying bills and...scary white bread. Look, I love you, and I'm not gonna let you fall into the pit of despair that Abby fell into. You either get happy, or I'm telling your momma and grandma on you."

Alexis patted one of her managers on the back. "How you doing, Chase? You doing all right?"

Chase took one look at Alexis's big toothy grin and backed away from her. "Are you about to hose me again?"

"Do you see a sprayer in my hands?" Alexis asked. "It's a beautiful day, isn't it? I'm happy. I'm very happy. Are you happy?"

"Did you take some kind of medicine this morning?" Chase asked warily.

"Nope." Alexis took a step toward Chase, and he backed away from her again. "Come here, man, I wanna talk to you."

Chase looked around to make sure Alexis hadn't dragged a hose over to where he was working. "What's up?" he asked nervously.

"Do you think I'm a grumpy, bitter person?"

"Um...no?"

Alexis held up a finger. "Let's try this again. Pretend you don't work for me and answer that question."

"I can't because I do, and I like that direct deposit in my bank every Friday."

Alexis pulled Chase's sunglasses off and said, "So your refusal to answer means the answer to my question is yes. Is that right? Look me in the eye."

"Would you just spray me with the hose and get it over with?"

"Answer the question!"

33

Chase backed away from Alexis again. "Well...there are days when you're kinda intense."

"Okay." Alexis pointed to her face. "I'm still smiling, it's all good. So how many days of the week do you find me intense?"

"Seven?" Chase held up his hands in surrender when Alexis's smile faltered. "I know when you're having a bad day because you get that line in the middle of your forehead. I mean, it's there all the time, but it's...it's shallow right now...or it was before I opened my mouth."

"You look like shit."

Stacy gazed up at her boss as he stepped into her office and closed the door. "Thanks, Wes, that's just what I needed to hear."

"What's going on with you?" Wesley Buchannan asked as he took a seat in front of her desk.

"Janey and I broke up."

"Ah," Wesley said with a nod. "She dump you, or did you dump her?"

"It was a mutual decision. I'm staying at Jason's house right now, and though I appreciate his kindness, I feel a little displaced. Every time I think of something I need, I have to go dig through a bunch of boxes for it."

"Go rent an apartment."

"I've considered buying a house, so at the moment, I don't want to commit to a lease." Stacy smiled. "I think I'd like to have a place out in the country, but the commute concerns me because the traffic in Baton Rouge is horrible. I like Jason's neighborhood, but the houses are huge. I don't need anything with four bedrooms."

"If you get one that big, I'll come live with you and pay rent."

"Don't tell me you and Sara are having problems," Stacy said with concern.

"No, she and I are fine for the most part. It's those damn dolls she collects. First they were in the spare room, now they're trickling into the den. I sit in my chair, and I feel like a dozen pairs of eyes are on me." Wesley shuddered. "Those soulless little bastards are creepy. The dog doesn't even like them. He gives the shelf they sit on a wide berth. Make sure the next woman you date doesn't collect anything with eyeballs. Hey, we've got the pool house, and since our youngest went off to college, it sits empty. You're welcome to it, rent-free."

Stacy smiled, genuinely touched by Wesley's offer. "Thank you, but Jason seems intent on keeping me. He hides my apartment guides."

"Well look, let me talk to the guys who handle residential. They take care of a lot of corporate apartments. They have people come in, live in a place for six months, and move on. You may have to wait for a little while, but you might be able to get one of those. You can have your own territory until you make up your mind on the house. You might get a good deal on the rent, too, though that's probably not a concern to you since you're so rich and all."

Stacy laughed at the longstanding joke. When she developed a good rapport with Wesley, she divulged that although her parents were wealthy, she wasn't. When they passed on, she stood to inherit the estate, which would be divided among her and her three sisters. Stacy didn't bank on that. She often did things to fall out of her parents' good graces. Unlike her Aunt Audrey, her folks didn't treat her sexuality as a novelty, and it was often a bone of contention. She had a decent inheritance from her grandfather, and she'd invested every penny as a nest egg.

"Yeah, I should just run out and buy a house and a new girlfriend to go along with it. I'm sure there's plenty of women out there who want to be kept by me."

"I can tell you one right now, and that's Stacy Lettow in purchasing. That woman swoons every time you walk by. You could grab her right up if you don't mind the fact you have the same first name. That's gotta be strange but convenient. You'd never mess up and call her by the wrong name."

Dear Me,

Talk about getting the wind knocked out of your sails when your best friend tells you you're turning into a grumpy hermit. She told me that at breakfast today, and I was in denial until I talked to Chase, that little fucker. I made myself happy by soaking his ass five times before lunch.

I did some soul searching, and I don't think I'm depressed, but I do think I'm becoming too comfortable with being by myself. I'm really beginning to enjoy the company of cats more than people, and that's probably not a good thing. Sprout and Ginger are so cute right now. Ginger's cleaning Sprout's head, and he's smiling. Sometimes he'll...yeah, I really need to get out more.

I think life would be simpler if people acted more like cats. Like if someone is prattling on about something I don't care about and I pop them in the forehead, they'd understand to walk away just like a cat does. A simple hiss conveys so much.

I will attempt to gradually release myself back into a social environment.

Me

Chapter Six

Stacy spent two months with Alana and Jason. Alexis visited Alana a couple of times, but Stacy made it a point not to be there when she knew Alexis was coming. She also deleted the link to Holt's Garden Center and stopped viewing Alexis's videos. It wasn't that she was angry with Alexis, but she knew it was sensible to let go of the fantasy.

"This is really nice," Jason said as he walked around Stacy's spacious new apartment. "I still think you should've bought a house."

"I have six months to make my mind up on that. This is one of our properties, and Wes helped me negotiate a short-term lease."

Jason ran his hand over the marble countertop on the island separating the kitchen from the living room. "You didn't have to be in any hurry. You weren't a nuisance, and Alana and I loved having you there."

"Don't get me wrong, I'm very grateful for the two months I stayed at your place, but I needed something to call my own." Stacy sighed happily as she looked around. "This suits my needs just fine, and my commute to work is much shorter." She pointed at a vase of flowers. "Look what your fiancée dropped by this morning. She's very thoughtful. I really, really like her."

"She's amazing, isn't she?" Jason said with a warm smile. "We talked last night after we helped you move, and we set a date."

Stacy's eyes flew open wide. "When?"

"September 12."

"This year?"

Jason nodded.

"Buddy, that's three months away. Your window for planning is very small."

"We're not going to have the typical wedding in a church, much to my mother's chagrin, I'm sure. Alana and I want to get married on the beach, barefoot in the sand. Do you remember going to Cape San Blas?"

Stacy thought for a moment. "You mean that place in Florida in the middle of nowhere?"

"That's the one," Jason said with a laugh. "Here's the glory of the plan. Mom may invite all her acquaintances, but most of them aren't going to make the seven-hour haul out there, and we don't want a big crowd. We want family and close friends to be there when we take our vows in a very casual ceremony."

"Has it changed? Are there hotels there now?"

Jason shook his head. "I went fishing out there last year, and it looks exactly the same as it did when we went there as kids. That's the other deterrent. There are plenty of beach house rentals, but the closest hotels are in Port St. Joe, maybe Mexico Beach, then there's Panama City. That's, I think, an hour away."

Stacy laughed. "I like it, but your mother is going to lose her mind."

"Uh-huh," Jason said with a grin. "Garret, the guy I went fishing with, has a few rentals on the cape. I talked to him this morning, and I snagged two side by side. They're huge, one of them has seven bedrooms, and the other has eight. You, of course, will stay in the one with Alana and me, and her family will stay with us too."

Stacy's right brow shot up. "And that includes Alexis."

"Yes, but by that time, I'm sure you two will be able to get along. Alana's with Alexis right now asking her to be her maid of honor. I'm going to go ahead and give you a heads-up. Alana wants you to be a bridesmaid."

"Oh," Stacy said, drawing the word out.

"You can't say no."

"Are you sure?" Stacy asked with crooked smile.

"Stacy!"

She threw her hands up in surrender with a laugh. "Joking. I would be honored."

Jason leaned on the bar and said, "I need a favor from you."

"Anything."

"I have to tell Mom about our plans tonight, and I want you to go with me."

"Oh, shit." Stacy grimaced. "Anything but that."

Alexis put a hand to her chest. "Me?"

"Who else would I ask to be my maid of honor?" Alana's face fell. "You don't want to do it?"

"Yes, I want to. Of course, I do." Alexis held out her arms. "Okay, bring it on in."

Alana laughed as she hugged Alexis tightly. "I was so afraid you'd say no because you have to wear a dress."

Alexis was grinning like the Cheshire cat until she heard the word dress. "So this is real? You're really gonna do this?" Alexis asked as Alana released her.

"I am." Alana held Alexis's gaze. "I've never been in love before, I know that now. My chest feels like it's gonna explode with all the feelings. He walks into a room, and my heart pounds. I wake up beside him every morning, and I have to touch him to remind myself he's real."

"I'm jealous," Alexis blurted out, truly surprised at what she was hearing. "I'm happy. I'm very happy for you."

"Thanks." Alana smiled, looking a little dazed, then she blinked. "I forgot to tell you, we're gonna get married in Florida on the beach. Jason and I don't want a big formal wedding. Ever since we told his parents we were engaged, his mother has been making all kinds of plans and telling us what we're gonna do. Jason's about to throw a monkey wrench in her planning, and she's gonna have a fit."

"It's your wedding, though. You and Jason should do what you want."

Alana sighed and took a seat on Alexis's sofa. "She's…a force to be reckoned with. We didn't want to have an engagement party, but Audrey insisted. Jason told her just to invite family, and you saw what that turned into. He's stressed about telling her, I can tell. He's gonna do it this evening, and he doesn't want me to go with him because he knows it's gonna cause a fight."

"You should probably respect his wishes on that," Alexis said as she sat next to Alana.

"I wish Audrey was more like Mom and her 'whatever makes you happy, dear' attitude."

Alexis laughed. "I remember when I told her I was gay. She was folding laundry, and I casually threw out, 'Hey, Mom, I'm pretty sure I'm a lesbian.' She never missed a beat. She folded one towel and grabbed another and asked how I knew. I told her I was in love with my dorm mate, and we'd been seeing each other for almost a year. Mom said, 'That cinches it. I'm happy if you're happy.' Grammy asked me if I'd caught it from sitting on the toilet seat in my dorm, and Grandpa claimed it was in the food they served in the cafeteria."

"You were really in love then. I remember how you used to look at Lily. Everything you felt showed in your eyes." Alana sighed. "I remember how devastated you were when y'all broke up. You lost a lot of weight, you didn't want to be around anyone, and it took you a while to come out of that. So tell me, is it really better to love and lose or not know love at all?"

Alexis thought for a moment. "I'd have to go with Shakespeare on that one. Are you worried that Jason might break your heart?"

"Karma, ya know? I've broken a bunch, maybe it's my turn."

"There's always that risk."

Alana's mouth fell open. "Couldn't you have lied?"

"Oh. No, Alana, he'll never break your heart, and you two will live happily forever and ever. You'll have pink ponies in your yard and cotton candy clouds above. Gumdrops and—"

"Asshole."

Alexis cracked up and gave Alana a little shove. "Stop scowling at me, you're gonna be fine."

"I was really beginning to think there was a curse on the Holt women," Alana said seriously. "Think about it. The only one who has ever had a lasting relationship was Grammy. I don't

40

think Mom is ever gonna fall in love. She says she's happy that way and it's her choice, but I don't know if that's true. Grammy thinks she's so scarred from what happened with our sperm donor that she can't ever let her guard down again. Is that what happened to you? Did Michelle hurt you so bad that you've given up?"

"No. I haven't...given up. I'm just doing my thing."

"You never talk to me about stuff like this. You haven't gone out with anyone in over a year, and I don't know if you're, like, scarred, either. I keep thinking if Jason dumps me, I'll be like Mom because that's what happens to us. Did that happen to you? I need to know," Alana pleaded.

Alexis placed a hand on Alana's shoulder and said calmly, "You're getting a little crazy, you need to chill." Alana stared at her, waiting for an answer, and Alexis sighed. "Michelle didn't scar me, and you're wrong. I've dated a few women since she and I broke up."

It was hard for Alexis to admit to Alana what she was feeling inside. She didn't want to appear weak or needy. Since childhood, she'd been building a tough façade.

"But you haven't seen anyone seriously," Alana argued.

"I'm not ready, I'm being more selective." Alexis shook her head. "I really don't have the time or the desire to screw around with something I know isn't gonna work out."

"But how do you know it isn't if you're not trying?" Alana persisted.

"You sound like Jaime," Alexis snapped. "I'll know the right woman when I meet her, okay?"

"How will—" Alana's mouth hung open in response to the rap she received on the forehead.

"That was a paw pat. It means I no longer want to continue this conversation. I didn't hit you hard, stop staring at me like that." Alexis stretched out her legs and propped her feet on the coffee table. "So what do you wanna talk about now?"

Jason pulled his car into a space in front of Stacy's apartment, put it in park, and sat staring straight ahead. His hair was mussed, and he looked as though someone had dragged his

41

body across a makeup counter. Mascara and eye shadow stained the front of his shirt. Stacy sat beside him, looking much the same, and she made no attempt to get out of the car.

"Jason…I love you, but don't ever ask me to break bad news to your mother again."

"For a moment, she sounded like she was speaking a foreign language." Jason squinted and shook his head slowly. "Words, they just kept spilling out of her mouth really loudly, then came the wailing. How does my wanting to get married on the beach translate into me hating her? How does this ruin her life?"

Stacy nodded. "When she clasped her face in her hands and said she knew the minute she gave birth to you that you would break her heart, I knew we were in trouble."

"I stood my ground, though…didn't I?" Jason asked nervously.

"Yes, you did," Stacy replied with a nod. "I was really proud of you, and the way you used the couch pillow to deflect the DVDs she threw at you was quick thinking." Stacy thought for a moment. "Did she call me a demon?"

"Yeah, but she took it back when I convinced her it was my idea, not yours." Jason swallowed hard. "I'm so glad Alana wasn't there to witness that. Her mother is so laid back, I don't think Allison would care if we told her we wanted to get married in her attic. When I go over there to have dinner with them, everything is so casual and warm. They use the same fork for the salad and main course, sometimes even dessert."

Stacy smiled. "That sounds really nice," she said and gazed at Jason. "Are you okay?"

"I'm good. Wait. When we left, Mom did understand that I'm not changing my plans?"

Stacy opened her door and laughed. "She threw a slice of pecan pie at you, so I'm ninety-nine percent sure the answer to that question is yes."

Chapter Seven

Sunday was Stacy's lazy day. She normally slept in, but she got up early that morning and worked nonstop until well into the afternoon setting up her new temporary home in anticipation of a visit from one of her oldest and dearest friends. When Ashley Archer knocked on the door, Stacy threw it open and practically leapt on her.

"You're crushing your present," Ashley said with a laugh as Stacy hugged her.

"I've missed you so much." Stacy gave Ashley another squeeze and dragged her inside. She grinned at the plant Ashley handed her. "You know I'm going to kill this, right?"

"No, you're not." Ashley held up a bottle of champagne. "Show me your new place, then let's drink this."

Stacy twirled in a circle. "This is the kitchen and living area, and my bedroom is through that doorway. It's tiny but temporary."

"Well, what it lacks in size, it makes up for in style." Ashley moved past the bar dividing the kitchen from the living room and noticed boxes yet to be unpacked. "Please tell me you have glasses somewhere."

Stacy set the plant on a table by the window and joined Ashley in the kitchen. "You've gotten spoiled. I remember a time when you and I drank right out of the bottle."

Ashley ran a hand through her short graying brown hair. "I've grown up, and I'm more sophisticated now. I eat my Apple Jacks out of a bowl instead of a Solo cup," she said and smiled when Stacy handed her a wineglass. "This will do."

"My champagne glasses are probably still at Jason's. I had to store some things there. I'm debating on buying a house, and this place came with a very short-term lease." Stacy opened the champagne, filled Ashley's glass, then her own. She raised her glass and said, "To sweet reunions."

Ashley tapped Stacy's glass and took a sip. "All right, out with it. What happened with you and Janey?"

"Let's go sit down." Stacy led Ashley to the sofa where they took a seat. "Let me see," she said with a sigh. "The last time we talked, Janey and I were on our second break. Nothing improved after that, we were still arguing and getting on each other's nerves. We finally had that one big blowout, and we realized it wasn't going to work, so here I am. Now let's talk about something fun. You mentioned a lot of travel in your future when we spoke on the phone. What's that all about?"

"Last summer after school let out, I sat around the house eating and gaining weight. I told myself I wouldn't do that again this year. So when Diane told me she was taking someone else's route for two weeks and it was going through Baton Rouge, I told her to get me on that flight. I'm going to spend a week with my sister, then I'll go up to Salt Lake and see my mother. After that, Diane and I are going to spend a week and a half in the Bahamas with some people she knows from work."

"It must be nice being married to a commercial pilot," Stacy said with a smile.

"Well, it is, and it isn't. We aren't in each other's hair all the time, but when I really want her to be available to do something with me, she's at work. While I was accepting my teacher of the year award, she was flying somewhere over the country." Ashley pointed at Stacy. "You need a pilot because you're a woman who appreciates alone time."

"I used to be," Stacy said with a wan smile. "I still am, but I miss having someone to curl up next to. Janey and I didn't do a whole lot of that over the past year. I've been lonely."

"Don't let that get you into trouble. Loneliness sometimes leads us to make bad decisions. Your taste in women is shit. Pick a good one this time based on her character and common

44

interests you share, instead of going for looks and how great she is in bed."

Stacy sucked her teeth. "Thanks, friend."

"All right, I'll say it. I told you so. I told you Janey was not the woman for you, and honestly, I can't believe y'all stayed together as long as you did. You mistook arrogance for confidence. Janey was rude and shallow. The only thing you two had in common was you were both female, and that's it."

Stacy nodded and sighed. "I thought opposites were supposed to attract."

"That's all they do—attract. If you actually want to enjoy a long-term relationship with someone, make sure you at least have some common interests." Ashley smiled. "Forgive me, I'm lecturing. What else is going on in your life?"

"Jason is getting married."

Ashley blinked rapidly. "Who? I'm sure you don't mean your cousin who swore he'd never be tied down."

Stacy laughed. "He met Alana eight months ago and proposed to her right off the bat. She comes from a completely different background, raised by a single mother who lived with her parents in what Jason describes as a tiny house. Alana didn't go to college, she's a hairdresser. You know my Aunt Audrey didn't approve of Alana at first, maybe she still doesn't, but she fakes it well. She made the mistake of saying something negative about Alana one day, and I have never seen Jason yell at anyone like he did Audrey. I knew his feelings for Alana were truly real then."

"Was Alana there?" Ashley asked with concern.

"No, but unfortunately, I was. Jason has never raised his voice to his mother before then, but he berated her so harshly I actually felt sorry for Audrey. Last night, he made me go with him to tell her that he has decided to get married on the beach on Cape San Blas, which means Audrey can't invite half of Baton Rouge as she planned. This time, she did the screaming at both of us."

Ashley laughed. "You and Jason always did like to keep it simple. I remember when we were in college and you invited me to your parents' house for some party they were having. I had to

45

wear one of your dresses because I didn't own anything I felt would be worthy of the event. Everybody was dressed so elegant, and there was so much expensive champagne and food, and I felt like a princess at a ball. I lost you, then I found you with Jason in one of the rooms playing video games. You had your shoes off, feet propped up, a Tootsie Roll hanging out of your mouth like a cigar. I could see the spandex shorts you were wearing under your dress. You didn't give a shit about anything happening at the party."

Stacy laughed. "No, my idea of a good time is still pizza and video games or movies with friends. You know, I often think of Dee and how we all thought she was so prim and proper until we got her to drink beer, and she belched the alphabet."

"And they weren't dainty little burps, either. She sounded like a bullfrog."

"I miss our college days," Stacy said with a winsome smile.

Alexis patted her stomach happily as she rode in the backseat of Jason's car. "I am so full. I got so engrossed in the movie I didn't realize I was eating your sliders too."

"Sure," Alana said as she glanced over her shoulder. "I guess you didn't realize you ate my slice of cheesecake, either."

"No, I was well aware of that." Alexis yawned. "I like that theater. I'll go see more movies now that I can stretch out in a recliner and have food delivered by pushing a button. Hey, thanks for inviting me."

Jason glanced in the rearview and smiled. "You're welcome. I hope you don't mind, but I have to run by Stacy's new place for a second before we take you home. I found the bolts that go to the frame of her bed, and she needs them."

"No problem," Alexis said as cheerily as she could manage.

Alana looked over her shoulder again and mouthed, *You behave.*

For Jason's sake, Alexis decided to try to take the high road. "So... how does Stacy like her new place?"

"She's happy with it for now," Jason replied. "I think she's going to get tired of it pretty fast because it's very small."

"She's thinking about buying a house, so she's just gonna live there for a little while," Alana added.

"Oh, cool. I really hope that works out for her." Alexis smiled as sweetly as she could when Alana glanced at her again. When they pulled up in front of Stacy's building, Alexis made no attempt to get out, figuring that Jason would simply drop the bolts off. When he got out of the car, Alana opened her door and said, "Get out, Lex, don't be rude."

"But I'm really good at it. I should probably wait here."

"Go inside, say hello, and be polite," Alana ground out. "You're gonna have to see her again, so you may as well bite the bullet now. Don't embarrass me in front of Jason."

Alexis got out of the car with a huff. Jason was waiting for them on the sidewalk. "Everything okay?"

"Uh-huh," Alana replied, then narrowed her eyes at Alexis.

They walked up to the door, and Jason knocked. Stacy opened it and looked completely stunned to see them all. "Hey...um—hey."

"Sorry to come by without warning." Jason held up the bag containing the bolts and a couple of wrenches. "I can have your mattress off the floor in less than five minutes."

"Oh, great, come in," Stacy said and stepped out of the way. "Jason, you remember Ashley?"

"Well, hey, girl, I haven't seen you in ages." Jason rushed over to hug Ashley as she stood.

Alexis stood back while Jason introduced Alana to Stacy's friend and listened to them talk about the upcoming wedding. She glanced at Stacy, who was staring at her. "Nice place, congratulations," Alexis said and looked away.

"This is my soon-to-be sister-in-law, Alexis Holt," Jason said, drawing her into the conversation. "Alexis, this is Stacy's best friend, Ashley Archer."

Alexis walked over to Ashley and said, "It's very nice to meet you."

"We're going to fix the bed," Jason said suddenly and dragged Alana toward the bedroom. "Y'all chat."

Alexis felt extremely awkward. Stacy did too, and they stared at each other for a moment, neither knowing what to say.

Ashley picked up on the tension and gazed at both of them oddly.

"Um…the last time I saw you, I think you were threatening to waffle my butt," Alexis said with a tight smile.

"And you called me a bitch."

"Oh," Ashley said wide-eyed and sat down.

Alexis held up a finger. "I used the playful sense of the word biatch. That's usually reserved for friendly chatting like when you see someone you know and you say, 'What's up, biatch?' Are you hearing the difference? I think it's in the dictionary."

"Uh-huh," Stacy replied with a nod. "Would you like some champagne?"

"No, thank you. We just went to the movie theater where you push a button on your chair and they bring you food. I pushed it a lot. I think I have a callous on the tip of my index finger." Alexis raised her voice slightly. "How's it going in there, need my help?"

"Almost done, we're fine," Jason replied.

Alana did, too, in a softer tone. "You idiot."

The room fell silent again. Alexis and Stacy remained standing, and Stacy asked, "Would you like to sit down?"

"No, I'm good. They're only gonna be a minute." Alexis pointed at the ivy on the bar. "Nice little golden pothos."

Ashley perked up. "Ah, you're a plant lover, too."

"Alexis owns a garden center," Stacy explained and took a seat on the arm of a chair.

"I bring Stacy a plant every time I visit, and she kills it." Ashley sighed. "I still hold out hope of making a green thumb out of her one day."

Alexis nodded. "That ivy is a good starter plant. Any idiot…" She inhaled sharply when one of Stacy's eyebrows shot up. "I mean, anyone can grow that particular ivy."

Alexis knew she'd offended Stacy again and tried to think of something nice to say as she took in Stacy's appearance. Stacy was clad in a T-shirt and gym shorts, and her hair was in a ponytail. She looked very youthful, so Alexis attempted a compliment. She smiled at Stacy and said, "You look like a little kid."

"Excuse me?" Stacy asked with a slight frown.

"You um…" Alexis cleared her throat. "You don't look how…ever old you are."

At least Ashley caught on to Alexis's intention and said, "I know. She's thirty-eight, and she still looks like she did in college. Some days, I hate her for that."

"Okay, the bed is up, and we're leaving so you can enjoy your company." Jason walked briskly back into the room with Alana right behind him.

Ashley stood abruptly. "Don't rush off because of me."

"We'd love to visit, but we have to get Lex to her shock treatments, and I promised my mom I'd cut her hair," Alana said as she pulled Alexis toward the door. "It was nice to meet you, Ashley."

"Likewise."

"I told you to be polite," Alana said once she and Alexis were outside.

"I did and stop treating me like a child. Let go of my arm. I could've gone off on that woman for leading living plants to the slaughter. I was gonna apologize for being rude at your dinner, but I didn't want to do it in front of an audience. I tried to be pleasant."

Alana laughed ruefully. "Well, that was an epic fail, biatch."

"Oh, there's a story I need to hear," Ashley said after Stacy closed the door behind Jason. "What is up between you and that woman?"

Stacy told Ashley about what happened at the engagement party and the night she had dinner at Alana and Jason's house. "I haven't seen Alexis since that night," she said and sighed. "I need to get her number from Alana to give her a call. I need to apologize for what happened at the party because I'm one of Alana's bridesmaids, and Alexis is the maid of honor. We're going to have to work together."

"She's really nice-looking."

"Yes," Stacy agreed with a nod. "Very."

49

"Are you attracted to her?" Ashley asked excitedly. "You couldn't seem to take your eyes off her, but I thought it was because y'all were about to fistfight."

Stacy gazed at Ashley for a moment. "I have to admit something to you. I think you're the only person on the planet who might understand aside from Jason, but I'm not ready to tell him this."

"Okay," Ashley said as she made herself comfortable.

"I kind of...stalked Alexis before I met her."

"Oh, shit, I need more champagne. Go get the bottle."

Stacy got up and went into the kitchen. "Long story short, Jason told me to go to Alexis's garden center website and check out Alana in a video, and that's where I saw Alexis." She returned and refilled Ashley's glass and her own before she took a seat on the sofa. "I developed this crazy crush on her the second I saw her. It was during the long break with Janey. I...had a lot of vivid sexual fantasies starring Alexis."

"What kind of videos does she have on her website?" Ashley asked with her brow furrowed.

"Gardening tips and advice." Stacy blew out a heavy breath. "Alexis became an escape for me. I made her into a fantasy lover who was perfect in every way. I offended her, and she's been a complete dick, and it couldn't have turned out better. I stopped watching her videos and fantasizing about her, and when she walked in here a few minutes ago, my pulse started racing, and I realized I'm really attracted to someone who despises me, and I kinda don't like her."

"Oh, girl, can you make your life any more difficult?" Ashley threw back her head and laughed.

Stacy smiled, then chuckled. "I'm so stupid."

Dear Me,

When I was in sixth grade, I developed a crush on Samantha Creel, who was in the eighth grade. She could play any sport, and she was one of the coolest girls in school. I felt like I had swallowed a vibrator every time I saw her. I walked into the bathroom once, and she and her friends were hanging out in there. I remember they all stopped talking and looked at me. I'd invaded their territory, and they didn't seem to know how they felt about that.

I walked into Stacy's apartment today, and it was just like being in that bathroom again with that vibrator rumbling around in my stomach. I should've done what I did way back then and just backed out of the door without saying a word.

Maybe that's why Stacy gets under my skin. Had I gone to school with her, she no doubt would've been one of the cool kids who didn't like little dorks like me. So many years have passed since my school days, and that little dork still lives inside of me. Apparently, that damn vibrator does too.

Okay, I can admit she's hot right here on paper I intend to burn. I really hate that. I finally meet a woman who makes that vibrator fire up, and I can't stand her. It's been so long since I've looked at someone and felt my insides jiggle. Why did it have to be her?

Me

51

Chapter Eight

"Firstborn is here, let the feeding begin," Alexis announced as she let herself into her childhood home.

"In the kitchen, sweetie," Elise replied.

Alexis strolled in and noted with disappointment that there was nothing cooking. Elise was sitting at the kitchen table and in front of a small easel with a canvas perched on it. She looked very intent as she painted.

"When did you start doing this?" Alexis asked as she moved behind Elise to see what she was working on. "And why are you painting a penis?"

"Shut your mouth, that's a banana," Elise retorted, completely flabbergasted.

"It's got balls, and it's flesh colored."

"Those are oranges, and I ran out of yellow, so I mixed a little white with the orange paint." Elise pointed to the canvas with her brush. "Look, you can clearly see the dish I sketched beneath it and...oh, dear Lord, it does look like a penis."

Alexis nodded with a grin. "And it doesn't look like it's lying on a dish. It appears to be rising to the occasion." Alexis picked up a smaller canvas and gazed at Elise's artwork. "What is this?"

"Why, it's a vagina, dear, surely you can identify that."

"No, this is clearly a flower, but I just don't know what kind it is." Alexis turned the canvas back and forth.

"It was going to be a rose, but the more I worked on it, the thing started to look like a gardenia. That's where all my yellow paint went." Elise sighed and dropped her brush into a cup of cleaning fluid. "Your mom is on a date, and I'm craving Chinese, so how about it?"

Alexis paid the delivery boy, then carried the bag of food into the kitchen where Elise had cleaned and set the table. "Here are eggrolls and your noodles and spicy chicken, you must be planning on killing a few roses tomorrow," Alexis said as she set out the containers.

"I'll have some peppermint tea after dinner," Elise said. "I'm glad you came over. We need to discuss your duties as maid of honor."

Alexis frowned. "Duties? I thought I was supposed to stand next to her and give her Jason's ring."

"Oh, no, there's much more involved." Elise tore open the containers and spooned food onto her plate. "You'll have to shop for her dress with her, you'll also have to help pick out the bridesmaids dresses. You'll have to plan and host the bridal shower and bachelorette party, coordinate the bridesmaids, but that won't be hard, there are only two besides you. You're basically Alana's right hand in all the preparations."

Alexis sank down slowly into a chair, her food cartons remained unopened. "Grammy, I don't know anything about that stuff. I've only gone to two weddings in my life, and I was ten years old at one of them."

"Your mother and I will help you. I'm sure Stacy and Rene will too. Stacy has a huge family, and I'm certain she's been in more weddings than you can shake a stick at, so she'll be a wealth of information."

"Stacy?" Alexis asked, still unable to connect the dots.

"Jason's cousin, the one you attacked with a badminton racket." Elise gazed at Alexis's confused expression. "She's one of the bridesmaids, didn't you know that?"

"No, and I didn't know about Rene either."

"Alana didn't discuss this with you when she asked you to be her maid of honor?" Elise asked in surprise.

"No, she asked me if I would do it, and that's all she said about it. I need to resign, this is way out of my league. I honestly thought all I'd be doing is standing there with her when she took her vows."

"You can't resign, silly. This is a big honor your sister has bestowed upon you. She wants you, her sister, to help her plan her big day. You can't let her down."

"Surely she knows that I don't know anything about this kind of stuff. I agreed to wear a dress! Isn't that enough?"

"No," Elise said firmly. "If you can run a business, you can do this."

"I don't like Stacy," Alexis snapped.

"You look and sound like a petulant child. Wipe that scowl off your face. Now I know Alana explained to you what happened at the engagement party, if you can't let that go—"

"Explained what?"

Elise's brow shot up, and she blinked rapidly. "The reason Stacy was rude to you."

"Alana hasn't told me anything about that. What do you know? Tell me now!"

Elise threw her napkin on the table and exclaimed, "My stars, you girls are terrible communicators. Get your sister on the phone and tell her to come over here right now."

When Alana walked into the kitchen, Alexis said, "You've got some explaining to do."

"About what?" Alana said, looking at Alexis and Elise.

"Honey, you haven't told Alexis what Jason told you about the engagement party," Elise said calmly.

"Well, I was hoping they'd talk it all out this past Sunday when we went to Stacy's apartment, but Stacy had company and Alexis…" Alana shook her head. "I can't relive that. It was so awkward."

Alexis narrowed her eyes. "Did you take me over there for that reason?"

"No, we had to give her the bolts." Alana shrugged. "And Jason and I thought it might be a good opportunity for you and Stacy to talk. We were both kind of hoping she'd explain her side of the story to you, and for once, you'd be open-minded."

"You tell me her story," Alexis said and folded her arms.

54

Alana smacked her lips. "Okay, it goes like this, Lex. When you walked up to Stacy at the party, she and Janey were fighting because Janey is insanely jealous, and she was drunk. Stacy was afraid if she was nice to you, Janey would lose it and cause a scene. She felt bad about that."

"Yeah, she sure seemed to be feeling guilty that night I had dinner at your place. She could barely say two words to me. Oh, wait, she did, she called me a shuttlecock."

"You were a shit that night." Alana changed her tone and made it flat. "'I sell plants and poo.' That was your contribution to the conversation. Shuttlecock means birdie, Alexis!"

"That was not what I said or how I said it," Alexis argued. "And hey, why didn't you tell me she was a bridesmaid the night you asked me to be maid of honor?"

Alana threw her hands up. "I hadn't asked her then, but when I did, she didn't have any problem when I told her you were the maid of horror."

"This really takes me back to the days when you girls were pre-teens," Elise said and bit into an eggroll. "I wanted to beat you both then too. Alexis, you're being difficult and childish for no good reason, and it needs to stop today, do you hear me?"

Elise's tone hit Alexis like a slap. "Yes, ma'am," she replied as some of the fire drained out of her.

"Alana, you need to be more forthcoming with information. Alexis is completely in the dark about your plans."

Alana pointed at Alexis. "This is why. I was really hoping if I kept them apart for a while, Lex would forget about being mad at Stacy."

"That would only work if you were marrying Jason ten years from now, but the wedding is a few months away." Elise waved a hand at the two of them. "Fix this."

Alana pursed her lips and asked, "Did Stacy say something unforgiveable to you that day?"

"No, but her girlfriend was a complete bitch."

"Right, she was, and that's why Stacy broke up with her. I am one hundred percent positive if Janey had not been there, you and Stacy would've hit it off immediately. She's really nice and

55

down to earth with a fantastic sense of humor. If you would just spend some time with her, you'd see that."

"Your sister holds a grudge like a mountain climber does a rope." Elise chuckled. "Just like her grandfather. It comes naturally to her, so, Alana, be patient and understanding. Did you also neglect to tell Alexis that we're going wedding dress shopping this Saturday, and Stacy is coming with us?"

"No," Alana replied, meeting Alexis's gaze. "I wasn't gonna make you do any of that because I knew you'd be miserable."

"You hear that, Alexis? Your sister who loves you is considering your feelings."

"All right, Grammy." Alexis gritted her teeth for a moment. "As maid of honor, that's one of my duties, and I wanna be there."

Alana bent down and kissed Alexis's cheek. "That makes me happy."

Elise smiled. "Oh, good, the adults are back."

"Grammy painted a penis." Alexis grabbed the canvas and held it up.

Alana's jaw sagged as she stared at it, and Elise got flustered again. "It's a banana!"

"Grammy, where are you getting your fruit from?" Alana asked.

Chapter Nine

When Alana invited Stacy to go dress shopping with her, she'd mentioned that Alexis wouldn't be going. Stacy had interpreted that as Alexis's refusal to be around her, so she didn't ask for Alexis's number and decided not to apologize. On Saturday morning, when Stacy opened her door to Alana, she was surprised to see Alexis standing beside her.

"Hey—" Stacy gawked at Alexis's blue T-shirt; it was identical to the one she was wearing right down to the muddy hiking boots design on the chest. Their jeans even looked the same. She recovered quickly and said, "Where's your shirt, Alana, didn't you get the dress code memo?"

"I must've missed out on that," Alana replied with a laugh.

"Come in, I'll just go change since we aren't all in uniform. I don't want you to feel awkward," Stacy joked with a smile.

Alexis went straight to the ivy that Stacy had moved to a windowsill. She snatched the plant and held it up to Alana. "Look at this! She's scorching it. The woman's an animal!"

"She probably didn't know any better," Alana whispered. "Put it down."

Stacy walked back into the room and noticed Alexis holding the plant. "Hey, why is it looking so bad?"

"You may as well have it on a rotisserie," Alexis snapped, then softened her tone. "Your ivy isn't happy in the direct sunlight coming from the window. They do like light, just not direct sunlight. You're watering it too much too, that's why it has some yellow leaves."

"I really don't want to kill it. Where do you suggest I put it?" Stacy asked.

Alexis walked around cradling the pot like a baby. "You have fluorescent lighting in your kitchen, they like that." She walked over to the window by the table. "Do you open these blinds a lot?"

Stacy shook her head. "Not really, it's just a view of a wall."

Alexis set the ivy on the table. "I would put it here on a plant stand. It doesn't like soggy soil. It'll tell you when it needs water because the leaves will droop. The best way to tell if it needs to be watered is to stick your fingers in the dirt to see if it feels dry. Now you can give it a dash of coffee—no sweeteners or cream—and that will really bring out the variegation in the leaves. If you make it happy and give it something to climb on, it'll grow all over the place. I have one in my loft, and it's taken over the railing. It's going to need a new pot. This container is too small, and it's root bound already."

"I'll take your advice because I'd really like it to be pretty when Ashley comes back into town," Stacy said. "So thank you."

Alexis nodded. "Welcome."

"Okay, let's move." Alana headed for the door. "Please don't get her started talking about plants. She'll give you the same lecture she gives me. 'Alana, are plants alive? Are dogs alive? Would you forget to give a dog water?'"

"Will it grow up my wall?" Stacy asked as she and Alexis followed Alana.

"Oh, yeah, give it something to attach to, and it'll go crazy if you take care of it. I won't bore you with the botanical name, but it's most commonly referred to as golden pothos or devil's ivy." Alexis grinned. "Your friend must've thought it would suit you. That was a joke, by the way."

"A sense of humor is a sign of intelligence," Stacy said as she locked her door. "I'm really surprised you were able to make a funny." She wrinkled her nose and smiled when Alexis shot her a look. "That was a joke too."

When they arrived at the bridal boutique, Allison and Elise were waiting for them in the parking lot. "Why didn't your mother and grandmother ride with us?" Stacy asked when she spotted them.

"Mom says she's worried Grammy will tire out before we're done, so she drove her own car. The truth is, Mom wanted her escape pod. She's really not fond of any place that doesn't have men in it," Alana replied.

Alexis tried to keep a pleasant expression on her face when she got out of her truck and gazed at the dresses on display in the windows of the boutique. She had never had a colonoscopy before but figured that procedure had to be infinitely more enjoyable than wedding dress shopping. After Stacy exchanged hugs with Allison and Elise, they all entered the shop. Alexis brought up the rear, feeling like a lamb being led to slaughter.

"Hi, my name is Alana Holt, I have a ten o'clock appointment," Alana said to the woman who greeted them.

Alexis leaned close to her mother and whispered, "Do you actually have to make an appointment to come in here, and why does it look like a funeral parlor? Where's the dresses?"

"Just go with the flow, Alexis," Allison answered softly.

A tiny waif of a woman walked into the foyer on a pair of extremely high heels. Her hair was wrapped around her head like a blond turban. "Hello, I'm Karen," she said in a soft voice and took Alana's hand. "It's so very nice to meet you. Please follow me to your suite."

Alexis leaned close to her mother again as they followed and whispered, "I seriously think we're in a funeral parlor, and we're about to be shown a body in a casket."

They were escorted into a windowless room with a seating area made up of couches and high-backed chairs facing a small dais. A rolling rack was against one wall and held what looked like a dozen dresses. On the opposite wall was a table that held trays of pastries and fruit, a carafe of coffee, and another carafe labeled "caution water extremely hot." There were cups on saucers and small serving plates.

Karen gestured toward the table. "Please make yourself welcome. We have assorted teas, coffee, water, and juice. Alana,

59

I have the dresses you requested, and I also brought out a few more for you to consider. I selected them with your venue in mind." Karen pushed the other dresses away from one in particular. "This dress was the one you chose online as your first choice. Would you like to try it on?"

"Yes," Alana replied excitedly.

Everyone else stood around when Karen took Alana into the fitting room, and once the door closed, Stacy said, "Jason gave me his credit card with explicit instructions. Regardless of the price, Alana is to get the dress she wants."

Allison melted. "He is so sweet."

"And brave," Alexis added. "Does Alana know that?"

"No, it's a surprise. He looked at them online with her, and there was one she really liked but thought it was too expensive. He bookmarked the page when Alana wasn't looking and emailed it to me. It's on my phone," Stacy said as she set it on the coffee table of the seating area. "If either of you can get Karen away from Alana, give her the phone, so she can pull the dress."

"Ladies, we have our mission," Alexis said with a serious tone. "Mom and Grammy have to find a way to distract Alana, so one of us can get to Karen."

Allison nodded. "Got it."

"I'm down with it," Elise said and set her purse on the floor. One of her brows arched when Alexis looked at her oddly. "What?"

"Down with it?"

"You know what that means. I'm game," Elise replied and straightened her blouse.

"Mom had an embarrassing incident at the store this morning, and now she's decided to learn urban slang," Allison explained with a smile. "She—"

"No, let me tell it." Elise cleared her throat. "I was in the checkout line at the market, and the girl working the counter pointed at my purse and said, 'That's straight dope.' I thought she had seen the prescription bottle in my bag when I opened it to get my wallet. There were rough-looking people in the line behind me, and I thought she'd announced that I was carrying drugs, and I got mad. I told her very loudly that all I had was antacids, and she ought not be accusing people of having dope, especially old ladies, and I wanted to see her manager. The woman working the other counter politely explained to me that the girl was complimenting my purse, straight dope means cool, stylish, or pretty. I was gonna learn Spanish to keep my old brain fresh, but the language of the youth is much more interesting."

"Keep it real, Grammy." Alexis held out her fist, and Elise stared at it. "You bump it with yours. It's like a high five."

"What's the going rate on a wedding dress nowadays?" Allison asked.

"I'm not really sure about beach wedding dresses." Stacy pursed her lips and stared at the ceiling as she thought. "I would guess somewhere between seven hundred to two thousand at this boutique."

"What?" Alexis practically yelled.

"Shh!" Allison shook a finger at Alexis. "Keep your voice low."

"Well, I'm sorry, Mom, that's crazy."

The fitting room door opened, and Alana beamed as she walked out and stepped onto the dais. "Okay, everyone, be honest and tell me what you think."

"It's...elegant?" Stacy shook her head. "No, it's..."

"Underwear." Alexis frowned. "It looks like something you would wear under a dress."

"It's a summer dress, designed for beach weddings," Karen explained. "It's a bit less traditional."

"Turn around slowly, honey, and give us the full effect," Elise suggested.

Alana turned and stared at her reflection in the surrounding mirrors. "I don't want a lot of heavy silk and lace, but I have to agree with Alexis, this one is too...well, there's not quite enough of it."

"Okay, very good," Karen said, maintaining her smile. "Let's try something else."

"I'm going to the restroom," Elise said as soon as Karen and Alana went into the changing room. "If she comes out before I get back, tell her to wait on me. Allison, come with me, I don't want to get lost."

Alexis and Stacy were in the room alone together. "I'm sorry for the way I behaved the night we had dinner," Alexis said. "I was rude, I apologize."

Stacy tucked her hands into the pockets of her jeans and rocked back on her heels. "Janey and I were fighting when you walked over at the engagement party. I'm very sorry for what she said to you, and I regret that I didn't say something to her then about it. I was afraid she would become even more obnoxious and cause a scene. I did intend to speak to you again that day and explain what happened, but I wasn't able to find you."

"I took a walk. I prefer small get-togethers where I at least know most of the people."

"Me too. I usually avoid my family's parties. I wouldn't have gone to that one if it hadn't been for Jason and Alana. I didn't know half the people there, either." Stacy laughed. "I was miserable, my shoes hurt my feet, and that dress was too tight. I was afraid to eat anything or bend over because I was sure the fabric would split. I went home and put on baggy shorts and ate cold pizza."

Alexis grimaced and rubbed the back of her neck. "I don't know anything about being a maid of honor, so any advice you can give me would be greatly appreciated."

"Well, you may not have as many duties as you'd normally have in that role. My aunt Audrey will take over just about everything. If that doesn't bother you, then you'll be fine. I'm sure Jason didn't tell her what we're doing today, or Audrey would've invited herself along." Stacy smiled when Alana walked out of the changing room. "That's very pretty."

"But is it too much?" Alana asked, looking unsure.

Alexis squinted. "Are you wearing shoulder pads?"

"No, that's how the dress is made. It gives the impression that the neckline plunges deeper," Karen explained.

Alana turned on the dais and looked at her reflection in the mirror. "I'm so sorry, Karen. I don't think I like this one, either."

62

"That's quite all right. We want you completely happy with your choice, and you may try on as many as you please. It's no inconvenience to me."

"Don't go yet," Alexis said when Alana moved toward the changing room. "Mom and Grammy are in the bathroom, but they wanted to see what you came out in next."

"Well," Alana began with a sigh, "regardless of what they say, it won't be this one. They'll be back by the time I put on the next one."

Alexis waited until Alana went back into the changing room and said, "She's stressing. She sucks her bottom lip in when she starts feeling pressured."

"I'll go talk to someone—where's my phone?" Stacy asked and looked around for it.

Alexis searched for it too. "I bet Mom and Grammy had the same idea. One of them probably took it."

"I think that's the only logical explanation," Stacy said as Elise and Allison walked into the room.

Allison smiled and handed Stacy her phone. "The dress is on the way."

Alana walked out of the changing room, and before she could get anywhere near the dais, all four of the women said, "No." She turned right back around.

"Karen, may I ask you something?" Allison waved at Alana, who paused in the doorway of the dressing room. "Go on, honey, I just want to borrow Karen for a sec."

When they had Karen alone, Elise said, "Your associate is bringing another dress, and it's a surprise. Would you make sure Alana tries it on after the next one?"

"Certainly," Karen replied with a smile, then rejoined Alana in the dressing room.

"She's so perky and happy. I'll bet she goes home and beheads stuffed animals just to cope with this job," Stacy whispered.

"I couldn't do it. After the third or fourth dress, I'd pick one out and tell the bride-to-be that was her only choice, and if she didn't agree, I would choke her a little bit." Allison winked. "Just a little."

A woman slipped into the room and hung a dress on the rack. She gave Allison a thumbs-up and slipped back out.

"Are we gonna eat when we leave here? If not, I'm about to put a hurting on the snack table," Alexis said, eyeing a croissant.

"I'm going to do that anyway." Stacy left the group and grabbed a pastry.

Alexis watched as Elise and Allison joined Stacy at the table. She did have to admit that Stacy seemed very down to earth and nice. She allowed herself a moment to gaze at Stacy's butt, then had to turn away when her internal vibrator made its presence known. She almost regretted that they had made peace. It was easier to keep a lid on her attraction to Stacy when she despised her.

Alana walked out again, obviously unhappy with the dress she was wearing. "Okay, y'all, I think this is the last one for today. I need to go back to the website and choose some different styles."

Alexis plopped down on one of the couches. "Don't sweat it. We'll stay here until you find the one you want. Try one more. The one Karen just took off the rack looks really pretty."

"Are you sure you don't mind?" Alana asked, looking as though she was about to cry.

"There's food and coffee, and this couch is comfy. It's all good, sis."

"Okay, one more," Alana said as she stepped off the dais. When she returned a few minutes later, she was met with a chorus of oohs and ahhs. "Now that is straight dope," Elise said with a huge smile. "Give me my props, people. I used the term correctly in a sentence."

Chapter Ten

"Oh, my God," Alana said with her eyes brimming with tears. "I can't. I can't get that dress, it's too expensive."

Everyone sat gathered around Alana on the sofa, except for Stacy, who knelt in front of Alana and took her hand. "Jason sent me the link to that dress because he knew you loved it, and he thinks you'll look even more beautiful in it. He doesn't care how much it costs. Is that the dress you want?"

"Yes," Alana replied with a sniff. "But I don't want him paying for it. Tradition says I'm supposed to be responsible for my dress."

"I'll buy it," Alexis said. She would've bought two of them if it meant they could leave the boutique.

Alana nodded. "Okay, I'm good with that."

"No, wait," Stacy said. "You two aren't having a traditional wedding, so there's no reason to stick to tradition here. Jason was adamant, he wants to buy the dress, so please let him."

Alana's face was flushed, and she closed her eyes. "I have to think."

Stacy stood and motioned for Alexis to follow her to the condiment table. She stood with her back to Alana and whispered, "That dress is fifteen hundred dollars."

"I feel faint, hold me." Alexis braced herself by putting a hand on the table.

"Help me convince your sister to allow Jason to buy the dress."

Alexis walked over to where Alana sat. "Jason's feelings are gonna be hurt if you don't let him pay for it. This is a gift to you, so you have to accept it, or I have to kill you."

"I can't believe we got a dress on the first day," Elise said with a smile and raised her glass. "To the thrill of the hunt, may we be as lucky next weekend when we search for bridesmaids dresses and may we get Mexican food again, too."

"Oh, yay," Alexis deadpanned and held up her glass to the toast.

"Hopefully, Rene will be able to come with us to shop for those. She had to work." Alana frowned. "She would've loved to have gone with us today."

Elise sighed and stood. "Well, I have to make another trip to the ladies' room."

"I'll join you," Allison said.

Alana jumped up. "Me too."

"We're gonna have to go through this again with bridesmaids dresses," Alexis said wearily. "What's the next hurdle after that?"

"The bridal shower. I suggest you ask Alana if she wants to have it here in town instead of at the beach. She may have friends who can't travel to attend the wedding. Either way, we have to get a guest list from her with addresses and phone numbers. The next step would be getting the shower invitations done and sent out."

Alexis pressed her margarita glass to her forehead. "I've never been to a bridal shower. What do people do at them?"

"Um…they play stupid games, and you have to supply prizes for the winners."

"Oh," Alexis whined and sank lower in her chair.

"They'll eat finger food and drink beverages you also supply."

"Shit." Alexis sank lower.

"Then she'll open her gifts, and you have to keep track of what she got and who it was from so she can send out thank-you cards." Stacy chuckled. "If you get any lower, you're going to be on the floor. Remember what I told you. Audrey will definitely

66

take this over. She lives for things like this. She'll want to host it at her house, and she'll have it catered. She'll foot the bill, all you have to do is agree."

"What's wrong with you?" Alana asked Alexis when she returned to the table.

"Stacy and I were just talking about your bridal shower. Do you want to have it here before you leave for Florida so more of your friends can come?"

Alana looked like a deer caught in headlights. "Do I have to have one?"

"One what?" Allison asked when they rejoined the group.

"A bridal shower," Stacy said.

"Why wouldn't you want one?" Elise asked. "That's when you get a bunch of gifts."

"Stacy, please don't take offense to this, but I don't know how well my friends will gel with your family. My girls are kinda wild and crazy," Alana said, looking really uncomfortable.

Stacy laughed. "Good because my people are stiff and boring. Don't stress or spend time worrying about what my family will think, and please don't let them stop you from enjoying everything that goes with a wedding. This is your celebration."

Elise poked Alana in the arm. "Have your shower, baby."

Alana nodded. "I'll think about it."

When they arrived at Stacy's apartment, Stacy didn't immediately get out of Alexis's truck. "Alexis, I need your phone number, so we can discuss the shower plans."

Alexis gave Stacy hers, then added Stacy's to her phone. "Stacy says we need a list of everyone you want to invite, and you still have to tell us if you want to have it here," Alexis said.

"I really don't want to have one at all. If people want to give gifts, can't they just bring them to the wedding?" Alana sucked her bottom lip in as her neck flushed.

Stacy was seated behind Alexis and could see the signs of stress on Alana that Alexis had mentioned. She reached up and patted Alana on the shoulder. "Hey, you don't have to do anything you don't want to, this is your show. We'll do whatever you want."

"Thank you, Stacy," Alana said with a weak smile.

"And thank you for inviting me."

"See you later, Stacy," Alexis said as Stacy got out of the truck. She waited until Stacy was in her apartment before she drove away. "All right, sis, tell me what has you on the verge of a nervous breakdown."

"I don't care what Stacy said, my friends can't mingle with the Kirklands. I already feel like they look at me like some gold-digging gutter rat. I can only imagine what they'll think when they see a bunch of hairdressers and bartenders." Alana sniffed as she fought back tears. "I wish Jason's family wasn't rich, that's the only negative thing about us. Everything else is perfect."

Alexis smiled. "You really do love him. Anyone else would consider wealth a positive."

"Jason isn't rich, his parents are. He won't inherit anything until they die. I think they hold that over his head, and I worry they might tell him they'll cut him out of the will if he marries me. I don't want him to have to make that choice. Either way, I lose. If he chooses me, he'll always know I stand in the way of his fortune, and eventually, he may resent me for that. This is precisely why I don't want my friends around them. My girls can get wild and crass. Sadly, that's what makes them so much fun."

"You heard Stacy. You don't have to have a shower if you don't want to."

"I don't even want a wedding." Alana sighed and rubbed her forehead. "I want to marry Jason, but I'd really rather do it in Mom's living room with just you, Mom, Grammy, and even Stacy. She's the only member of Jason's family I feel like I can talk to and be friends with. She doesn't want to be around them, either. She only sees them on the holidays, and Jason says even then she won't stay long. I think her parents and sisters tolerate her being gay, but they don't like it. Jason told me Stacy's mother claims Stacy acts gay because she's rebellious and wants to hurt them."

Anger swept over Alexis. "Jaime's parents claim the same thing. I guess that's the only way a Southern Baptist can rationalize their kid being gay. She tried to make them understand a hundred times, she pleaded with them, but that's the story her folks are sticking with. She doesn't see them much either."

Alana glanced at Alexis. "I noticed y'all seemed to be getting along. Did you talk to her?"

Alexis nodded. "We made nice. I apologized, she apologized, it's all good."

"I'm glad," Alana said with relief. "Thank you. Stacy means a lot to Jason, and I really care about her too. She's a genuinely nice woman, and I think you two will become good friends."

"Maybe so, but I did kinda enjoyed the night we fought during badminton. She's got some fire. I bet her temper makes mine look like a puff of smoke."

"I never saw it when she stayed with us, then again, I don't provoke her like you do." Alana was quiet for a moment and asked, "Do you think she's pretty?"

"Yeah, she's very pretty."

"Do you think...would you go out with her?"

Alexis glanced from the road. "You're about to get another paw pat on the forehead."

Alana laughed softly. "I was just curious. When I first met her, I thought you and her would make a good match. You're both funny."

Dear Me,

I went wedding dress shopping at a former funeral parlor today. I'm certain that's what that place was before they turned it into a boutique. Instead of viewing a dead body, you watch a live one change clothes a lot. It had the same effect on me as a funeral. I wanted to cry, and I couldn't wait for it to be over.

So Stacy and I have reconciled. She's going to help me with my maid of horror duties, which are extensive. That means we're gonna see each other a lot, and I'm not sure how to feel about that. Without my wall of resentment toward her, I'm very vulnerable because she makes my vibrator go crazy. It hasn't hummed like that in a long time. Stacy is incredibly attractive, but maybe the reason I feel drawn to her is that I know I can't have her. She's wine and cheese, and I'm beer and nuts, even though I don't like beer. No, I'm chips and margarita.

Me

70

Chapter Eleven

Stacy was on a mission. She was going to buy a larger pot for the ivy Ashley had given her. Where better to shop than Holt's Garden Center where she'd ask the owner how to go about repotting a plant? That was at least what she told herself her intentions were. Buried beneath the lie was a desire to see if Alexis was anything like the fantasy woman Stacy had created in her head.

She turned into the parking lot of the garden center and was stunned by the amount of cars there. The place was bustling with activity on a Sunday morning. People were loading their vehicles with bags of soil and plants. A couple of employees dressed in green T-shirts with the store's logo were stuffing a fountain into an SUV.

Stacy got out of her car and walked through a gate into a greenhouse filled with tables covered in flowering plants. As she gazed at the throngs of people moving around her, she realized she'd chosen the wrong day to visit the garden center. If she were to find Alexis, she probably wouldn't have a spare moment to chat. As Stacy moved through the crowd, she heard a familiar voice.

"To keep your butterfly bush showy, you'll have to do something we call deadheading. As you can see, the flowers are gone, and what's left behind is an old yucky brown thing. So I'll clip it off just before the leaves on the branch, like so. Give it a couple of days, and you'll see new buds coming in. It's that simple, ladies and gentlemen," Elise said with a smile.

The small crowd gathered around Elise began to disperse, and Stacy made her way over to her. "Good morning, Elise. I wish I would've gotten here sooner, so I could've heard your lesson."

"Well, hello," Elise said and pulled Stacy into a warm hug. "I'll give you all the gardening advice you want anytime."

"I don't think I'm ready for a garden, but I am about to repot an ivy per Alexis's advice. I thought I'd come here to get the pot, a stand, and whatever else I'll need for that job."

Elise took Stacy's hand. "Thank you for what you did yesterday. Alana loves that dress."

"That was all Jason, I was only his assistant," Stacy said with a smile.

"You should join us for dinner sometime—matter of fact, we're getting together Tuesday night. You'll come, won't you?" Elise asked, still clutching Stacy's hand.

"Um…sure. What should I bring?"

"Just you, sweetie. We eat at six, so don't arrive fashionably late." Elise looked past Stacy and said, "Alexis, look who I have here."

"Herbicide on two legs is in our midst. Grammy, make sure she doesn't touch anything with her black thumb," Alexis said as she joined them.

Stacy grinned. "Hey, I'm trying to turn over a new leaf. I'm here to buy a pot and some dirt for the ivy."

"Alexis, I'm going on break in your house on your couch," Elise said and gave Stacy another hug. "Make sure she gives you the family discount."

"Grammy, don't turn my thermostat up to eighty again. I washed your favorite blanket, it's on the back of the couch," Alexis called after Elise as she walked away.

"You live here too?" Stacy asked.

Alexis pointed to the far corner of the sprawling nursery. "My house is behind the fence over there."

"This place is huge, and there's so many people it looks like an outdoor festival. You must be thrilled."

"Oh, I am," Alexis said with a big smile. "It's early summer, and everybody wants to get outside and work in their yards. This is my busiest time of year."

"I shouldn't keep you then. Would you point me toward the pots and the dirt?"

"You're not keeping me from anything." Alexis shrugged. "All I do is wander around and answer questions on days like this."

Stacy's gaze swept over Alexis, who was dressed in a green T-shirt and blue cargo shorts with a radio clipped to her belt. "I'd really like to see your place. Do you have time to give me a tour?"

"Sure," Alexis said happily.

"Okay, why are some of the plants in the greenhouses and others out here in the open?" Stacy asked.

"The area you came through to get in here isn't really a greenhouse, it's open on all sides as you can see. Those are bedding and vegetable plants on those tables. Houseplants are inside the store." Alexis turned and pointed at sections of plants out in the open that seemed to go on for miles. "These are shrubs, roses, and trees," she said as she walked and Stacy followed. "The greenhouse to your left is for shade-loving plants. This is my favorite area over here."

They walked between two greenhouses and entered an area shaded by a large tree. It was like entering a rainforest, fountains were everywhere surrounded by tropical foliage. Stacy sighed as she knelt beside a koi pond and watched the fish swim around. "This is very soothing," she said with a smile.

"It is until my cats, Ginger and Sprout, come over and try to go fishing. We're constantly running them out of here."

"This makes me want to buy a house even more," Stacy said with a sigh.

"You buy a house, and I'll make you a Zen garden. I have one at my place, and that's where I drink my coffee in the mornings. I live in the middle of a bustling commercial area, but you'd never know it in my gardens."

Stacy stood and followed Alexis back into the main area with the plants and shrubs. "What got you into this?"

"My grandparents. Grammy has always loved flowers, and my grandpa enjoyed fruit trees and vegetable gardening. My toes were in the dirt before I was out of diapers. I owe all this to my grandpa. I wish he was here to see what I did with the plot of land he helped me buy. There was nothing out here but the house. As far as you could see, it was all pasture and wetlands. Now everything around me is strip malls, neighborhoods, and competing drugstores on every corner."

"It's lovely. You and Elise seem to be very close. Is it fun to work together?" Stacy asked.

Alexis picked a dead leaf off a bush as they strolled past it. "She doesn't actually work here, but I'd love it if she did. She'll come in every so often on days of her choosing, and we'll set up her table where she likes to dispense advice. I heard her tell a woman earlier today if she couldn't get her husband out of his recliner to mow the grass, she should take the chair into the yard and burn it while he's at work."

Stacy laughed. "I think she's adorable. I wish my grandmother was full of life like her."

"Is she sick?" Alexis asked gently.

"No, she's a jerk. My maternal grandmother was very sweet, but she died when I was in my teens. Lucinda—she does not like to be called Lucy. Jason and I call her Lucifer behind her back. She is perpetually unhappy, and she doesn't like anyone else to be happy, either. She can suck the joy out of a room in a heartbeat."

"I'll bet Christmas at the Kirklands' is a hoot."

"Only if you're heavily sedated," Stacy said as she and Alexis meandered along the rows. "I love my family, but we're all happier if I keep my distance. Jason is the only exception. I'm gay, I don't like to dress up or go to dinner parties, I don't care about social status, so I don't really fit in. I'm the oddball Kirkland."

"You don't sound odd at all to me," Alexis said with a smile.

Stacy glanced at her. "So I'm no longer a butthole cock?"

"I've taken you out of that category for now, but I'm keeping a close eye on you in case I need to put you back in, so don't kill that ivy."

"I'll do my best not to commit herbicide." Stacy stopped and pointed at a plant. "That looks like marijuana."

"Yeah, that's exactly what it is. This is a full-service garden center that caters to all interests."

"I'm pretty certain marijuana doesn't make red flowers, wise ass. What is it really?" Stacy asked with a smile.

"It's a hibiscus." Alexis frowned when a voice came through the radio hooked on her belt. "Lex, I need the keys up front, please."

Alexis grabbed it and replied, "On my way."

"I should let you get back to work now," Stacy said with an apologetic smile.

"Walk with me up to the front, and we'll find a pot for that ivy."

Alexis grabbed a cart and put a bag of soil into it. Stacy picked out a pretty ceramic pot and a stand to place it on, then she was ready to check out. Alexis went with her, and once the clerk gave the total, Alexis said, "Code NC this one." Then she strode out of the store with the cart.

"There's no charge for this, ma'am," the clerk said as Stacy was about to swipe her card.

Stacy stared at the woman in surprise, then realized that Alexis was nowhere in sight. "Uh...thank you." She found Alexis outside and said, "Hey, you have to let me pay for those things. That's why I came here. I wanted to support your business."

"It's a housewarming gift, and I want to give that little ivy a fighting chance." Alexis grinned. "Where's your car?"

"It's the red Maxima parked way over there to the left."

Alexis pointed at a convertible BMW. "I really thought it was that one. I'm so glad I didn't walk over there and put your stuff in it."

"Okay, let's get something straight," Stacy said as she followed Alexis. "I make a good living, but I work hard for it.

Yes, my family is wealthy, but that doesn't show in my bank account, and it won't until they're dead."

Alexis stopped walking and gazed at Stacy. "I didn't mean to offend you."

"You thought I was a rich snob when you met me. I just want to make sure you know I'm not. Let's be clear on something else. If I come back here to shop, I don't expect anything for free. I do, however, want the family discount."

Alexis chuckled. "All right."

Once Alexis had everything loaded into the trunk of Stacy's car, she said, "We're getting together at Mom's Tuesday night for dinner. Jason's coming, so you should too."

"Elise already invited me."

"Good," Alexis said with a nod. "Then you have to come, Grammy has spoken."

Stacy's stomach started doing somersaults as Alexis gazed at her. "She told me not to bring anything, but I want to. What do you suggest?"

Alexis laughed. "You can't go wrong with chocolate."

"Okay, and thank you for the gifts." Stacy gave Alexis a quick hug and stepped back. "I'll see you Tuesday then."

"I think I need psychiatric help," Stacy said when Ashley answered her phone.

"I do too. I'm at my mother's house, and she has bought a karaoke machine. I never dreamed there were so many ways to butcher *I Will Survive*, but Mom has found at least a dozen of them. If I hear that song again, one of us may not *survive* this visit." Ashley blew out a breath. "Tell me what traumatic thing is going on in your life, free me from this musical torture chamber."

"Remember when I told you I made a fantasy woman out of Alexis?"

"How could I forget, biatch?" Ashley replied with a laugh.

"Long story short, we went dress shopping with Alana, and Alexis and I made peace. I wanted to see if she was anything like the fantasy woman I'd made her into, so I went to her garden center today. It was very busy, but she took the time to show me around and chat a little. I found her engaging, interesting to talk to, and very sweet. She refused to let me pay for everything I got to repot the ivy you gave me. I know this sounds crazy, but I think she may be exactly like the fantasy Alexis I created in my mind."

"Most women would be happy about that," Ashley said as music played in the background. "You sound like it's a bad thing."

"It's strange, and I'm kind of scared—"

"You want to know what's frightening? An eighty-year-old woman in hot pink spandex pants singing ...*Baby One More Time*. My mother is going Britney Spears on me. She's air humping, that's just not right."

"I'm sorry. You're visiting with your mom, and I shouldn't be interrupting with my issues."

"No, no! You're not. I'm thrilled to hear words that aren't being sung." Ashley cleared her throat. "You have my undivided attention. Please talk to me."

Stacy sat on her couch and pulled her knees up beneath her chin. "I spent a lot of time with the imaginary Alexis in my head, so when I'm with the real one, there's a feeling of familiarity. In my fantasies, I've thrown my arms around her and kissed her hundreds of times. When I was at the nursery and I was saying goodbye to her, I almost kissed her. I realized what I was doing when I reached for her, so I ended up giving her an awkward slap hug. She just stood there staring at me as though she didn't know what was happening to her."

"What's a slap hug?"

"I just kinda reached around her with one arm, with our bodies barely touching, and I slapped her on the back." Stacy winced. "A little harder than I meant to."

Ashley cackled. "Oh, my God, I wish I could've witnessed that."

"She may have security cameras," Stacy said with a laugh.

"You obviously spent a lot of time with fantasy Alexis."

"I'm embarrassed to admit I did. My imagination was so much better than my reality. Fantasy Alexis didn't try to manipulate me into feeling guilty for not bending over backward

77

for her whims. She communicated with me, instead of leaving clues for me to decipher what she wanted. I, of course, was a much better person too. I had infinite patience, I was romantic and sweet. I didn't roll my eyes once."

"Sweetie, it's time to embrace reality," Ashley said kindly.

"I have. I haven't been to fantasyland since I met the real Alexis face to face, and I don't watch her videos. I feel like I already know her, though, and it's kind of weird."

"What kind of career did she have in your fantasies?" Ashley asked.

Stacy laughed as her face warmed. "Her job was to please me."

"I have that one too, but it involves a plethora of actresses who find me utterly irresistible." Ashley laughed. "They keep me company sometimes when Diane is gone."

"So I'm not weird?"

"Oh, yeah, you are because you've taken fantasy to a whole different level. It's like one of those video games you play where you build an entire kingdom. You know, that might be why your mind works like that. I hope you don't think I'm minimizing your concerns, but I think as you get to know the real woman, everything you have filed in your mind will change."

"And hopefully while that happens, I won't do anything horribly embarrassing."

Ashley laughed. "Would you please wear a body camera whenever you're with her, so we can drink more champagne and watch whatever slip-ups you may make?"

"You're the only one I'd watch them with," Stacy said with a smile.

"Help me out. Tell me how to kindly let my mother know she's tone deaf."

"I don't think I would tell her that unless she was planning to take her show on the road. It obviously makes her happy, so why ruin it for her?"

"There's the woman I know and love," Ashley said with a laugh. "Sensible and kind, although I think if you were here, you wouldn't be either of those lovely things. Fine, I won't crush my mother's spirit, but I am going to find some earplugs."

Dear Me,

Stacy came by the garden center today. The damn vibrator went off again as soon as I saw her, and now it feels like it's hooked up to a car battery. I was talking to a customer about sasanquas, the crowd parted, and there was Stacy. She had on a pair of blue jean cutoffs and a tank top, and she wasn't wearing any makeup. She looked prettier than I'd ever seen her.

Right in the middle of my busiest day of the week, I dropped everything and showed her around. The sun hits her eyes, and they just glow. Pretty, too damn pretty. I felt like we were having a moment. She smiled at me a lot, and it made me offer things like building her a Zen garden. I'm weak. I'm like putty around her. I felt like a puppy loping along beside her, silently begging for a pet. I did get one, but it was kinda violent.

I didn't let her pay for the stuff she wanted. I took it out to her car and loaded it for her. We chatted for a minute, then she moved in like she was gonna hug me, but all of the sudden froze when we got close. She kinda rapped me between the shoulder blades with the heel of her hand, and I burped. I'm pretty sure she noticed because she stared at me awkwardly and nearly ripped the door off her car trying to get into it.

I thought we'd had a moment in the garden center until that hug. Those are the kinds of hugs a woman gives when she's trying to be nice, but she doesn't want you to get the wrong impression and read too much into it. In short, I don't think the attraction is mutual.

Oh, Me

Chapter Twelve

"Alexis, check the pasta, and don't throw a string of it at the wall like Momma does. You know when it's ready," Allison said as she finished up the salad she was making.

"It's time to drain it." Alexis took the pot to the sink and asked, "Where is Grammy?"

"She's putting the last touches on the fruit bowl painting. She wants to show it to us tonight, and she's expecting feedback. Regardless of what it looks like, be prepared to praise it, or she'll be crushed."

Alexis grinned as she poured the pasta into a strainer. "Oh, I can't wait to see the pecker platter."

"It does look like a penis, doesn't it? I've always wondered who I'd inherited my freaky side from because both of my parents have always been so conservative. Apparently, it's my mother. She's expressing her sexuality through fruit, and I don't think she realizes it. Oh, the bread!" Allison dashed to the oven and ripped open the door. "Just in time," she said as she grabbed hot pads and took out the pan.

"Since when do you worry about burning the bread? I've eaten charred chunks all my life, and I've come to expect it."

"Jason and Stacy are eating with us, so you'll have to get over your disappointment or set a couple of rolls on fire."

"We're here, let the feeding begin," Alana announced as she, Jason, and Stacy came through the front door. "Why don't I smell bread burning?"

"Ha!" Alexis said and laughed when her mother swatted her with one of the hot pads.

Allison greeted everyone who came into her kitchen with a hug and a kiss on the cheek. Stacy got two kisses when she placed a chocolate cheesecake on the counter. "Everyone, I'll put the salad and bread on the table, but we'll form a buffet line for the spaghetti," Allison said and handed Stacy a plate. "You'll go first."

Stacy began by putting a small dab of pasta on her plate, but Jason grabbed the spoon and said, "Uh, no, let me show you how we do it here." He dropped a heaping spoonful onto Stacy's plate.

"I'll help you with the sauce," Alana said and ladled it on thick.

Stacy stared at something that didn't seem right on her plate. "Is that an egg?"

"Yes! Eggs!" Jason exclaimed. "I love the eggs!"

"Mom puts all kinds of things in her sauce," Alexis explained. "Pork chops, chicken, and boiled eggs."

Elise strode into the kitchen and put a hand on Stacy's back. "I'm so glad you're here, you follow me." She led Stacy to the table and seated her next to her own spot.

Once everyone was gathered at the table, they joined hands, and Allison said, "Momma, make it short."

Elise bowed her head and said, "Dear God, we thank you for the food on this table and our family gathered around it. Father, we ask that you bless it and make it good for our bodies. We thank you for the shower we got this afternoon, and now I won't have to go outside and fight with that infernal sprinkler system that Alexis says she'll fix but never does. Lord, I thank you for the perm that Alana's gonna put in my hair, even though she doesn't know about that yet. I pray it doesn't irritate my scalp this time and make it flake. Lord, now you know I'm gonna eat that cheesecake that I saw sitting on the counter, and I pray that you don't allow those calories to rest on my already wide hips. If you really wanted to, you could make those calories just disappear. I'd appreciate—"

"Momma!"

"Amen."

81

"Oh! I didn't pour the wine," Allison said and started to stand.

"Got it, Mom." Alexis hopped up, grabbed the bottle, and went around the table filling each glass.

Jason watched with a smile as Stacy took her first bite. "Amazing, isn't it?"

Stacy chewed and swallowed. "This is outstanding. Allison, my compliments."

Allison looked genuinely pleased. "Thank you, I'm so glad you like it. Jason always seems to enjoy it."

"Let me tell you what he did to me," Alana said to Stacy. "The last time Mom made this, she packed up a huge container and sent it home with us. The next day, Jason took the whole thing to work with him, and I didn't get any. Then he tells Mom and Grammy that I ate it all and didn't share, and they believed him. Not only did I not get any of the leftovers, I got fussed at for hogging them."

Stacy smiled. "I'm not surprised. He told my mother that I was wearing his underwear when we were kids."

"Because you were, and you weren't giving them back," Jason said.

"You didn't have to tell on me," Stacy shot back with a laugh. "I was so jealous of your underwear. I coveted your little superhero boxer shorts. I couldn't feel tough playing basketball with a princess creeping up my butt."

Alana tipped her wineglass toward Stacy. "You should've done what Alexis did and went commando. She didn't want to have anything to do with panties."

"I'd find them everywhere," Allison added. "I had to stand in her room with her and make sure she put everything on before school. Then while I was doing Alana's hair, that little scamp would take the underwear back off and hide it. I found panties in the umbrella stand, slippers, the rubber boots my dad used to keep on the porch. You couldn't open anything around here without panties popping out."

Alexis shrugged. "It's like Stacy just said, they creeped. I was a child of action, and I couldn't run around with a bunch of underwear in my butt crack. I don't know why y'all didn't understand that."

"I love the conversations we have here over dinner." Jason shook his head. "You can ask Stacy, when our families get together for a meal, it's so dull. Conversations are about business, stocks, and who died."

Stacy laughed. "After an hour of that, you want to die just to get out of there. That's why I seldom go to my parents' house for dinner."

"Y'all must think we're complete savages," Elise said. "We do have manners, and we use them in public, but here at home, no one gets out of whack if there's an elbow on the table."

"It's more about enjoying your time together, right?" Stacy said, gazing at Elise.

"Exactly."

Stacy smiled warmly. "Well, thank you for having me. I'm thoroughly enjoying this wonderful food and the company."

"You shouldn't be cleaning dishes. Alana's supposed to be in here," Alexis said as Stacy put a plate into the dishwasher.

"I asked her to let me do it to show my appreciation for a great dinner. You got the raw end of the deal. I hate scrubbing pots. Oh, and I just want to tell you, I did a good job of potting the ivy, and I think it seems healthier already. It was fun until I had to clean all the dirt off my kitchen table."

"Very good," Alexis said with a smile. "If it survives a month, I'll give you another one."

"Is that like a Holt's reward program thing?"

Alexis continued to smile and shook her head. "Motivation not to commit murder."

"I don't intentionally kill them. I think I overwatered some, and others I didn't water at all. I'm hoping to find the balance on this one. I'm sure I will now that I've been offered an incentive."

The pot Alexis was washing slipped from her hands, and it landed in the soapy water, which splashed up on her. "Shit, it's in my eyes," she said as they burned. She turned the water on and rinsed her face while Stacy grabbed a towel.

Alexis stepped back from the sink, blinked rapidly, and almost tripped over the open dishwasher door. Stacy grabbed her by the arm. "Keep blinking, they'll tear more."

"I can't believe how bad it burns. Mom must've poured half a bottle of soap into that water." Alexis clamped her eyes shut, and tears pushed out of her closed lids.

Stacy had enjoyed two glasses of wine with dinner, and it had dulled her senses. It seemed perfectly natural to kiss Alexis's closed eyes, and she was about to do that when Jason walked into the kitchen with an empty glass. Stacy froze, lips puckered an inch from Alexis's face, then stepped back. "She has soap in her eyes," Stacy explained as Jason gazed at her with a grin.

"Let Stacy blow in them, Lex. It'll make them tear more," Jason suggested.

"I was about to do that—that's what I was going to do when you walked in. I was going to blow," Stacy spat out rapidly and nodded. "That's what I was going to do."

Alexis shook her head and wiped her eyes with the back of her hand. "I'm okay now."

Jason continued to smile at Stacy until she looked away and said, "Elise wants y'all to come in the living room for a showing."

Alexis followed Stacy into the living room where everyone was gathered. Elise was standing in front of the TV with her hands folded. "I have begun painting again, after giving it up years ago. I've finished my first piece, and I'd like to show it to y'all. I need honest and sincere feedback, so please don't be afraid of hurting my feelings."

The room was completely still as Elise picked up the canvas leaning against the TV stand and turned it. No one said a word as they stared at it. Alexis watched Stacy and smiled when Stacy's brow slowly began to rise.

"The...um...the shading is really nice, Grammy," Alana said.

Allison nodded. "It looks great, Momma. I like it."

Elise set her gaze on Alexis. "Be honest with me, dear."

"Well, Grammy, you still have a stiff penis in a bowl, and now you've added pears that look like two breasts."

"Alexis Leigh!" Elise said and put Stacy on the spot next. "Sweetie, you give me your opinion. Do you see a...male member?"

Stacy's mouth fell open, and she made some sort of strange circular nod. "You asked for my honesty, so I have to tell you there's a penis in your bowl."

"You see that because Alexis said it," Elise argued. "Jason, Alana, what do you see?"

Jason clamped his lips together tightly, then said, "I don't see a penis, but I see two very voluptuous breasts beside an apple."

"Grammy, I think you're subconsciously painting nudes and using fruit," Alana said seriously.

Elise turned the canvas and studied it. "All right, I'll admit when I first started working on this, the banana was flesh colored, and it did look like a...doodle. But now it's yellow, and I clearly see a banana."

"An erect banana," Alexis said with a laugh.

"Momma, I love it, and I want you to hang it up right here in our living room." Allison pointed to a spot on the wall. "It would look perfect there."

Elise shook her head. "No, I'm gonna redo it."

"No, don't. Grammy, that's what was in your mind and on your heart when you painted it," Alana said seriously. "That's what art is, it's an expression. You expressed yourself erotically. I vote you leave it the way it is."

Alexis raised her hand. "I second."

Everyone's hands went up. "That seals it, Momma. We took a vote, so leave the penis in the bowl," Allison said with a smile.

Chapter Thirteen

"And over there is where we had a tire swing." Alana pointed into the darkness. "That's where I got my first kiss and Lex punched her first boy, right after my kiss."

"Wanna take me on?" Stacy pointed to the dusty Ping-Pong table sitting on the patio.

"You two really shouldn't play any game that requires rackets or paddles." Jason took Alana by the hand and led her to the door. "We're going back inside before the carnage begins."

"I think we can handle a game of Ping-Pong without bloodletting." Alexis walked over to the table and looked beneath it. "There should be paddles and balls in the box under here. Do you want to play for points or for the enjoyment of the volley? Alana and I used to see how long we could hit it back and forth until someone missed."

"Let's do that," Stacy said when Alexis handed her a paddle and the ball. She served when Alexis was ready, and the volley began. "I think it's sweet that you defended your sister's honor against that boy who kissed her."

Alexis laughed. "That's not why I did it. I traded him a box of Hot Wheels, a Water Wiggle, and a pack of gum for a skateboard he didn't deliver."

"We weren't allowed to have skateboards or skates. My oldest sister Liz got a pair of skates for her birthday one year and broke her arm. She ruined it for the rest of us. I think my parents would've encased us in Bubble Wrap if they thought for a second they could keep us in it. When I went off to college, I made up for all my years of being overprotected. If someone dared me to do something, I'd do it. That's how I ended up with thirty-eight stitches in my hip. There was a party at a frat house, and they had a rope swing. I was drunk, and I lost my grip on the rope. The flight into the hedge was glorious until I landed and was stabbed by a branch." Stacy laughed. "Here's the really sad thing, I was so proud of my stitches after the pain medication kicked in. I felt badass for the first time in my life."

Alexis missed the ball and stared at Stacy. "You could've just bought a leather jacket and biker boots if you wanted to look tough and spared yourself the pain."

"No, I had to have the experience, that's the point. I felt like I'd been living in a bubble, and I was finally free to do stupid stuff like everyone else." Stacy grinned. "I was really good at it too. Everyone called me Stacy Stunt."

Alexis started the ball going again. "Oh, all right, I get it now. You were spreading your little wings."

"Yes, I was flapping all over the place, and I survived. I'm sure you had your moments of rebellion too."

"There was not a whole lot to rebel against," Alexis said as she played the ball off the wall. "I mean, I did things like sneak out of the house when I was a teen…well, twice. I got caught the second time by Grammy, and she nearly pulled my ear off. After she lectured me for an hour and made me feel terribly guilty— she's a master at that when she wants to be—I didn't try it anymore. That was during my angry period because I was beginning to realize that I was a lesbian, and I didn't want to be different. "I think Grandpa had me figured out before I did, or at least he knew I was struggling with something. He'd tell me no matter what I did he'd always love and support me. When I finally did come out years later, he made a joke about me catching it from the cafeteria food in college, and he never treated me any differently."

"I would've liked to have known him," Stacy said, envious of the obvious bond.

"He was cool." Alexis found the ball and started it going again. "So what other crazy things did you do in college?"

"The typical stuff. Parties. I discovered my love for women then, too. After school, I settled into adulthood and became pretty dull after that."

Alexis smiled. "I wouldn't call you dull."

"That's because I'm armed with a paddle, and I think you know I'll use it."

Alana glanced out the window and said, "Oh, shit! They're sword fighting with the Ping-Pong paddles." She threw open the back door prepared to fuss at Alexis and was relieved to find the battle was good-natured.

Alexis faked Stacy out with a swing, and when Stacy reacted, she slapped Stacy's butt with the paddle. "I'm up two points," she said and dodged a hit.

"What's going on?" Elise asked when she joined the others in the doorway.

"They're spanking each other, and they seem to be enjoying it," Alana replied drolly.

"Stacy, it's time to say good night to your friend and help her pick up the toys," Jason said. "Tomorrow is a workday."

When Alexis got home that evening, she spotted a familiar car parked in front of her house. She hopped out of her truck excited about seeing her buddy, and the silence that usually greeted her when she came home was gone when she went inside. The TV was blaring, and Jaime had the blender going as Alexis walked into the kitchen. "Hey! Which one of the cats let you in here?"

Jaime switched off the blender and sighed. "Surprise, I'm homeless."

"What?" Alexis asked as she walked over and hugged her.

"I wasn't due to get off the rig for another ten days, but my relief has to have surgery in two weeks, so my shift was split again to cover his. I didn't tell Rachel I was coming home, but instead of surprising her, she got me. Some ugly dyke bitch was laid up on my couch watching my TV, and she's been sleeping in my bed like some fugly Goldilocks with Rachel."

"What?" Alexis couldn't believe what she was hearing.

"We're done." Jaime's face flushed as she blew out a breath. "I hope you don't mind I let myself in."

"I'm glad you did, and you know you're always welcome," Alexis said and gave Jaime another hug.

"On the ride home, all I could think about was having Rachel in my arms and making love to her. Somebody else took care of that for me. I'm sexually frustrated and pissed off, so I decided to make margaritas."

"Whatever you want," Alexis said with a smile. "I'm certainly happy to see you. I'll even have sex with you. We can wear bags on our heads, so we won't know it's us. I'll staple Megan Fox's picture to yours, and you can put whoever makes you happy on my bag."

"I can always count on you to make me laugh." Jaime gave Alexis a hug and stepped back with a disgusted look. "Why do you smell like a wet dog?"

"Oh, sorry. I got into some vicious Ping-Pong at Mom's."

Jaime took two glasses from the cabinet and said, "And here I was hoping you were out on a date."

Alexis's mind went to Stacy for half a second. "I'm getting to the point where that might be appealing again."

Jaime filled a glass and handed to her. "Has Alana dumped Jason yet?"

"She's really gonna marry him, she's finally in love."

Jaime glanced at Alexis as she poured her own drink. "Are you shitting me?"

"I shit you not. You should see them together, the little smiles they give each other. She can't stop touching him, and he's the same with her. They met, and it was like bam."

"Then there's still hope for us." Jaime tapped Alexis's glass with her own and raised it. "To us."

Alexis drank to the toast, then they went into the living room. Jaime took the sofa, and Alexis sat on the hearth because she did stink. She really wanted to go take a shower, but she felt Jaime needed a shoulder even if it was smelly. "Do you know this Goldilocks?"

"Nope. Rachel admitted to meeting her online. It wasn't something that just happened, Rachel went hunting for someone to screw behind my back." Jaime took a drink and sighed. "I asked her if she was planning on leaving me for this woman, and she said no, it was all about sex. Then she blamed me for taking the rig job and being away from home. If you recall, she was the one who talked me into taking it in the first place because it paid twice as much as I made working on an ambulance. I hate being on a rig, I can't tell you how boring it is, but the money sure made her life easier, and this is how she repays me."

"That's shitty," Alexis said, knowing there was nothing she could say that would make any difference.

"Yeah, it is. I walked in the door and saw that heifer laid up on my couch buck-ass naked, and I couldn't believe what I was seeing. I just stood there with my stupid mouth hanging open, and Rachel walks into the room stark naked. I just paid that couch off, and they fucked on it!"

"Gross."

"And she was a big ol' bitch. She had to be at the very least six feet tall. When she jumped up, she just kept going, and I thought she was gonna get hit by the ceiling fan. She was horrified of my little five-foot-four-inch ass, though, and I didn't even say a word. She started running around the living room grabbing clothes, then I watched her bare ass cheeks bounce through my kitchen. She was so freaked out she forgot her keys and her phone, so she had to sit in her car because she couldn't go anywhere. Are you laughing?"

"I can't help it," Alexis said and bit her lip.

Jaime glared at her for a second, then snorted. "She probably had heat stroke. The windows were rolled up, the doors were locked, and she was sweating buck shots."

"Did she even know about you?"

"Fuck yeah, pictures of me and Rachel were still all over the house—well, they were. I grabbed every one I could and threw them in the trash while Rachel followed me around trying to explain everything away." Jaime inhaled deeply and took a drink. "I can't talk about this anymore. What's been going on with you? Tell me something to take my mind off her, or I'm gonna go over there and really tear up some shit."

"Um...I'm gonna be Alana's maid of honor. I have to go with her this Saturday to pick out bridesmaids dresses."

Jaime stared at Alexis for a moment and began to cackle.

"I have to plan a bridal shower and a bachelorette party," Alexis said and grinned as Jaime guffawed. "I'm so happy this news makes you feel better. They set a date, September 12, so everything is kind of crazy. Oh, and they're gonna do it in Florida on some cape."

Jaime scrubbed her face and yawned. "I feel like we haven't talked in ages. They kept throwing shifts at me, and I was taking them because I wanted...I was gonna take Rachel on a trip. We always wanted to go Belize. Fuck, I have to start over." She held up a hand when Alexis stood and took a step toward her. "Don't hug me. I'll start crying, and I won't stop, and you stink."

"How about I refresh your drink instead?" Alexis went into the kitchen and grabbed the pitcher off the blender. Her heart sank with sadness when she returned to the living room and Jaime was drying her eyes. Alexis scrambled to think of something to make her laugh as she refilled Jaime's glass. "Did I tell you that Jason's cousin Stacy is also a bridesmaid?"

"Are you asking yourself at this point if Alana secretly hates you?" Jaime said with a chuckle and took a healthy drink from her glass.

"I suppose the thought crossed my mind, but Stacy and I have called a cease-fire, and she's really not all that bad. It turns out, she didn't mean to snub me—well, yeah, she did, but she didn't want to. She was fighting with her now ex-girlfriend when I walked up at the engagement party. It was just bad timing."

"Is she cute?"

"Very pretty," Alexis replied as she set the pitcher on the coffee table.

Jaime smiled. "This could turn out to be something interesting."

"She broke up with her girlfriend a couple of months ago, so you know what that means."

"Yeah, she's single," Jaime said before she took another drink.

"But probably not ready to date."

"Not everyone is like you, Lex. Some don't need an entire year to get over someone else."

"I was over Michelle before we ever broke up. That was our problem."

Jaime's eyes narrowed. "Are you trying to justify her cheating on you and basically rubbing it in your face?"

"No, she was wrong for that. She could've left me, but no, she had to prove a point first."

Jaime stabbed a finger at Alexis. "What Michelle did to you was cold-hearted, period. Now all three of us can say we came home to find our girlfriends in bed with someone else."

"Three of us?"

"Yeah, I'm seeing two of you."

Alexis smiled. "Are you hammered already?"

"I poured a whole bottle of tequila into the pitcher," Jaime said with a slight slur.

Alexis took a sip of her drink and grimaced. "Yeah, they're a little potent."

"I'm gonna quit the rig." Jaime squinted. "But you know, maybe it's not a good time to quit. I'm single now, and I could pay off a lot of shit. It's so boring, though. No, I should quit. Should I?"

"Think on that for a while when you're sober. Don't make any major decisions for a few days at least."

"Good advice," Jaime said with a nod. "I'll quit. We're gonna have to go out now. Hey, let's go to the bar Saturday night, take a cab, and get trashed."

"You may not think that's a good idea when you wake up in the morning," Alexis said as she watched Jaime pick up the pitcher and drink from it. "If we do go out, I'll have to keep a clear head, otherwise you'll spend all your money on booze and probably bring home someone scary."

"We go, we dance, we flirt. I'm not in the market for anyone right now, but I want you to take pictures of me dancing my ass off with a lot of different women, so I can post it all over the 'net for Rachel to see. Why is there a pillow on your mantel?"

Alexis smiled up at her orange tabby. "You need to back off the tequila. That's Ginger. She's waiting for you to pass out, so she can wrap herself around your head."

"Take a picture of that too." Jaime grinned. "I wanna be seen in bed with another woman even if she's orange…and a cat."

Dear Me,

I have a roommate. I couldn't get her upstairs to the spare bedroom. As I write this, she's lying on the couch with Ginger wrapped around her head, and Sprout is on her chest. Ginger is comforting her, Sprout is an opportunistic shit that's always looking for a warm bed.

I feel sorry for Jaime. I wasn't in love with Michelle, but it was still like a blow to the chest to find her in our bed with someone else. Jaime is in love with Rachel, and she's gonna suffer for a while. I know I can't do or say anything that will ease her pain, but at least I can give her a place to stay.

I don't know why we pursue love. It usually ends in suffering. Even if you're not dumped and have a happy ever after until old age, there's always death. The really suck-ass thing about love is when you don't have it, all you can think about is getting it. Knowing all this, I still want it to come to me. I want to feel what Alana described. I want to feel like my chest is gonna burst open with all the emotion.

In hindsight, I'm glad I never felt that way about Michelle. Then again, if I had, I would've treated her better, and she wouldn't have cheated on me. I'd like to think that's true, but I wonder if maybe my subconscious knew something that I wouldn't allow myself to see. Maybe something in my brain held my heart behind its steel walls to protect me. And that brings me right back to my fear of being incapable of falling in love. Maybe I don't ever feel anything because some internal protective measure wants to keep me from suffering like Jaime is now. I wish it would do something about that fucking vibrator!

Me

Chapter Fourteen

"What're you doing downtown?" Stacy asked as she walked alongside Jason toward their favorite café.

"I had a meeting with a client that began at eight this morning. I didn't think he'd ever stop talking, but when he finally did, I realized it was lunchtime."

"I'm glad you dropped in to see me. I was contemplating a leftover salad from yesterday and wishing I had Allison's spaghetti." Stacy blew out a heavy breath. "That stuff was delicious."

"She's an amazing cook. Alana not so much, but she's getting better," Jason said with a laugh as he opened the door to the café for Stacy. "I can't say anything because my idea of cooking is ordering pizza."

They chose a table near the windows, and after they ordered their food, Jason asked, "So what did you think of family time with the Holts?"

"They're really nice people," Stacy said with a smile. "Time with them made me think a lot about our family, and I have to wonder what's wrong with us. Allison hugged me good night, even though I was sweaty. My own mother wouldn't have done that. She barely hugs me when I'm clean, and she gives those stupid air kisses. My dad hugs by putting his hands on my shoulders and keeping me at arm's length. I remember riding on his shoulders when I was little and sitting on his lap. Mom used to lie in bed with me and read a story when it was time for me to sleep. When did my parents become the aloof robotic creatures they are now? Yours are the same way, what happened?"

Jason took a drink of his tea, his brow furrowed as he thought. "I think it began when they got involved in politics, at least it did for my dad. He and Mom started throwing parties for people they considered important, and they changed. You and I are the youngest in our families, so maybe they think they've raised their kids, and they can be someone else now."

"Maybe so," Stacy said with a thoughtful expression. "My kids will get real hugs."

"You better get started on them. You and Alana aren't in your twenties," Stacy said. "Be warned, I will spoil them. I'll be their favorite aunt."

"On our side of the family, sure, but you may have some competition in Alexis. Let's talk about her. Why didn't you tell me you two have something going on?" Jason said with a frown.

"Because there isn't anything."

"I saw you about to kiss her in the kitchen the other night."

"That was a blow," Stacy lied and looked as innocent as she could. She wasn't sure how she would explain what she was actually doing.

"Liar. Why are y'all hiding this?"

"What you saw wasn't..." Stacy sighed. "She doesn't know I'm interested in her."

"Aw, man." Jason sank down in his seat. "You were making a move, and I ruined it."

Stacy shook her head. "I wasn't doing that, either. She was hurting, and I...reacted. I was just going to kiss her to make her feel better. I had wine, I wasn't thinking clearly."

Jason looked confused. "Would it have been so bad to kiss her like that? You like her, why not?"

He did have a point. Stacy realized she could've kissed Alexis and broke the ice, but she was so surprised at her own compulsion. "Why is she single?"

"I don't really know. Alana did mention that Lex went through a bad breakup a while back, so maybe she's not ready yet. I'd like to get to know her better, but until recently, she was kind of standoffish. Well, I guess a better word would be guarded." Jason smiled. "The Holt women are magical creatures, you meet them, and you're hooked. I enjoyed my status as

96

eternal bachelor, but after three dates with Alana, I had made up my mind she was the woman I was going to marry. I'm not surprised at all to hear that Alexis has caught your attention. I think they're witches, good ones that cast powerful spells."

Stacy grabbed her water glass when the server set it on the table and took a drink. "Hey, let's keep this between us for now, promise?"

Jason nodded. "Sure."

Any other time, Stacy wouldn't have cared if everyone knew her interests. She had no problem with asking women out, and she'd dealt with a few rejections. This time, everything felt different. The real Alexis was a lot like her fantasy, and Stacy didn't know how she'd react to Alexis's rejection if it came. She wanted more time to see how much more in common the real Alexis had with the dream version before she revealed her cards.

"Are you going to ask her out?" Jason asked, pulling Stacy from her thoughts.

"She hasn't given the signal a woman uses to let someone know they're open to more than just being friends."

Jason's jaw sagged. "Y'all have a signal for that and you didn't tell me? You just let me wing it all those years?"

"You didn't appear to have any problems picking up women." Stacy shrugged. "I thought you knew about it."

"Well, what do y'all do, throw a thumb up?"

"Centuries ago, women got together and decided upon a certain look to give as a signal of interest. They passed it on to their daughters, and it has continued throughout generations across all continents. Jason, you are the very first man to receive this sacred secret knowledge."

"You sarcastic jackass."

Stacy had a good laugh at Jason's scowl. "Seriously, there are cues, everybody uses them. I know Alana looks at you a certain way when she wants you to kiss her. You haven't noticed that?"

"Yeah, she stares me in the eyes, and she does that little crooked grin thing." Jason sat back and folded his arms. "Let me see yours."

Stacy set her chin in her hand, and with a slight smile let her gaze linger on Jason's mouth for a moment, then slowly rose to meet his eyes. "See, it's subtle."

Jason frowned, then shuddered. "I feel really gross. That was very provocative. Don't ever look at me like that again."

At noon, Alexis hiked back to her house to check on Jaime, who was still asleep on the couch with Ginger wrapped around her head. Jaime was flat on her back, mouth wide open, arms and legs everywhere. Alexis tugged on one of her eyelids and said, "Are you still alive?"

"Water," Jaime rasped.

Alexis picked up the bottle she'd left on the coffee table for her and opened it. "You want me to just pour it in, or do you want to sit up?"

Jaime made an attempt to move, but Ginger slapped her on the forehead. "I tried to get up to pee earlier, and she did that. Is she gonna rip my face off?"

"No, maybe just an eyebrow," Alexis said with a laugh and picked Ginger up. "You want something to eat?"

"Not yet." Jaime slowly sat up and took the water from Alexis. She drank a sip, then gulped it. "Why did you let me do this to myself?"

"I think you needed it, and I'm very sorry that you slept on the couch. I tried to get you up and to the guest room, but you were like a slippery Gumby doll. After I took a shower last night, I came down here to check on you, and I had to watch your chest rise and fall to know you were alive." Alexis laughed. "You know, I only drank half of my glass and I woke up with a dull headache. I can only imagine what you're feeling."

Jaime smiled weakly. "Like hammered shit." She picked up her phone and stared at it. "I have twenty-seven text messages. Wanna guess who they're from?" She tapped the screen and read. "Half of these are 'please forgive me.' The rest of them are about couples counseling, she wants us to go."

"Put down the phone, and let me give you some advice." Alexis took a seat in her recliner.

"Hit me."

"Give yourself some time to process this before you commit to doing anything."

Jaime nodded and grimaced. "I woke up earlier wanting to be in bed with her. We weren't even together a year, but I loved her. I don't know if this is something I should or even could forgive."

"Again, that's not a decision for you to make right now. You're kind of in shock. Give your brain some time to start piecing things together." Alexis shook her head. "No major life decisions for at least a couple of weeks. Don't quit your job, don't agree to go to counseling with her. Don't even talk to her for a few days. Let her be miserable too."

"I can't say a hundred percent I won't get weak and call her." Jaime patted her chest. "I'm being honest."

Alexis held up a finger. "Okay, when you feel wimpy, think of something that she did that grated your nerves to no end. What've you got?"

"She slept with an ugly dyke while I was at work."

"Besides that."

"She cut her nails at the kitchen table," Jaime said grudgingly. "She didn't put the lid back on the toothpaste, and there was always hair stuck to the tube. Matter of fact, there was hair everywhere, she sheds like a dog. She was hot-natured and kept the house subzero. She never took out the trash. I would come home and the whole house would stink."

"You don't have to put up with a stinky house anymore or fingernail clippings on your kitchen table. There won't be hair in your toothpaste. Do you see what I'm saying? You don't have to put up with that stuff anymore. Single is not all bad. I put something on the kitchen counter and no one moves it, except for when Ginger gets up there, even though she knows she's not supposed to," Alexis said, eyeing the orange tabby, who stared back at her unrepentant.

Jaime nodded. "Focus on the positives, that's good. I don't have to suck her toes anymore!"

"You...you...you what?" Alexis asked aghast. "You put part of a foot in your mouth and sucked on it?"

"When they'd just been cleaned," Jaime retorted. "It turned her on."

Alexis snorted. "Has she ever sucked yours?"

"Changing the subject." Jaime averted her gaze. "We're going out Saturday night. You will be my guardian and not let me go home with any strangers. You will also take away my wallet if I look like I'm about to run a tab."

"Will you suck my toes, so I can understand the appeal?" Alexis asked, enjoying the flush on Jaime's face.

"I have a hangover, and I feel like I'm dying, but if your foot gets anywhere near my face, I will beat your ass."

Chapter Fifteen

"Oh, poor Jaime," Alana said sadly Saturday morning as she and Alexis drove to pick up Stacy. "I know she's thankful she has you to lean on."

"Yeah, but I think I'm getting the better end of this bargain. She cooks, she cleans, there's food in the fridge. The only drawback is she wants to go out clubbing tonight."

"It'll be good because you haven't been out in ages, maybe you'll meet someone."

"I'm not going to meet anyone. My job tonight is to make sure Jaime doesn't get plastered, take home some stranger, and suck her toes," Alexis said with a grin.

"You should invite Stacy," Alana suggested. "She went through a breakup recently too, and who knows, she and Jaime might hit it off."

The latter part of Alana's comment hit Alexis like a slap, and she was surprised at herself for taking offense. As bad as she felt for Jaime, she didn't want her taking solace in Stacy's arms. "Jaime isn't anywhere near ready to date anyone."

"You know the saying, if you wanna get over someone…get on top…or maybe it's get under someone else. They're both in the rebound stage, so they can bounce off each other."

"Nobody's bouncing on anybody," Alexis snapped. "I'm telling you, Jaime isn't ready for that."

"All right, simmer down, Ms. Protective."

When Alexis and Alana arrived at Stacy's apartment, Stacy threw open the door, grabbed Alexis by the arm, and dragged her inside. "Come look at the plant," she said excitedly.

Alexis walked into the kitchen and smiled at the ivy sitting in its new pot. It looked healthy and was sporting a couple of new leaf shoots. "Oh, yeah, it's gonna grow now. Good job on the repotting."

"Thanks," Stacy said, looking pleased with the praise.

"Oh, no," Alana said as she joined them in the kitchen. "Lex has recruited you into the green thumb club. It's like a disease that starts off with one plant, then your house fills up with them, and they're growing all over everything."

Alexis pointed to the ivy. "Look what she did. Can't you see the difference in this little baby in one week? Stacy's already got a green thumb, she just didn't know it."

"That's right." Stacy strutted around in a circle with her thumbs up. "It's alive! Alive! I am the keeper of the green. I'm gonna win a prize."

Alana set a hand on Stacy's shoulder and smiled. "Sweetie, you need to get out more."

"I thought your other bridesmaid was coming—Rene, isn't that her name?" Stacy said as they walked into the same boutique where Alana had gotten her wedding gown.

"She is, she's running late." Alana looked at her watch. "Okay, I tried to make this easy and picked out a few dresses online, but after last week, I'm not sure my choices are all that great."

"Hello, Alana," the hostess said as she greeted them. "Gwen is your consultant today."

A very austere-looking woman wearing a black pantsuit approached Alana. Her hair was long and silvery white, and when she smiled, it looked like a sneer. "Hello, ladies, please follow me," she said in a low, smooth voice.

They went to a different suite this time, but it was set up the same as the last one. Alexis went straight to the refreshments and poured herself a cup of coffee while Gwen showed Alana

102

the dresses. "Do you have plans for this evening?" she asked when Stacy joined her.

"Um...no?" Stacy said, caught off-guard by the unexpected question.

"My best friend and her girlfriend broke up recently, and Jaime wants to go out to a bar, get sloppy drunk, and make a fool of herself. It should be moderately entertaining to watch. I'm her designated driver and guardian, would you like to join us?"

"Yes, sure. Are we going to a lesbian bar?"

Alexis nodded and sipped her coffee. "Jaime wants to have pictures taken while she's partying, so she can post them on her social media sites to piss off her ex. Don't worry, you don't have to be in any of them if you don't want to. I'm certain Jaime will find plenty of party girls to pose with her, she has that kind of personality."

"Are you her wingwoman?" Stacy asked with a smile.

"No, I'm the anti-wing. If she gets plastered and tries to go home with a stranger, my job is to stop her."

The door to the suite flew open, and Alana's dearest friend Rene came in like a big-breasted tidal wave. She threw her purse on one of the couches and pulled Alana into a hug, and they bounced around in a circle while Rene sang, "You're getting married, we're shopping for dresses, this is so real."

Gwen was still holding one of the dresses and watched the pair celebrate with a bored expression. She turned toward Alexis and said, "You look like a size eight to me, which is what we need for this particular dress. Join me in the dressing room, please."

"Wait, I'm here to say yea or nay." Alexis shook her head vehemently. "I'm not trying anything on."

Rene pointed at the door. "Alexis, get your ass in there and put on that dress." She walked over to Stacy, pulled her into a hug, and said, "I'm Rene Hardy, it's so nice to meet you, Stacy. I've heard all about you. Alexis, are you still standing there gawking?"

"Well, I don't like that one. There's no straps, and something is gonna jump out," Alexis argued.

"A bra is made into the dress, and it's very supportive."
Gwen pointed at Alexis, then to the dressing room. "You, in there, now."

Alexis looked as though she would protest, then marched into the room. Gwen followed and closed the door behind them.

"What kind of shoes are we wearing?" Rene asked.

"None, it's a beach wedding. We'll be barefoot," Alana said with a smile. "That's a real bonus for Lex because she doesn't wear heels."

"Hey! Oh—hey! Women buy me dinner before they do that," Alexis could be heard saying from the dressing room.

Stacy clamped her lips together tightly to keep from laughing and gazed at Alana. "This definitely isn't her idea of fun, is it?"

Alana shook her head. "No, she'd rather be run over by a truck."

"Stacy, are you married?" Rene asked.

"Oh, no," Stacy said with a laugh.

"Stacy's a lesbian, like Alexis," Alana added.

"I know, you told me that already." Rene grinned. "But we can ask them that question now."

The door to the dressing room flew open; Alexis marched out in socked feet, got up on the dais, and spun once before heading back toward the dressing room. "Whoa, tiger," Alana said with a laugh. "Let me at least see the dress on you."

Alexis huffed and went back over to the dais. "I feel naked, and I was groped," she said with a look at Gwen.

"I've lifted firmer," Gwen quipped and brushed her nails on the lapel of her jacket.

"That is adorable," Rene said with a breathy sigh. "Turn around."

Alexis stood with her hands on her hips, eyes to the ceiling, and turned. The strapless dress was yellow and had a ruffled hem that hung around Alexis's knees. It was very simple-looking, yet delicate. It showed off the muscles in Alexis's shoulders and arms. Stacy was enthralled.

Alana tapped Stacy on the arm. "What do you think?"

"Lovely." Stacy thought it was perfect, but then she glanced at Rene and tried to envision her in the dress with her pair of what she speculated were double D's. She tried to think of a tactful way to say that this particular dress may not work for all of them, but Alexis beat her to it.

"Rene, this dress can't handle your girls. They'd be out and mingling with the crowd in a heartbeat."

"They're not as big as they look." Rene smiled and stood up straight. "I have on a pushup bra."

"Why would you want to push that much flesh up?" Alexis asked wide-eyed.

Rene laughed at Alexis as though she were insane. "I'm proud of my girls."

Alexis opened her mouth to retort, but she saw Stacy shaking her head. "Have we looked at me enough?" she said drolly.

"I want to take a picture." Alana went to her purse to retrieve her phone, but when she turned, Alexis had escaped into the dressing room.

"Might I suggest we have Rene try on dresses first, and if they suit her figure, we'll have the rest of the bridesmaids try on the same thing?" Gwen said.

Stacy nodded. "I think that's a good idea."

"What is your dress size?" Gwen asked.

Rene made a flourish with her hand. "I'm a ten, baby."

Stacy thought she saw Gwen roll her eyes before she walked over to the rack. "I'm going to pull some of the choices you've made in a size ten. I'll be right back. Please help yourself to some of the refreshments."

Alexis came out of the dressing room while everyone was making themselves a cup of coffee and asked, "Where is Ester the molester?"

"She went to get more dresses in Rene's size." Alana smiled and patted Alexis's cheek. "You looked really sweet in that dress."

"I thought I looked like a baby duck missing half of my down. That woman grabbed one of my boobs and tried to rearrange it. She didn't even tell me what she was gonna do first,

105

she just went at me. I almost slapped her." Alexis grabbed a cup and pointed at Stacy and Rene. "I'm warning y'all, Gandalf is a groper."

"I'm so excited for you, baby girl," Rene gushed. "I *love* weddings. My own went by in a blur because I had to take Xanax. I was so nervous, I couldn't eat for days before the ceremony because if I did, I'd throw up." She put a hand on Alana's arm. "Do you remember that?" Rene didn't wait for an answer and went on. "All the women in my family wanted to help dress me, do my hair and makeup the day of the wedding, and they were all fighting. Mom was teasing my hair so hard she yanked some out of my head. I felt like I was being pulled in a million different directions. My dad picked up the groom's cake from the bakery and didn't check it. What was supposed to be red velvet was German chocolate, and Jared hates coconut." Rene sighed. "The only clear memory of that day aside from what all went wrong was walking down the aisle. I looked at Jared and thought, I'm gonna pass out or shit my dress before I even get to him."

"Why am I doing this?" Alana asked and looked panicked. "I don't want to be the belle of the ball. I don't want my hair teased. I don't want a bunch of people staring at me...I can't breathe."

"Sit down, I'll get you some water," Stacy said with concern.

Alana shook her head and backed toward the door. "No, I have to talk to Jason. I have to do it right now."

"Oh, shit," Alexis breathed out when Alana ran out of the room. "Rene, stay here and tell Gandalf we'll have to get back with her."

"No, no, it's not your fault," Alana said with a sniff as she talked to Rene on the phone in the one place that brought her peace—an ice cream shop. She'd left the table where she'd been sitting with Alexis and Stacy to speak to Rene, but they were eavesdropping.

"It was her fault," Alexis whispered. "You don't tell a bride-to-be she's in danger of shitting her dress on the aisle."

"Does Alana have issues with anxiety?" Stacy asked softly. "Not usually, but I can tell you she doesn't like being the center of attention. It makes her very uncomfortable. She's probably gonna need a pint of mint chocolate chip before she can go back to that dress shop."

Stacy gazed at Alana. "Poor girl, she looks so upset. Do you think...she's having doubts about marrying Jason?"

Before Alexis could even mull the question, Alana ended her call and returned to the table where she dissolved into tears again. "I love Jason so much," she sobbed. "I want to be his wife, but this is too much, it's too much for me. Invitations, dresses, and showers, why do we have to have this shit?"

"You don't." Alexis shoved a spoonful of her cherry cheesecake ice cream into Alana's mouth. "Tell Jason you want to elope."

"He already knows I'm having a problem with this. That's why he wants to do it in Cape San Blas so the ceremony will be smaller. He's been so sweet, I can't ask him to run away with me," Alana blubbered. "His momma would be so mad."

Alexis glanced at Stacy and said, "Help."

"She's right, Audrey would be pissed."

Alexis smacked her lips. "Um, Stacy, that's not what I call helping."

"But I was going to say, it's your wedding, and it should be what you and Jason want it to be. He doesn't care about all the pomp and circumstance, he just wants to marry you," Stacy said and blotted Alana's face with a napkin. "Talk to him."

Alexis shoved another spoonful of ice cream into Alana's mouth. "Eat fast, it'll freeze your brain, and you won't have to think about anything anymore."

Chapter Sixteen

Alexis was dressed and pacing. She'd told Stacy when she'd dropped her off earlier that day that she would be at her apartment to pick her up at nine thirty that night. It was a quarter till nine, and Jaime was still in the shower. Alexis had already sent Stacy a text and warned her they might be a few minutes late, but it still grated her nerves not to be on time.

Jaime walked into the living room wearing only a towel, and her hair was dripping. "The next time I tell you I'm going to spend the day with my sister, don't let me. Would you check my hair for Silly String? I washed it twice, but I don't know if I got it all out."

"I don't see or feel any," Alexis said as she ran her hands through Jaime's short locks. "What's your ETA on getting ready?"

"I just need five minutes, I'm not gonna dry my hair." Jaime rushed back down the hall to the bathroom. "Lex, I can't thank you enough for letting me stay here, otherwise I would've been on Sue's couch with their dog and ground-up potato chips. She only has three kids, but I swear a dozen jumped on me as soon as I got there. Sticky-fingered little brats can't talk in a normal tone, either, all they do is scream," she yelled from the bathroom.

Alexis looked at her watch. "I'm glad I could save you from being chip-encrusted."

"I'm sorry I got here so late. One of the kids got a hold of my keys and hid them in the dishwasher. I bribed another one with five bucks, and he told me where to find them. How'd the bridal dress thing go?"

Alexis walked into the hallway and leaned against the wall. "It was a disaster. Alana's friend Rene showed up and started talking about everything bad that happened at her wedding, and Alana freaked. She ran out of the building, and I had to take her for ice cream."

"You're shitting me," Jaime said as she stepped into the hall wearing her jeans and a bra. "Did she call off the wedding?"

"I don't think so—what is that thing on your chest?"

Jaime looked down. "A bra?"

"You're not sure either? How old is that thing, and was it originally white?"

"Hey! It's comfortable," Jaime said before she stepped back into the bathroom.

"You better be glad you're not taking anyone home. If I was undressing someone and saw something like that on her, I'd run."

Stacy opened her door to Alexis and smiled. She gazed at Alexis's boots, faded jeans, and snug-fitting dark blue T-shirt, and wanted to sigh. "Where's Jaime?"

"In the truck on her phone with her sister. Jaime visited with her today, and one of Sue's kids took a hundred pictures of his baby junk with the camera on Jaime's phone." Alexis's gaze flickered over Stacy. "You look nice. Are you ready to go?"

"Yes," Stacy said, feeling like a kid going out on a first date. Her hand shook slightly as she grabbed her keys from the foyer table. Alexis stood by her as she locked up. "Do you like kids?"

"When they're somebody else's."

"I feel exactly the same way," Stacy said as they headed for Alexis's truck. "They make me nervous when they start swarming."

Alexis opened the front passenger door for Stacy, and when she climbed in, Jaime said, "She made me get in the backseat. You rate higher on her chain of friends tonight. I'm Jaime, it's nice to meet you, Stacy."

"A pleasure to meet you too," Stacy replied with a smile.

"I'll be happy to ride back there if you prefer to sit up here."

Alexis opened her door, climbed in, and said, "Jaime, I thought I told you to get in the back."

"I am in the—oh, you made a funny. I'm gonna ignore you for the rest of the ride. Stacy, how're you coping with having to spend so much time with Alexis?" Jaime asked.

"It's hard, but I'm muddling through. How long have you known her?"

"Um, I met Alexis...I guess it was about eight years ago when we used to play on the same softball team. Hey, would it be too personal to ask how you're handling your breakup? I just went through one, and I'd like to know when the desire to pull the stuffing out of the teddy bear she gave me will fade."

Alexis gritted her teeth and glanced into the rearview, wanting to choke Jaime. She hadn't mentioned to Stacy that she'd told Jaime her personal business.

Stacy took it in stride, though. "I'm very sorry. How long were you together?"

"About eight months. I don't know if Alexis told you, but I'm a paramedic and I work offshore on a rig. My ex decided to find someone to occupy her time while I was away. I came home this week and found them naked together. I was instantly homeless, but Lex took me in."

Stacy groaned. "Wow, that's a fresh wound. You're probably going to want to kill stuffed animals for a while. My breakup sort of lasted about a year. We just made it official a couple of months ago. I didn't experience the shock you suffered, so I can't give you a definitive answer."

"At least my ex and her giant were done. Lex walked in on her girlfriend performing a certain oral act on another woman."

Alexis smacked the steering wheel with her hand. "Thank you for sharing one of the most humiliating moments of my life."

"You shouldn't be the one embarrassed, Michelle was the one with a sock hanging out of her ass," Jaime said quickly. "Tell Stacy the story."

110

Stacy gazed at Alexis and said, "I think I want to hear about this if you don't mind. The sock has piqued my curiosity."

"I got off work at my usual time and walked over to the house and noticed a car I didn't recognize in the driveway. I go in expecting to find Michelle and her company in the living room or kitchen, but they weren't there. I was about to check the back deck when I heard moaning. So I go down the hall, open our bedroom door, and find Michelle's naked ass in the air, and there was a sock stuck right in her butt crack. I couldn't help but zero in on that sock, it was just hanging there like a tail. They were really into what they were doing, and they didn't even notice me at first. I just kept staring at that sock, wondering how it got there and how Michelle couldn't feel it stuck to her ass. I was even tempted to pull it off. I think I was truly in shock, then I yelled, 'If you were doing that with me, I bet you'd notice you have a sock in your ass!' Then I slammed the door and walked out."

Stacy covered her mouth with her hand, but her body shook with silent laughter.

Alexis shook her head. "Every time I thought of Michelle after that, I saw that sock stuck to her ass like a giant cotton hemorrhoid with stripes."

"And get this, Stacy, Michelle brought that woman to the house knowing Lex would catch them." Jaime smacked the seat. "What a bitch."

Alexis glanced at Stacy. "That was her way of saying we were through, and I got the message loud and clear."

"How long ago was that?" Stacy asked.

Alexis chuckled. "Long enough for me to be able to laugh now about that misplaced sock."

"Hey, y'all, I've got a hundred bucks in my pocket. If I start buying drinks for everybody and run out of cash, please don't let me take out my wallet." Jaime sucked her teeth. "Don't let me take my clothes off either."

The club was small, the music was loud, and the steady thump seemed to pulsate through the floor into Stacy's shoes. There was a moderate crowd, mostly very young, but she was

111

pleasantly surprised to see quite a few women her age or older. She wasn't looking to pick anyone up, but she didn't want to feel like a dinosaur either. She followed Alexis and Jaime to the bar where Jaime squeezed between the people gathered there and flagged down a bartender.

Alexis leaned in close to Stacy's ear and asked, "What would you like to drink?"

"Abita Purple Haze."

Alexis turned and told Jaime what she and Stacy wanted; Jaime relayed it to the bartender with a couple of add-ons. When Alexis turned again, she handed Stacy the beer and a shot glass. Stacy held up the shot glass. "What is this?" she yelled over the music.

"It's called Just Shoot Me," Jaime replied. "Very smooth, and it'll kick your ass."

"Okay, I can only do this once, though, and the next round is on me." Stacy downed the shot and shivered from head to toe.

Jaime did her shot and chased it with a beer. "Now we'll feel loose," she said and grinned at Alexis. "Hey, at least you get to drink for free."

"All the ginger ale I want, woohoo," Alexis said with a laugh.

Jaime leaned in close to Stacy. "You're already getting a lot of looks. Don't turn around yet, just look casually at the table on the wall behind you. There's a woman staring holes in your butt, and I think her friends are encouraging her to come say hello."

"Thanks for the heads-up." Stacy wrapped her arm around Alexis's waist and said into her ear, "Do you mind if I use you to ward off anyone who might be interested?"

"Not at all. You want me to glare at anyone in particular? I can puff up and make myself really scary."

Stacy laughed. "No, I'll just hang on you, that should be enough."

Jaime turned away from the bar with another shot and downed it. Alexis poked her in the shoulder. "You better slow down, or you're gonna be sloppy drunk before midnight."

"I'm good now." Jaime nodded. "Very good. I see an open table near the dance floor, y'all wanna grab it?"

112

Alexis nodded and took Stacy's hand as they made their way through the crowd. Stacy grinned goofily. It had been a long time since she'd had hard liquor, and she was already feeling a little fuzzy in the brain.

"I'm glad you saw this because this place is about to get packed." Alexis nodded at the people pouring in the door. She set her giant designated driver cup in the middle of the table. "Our territory is marked."

Stacy smiled and sat in the chair Alexis pulled out for her. The real Alexis was acting just like the fantasy version; she was being chivalrous and protective. They were pretending to be a couple, and there was alcohol involved. Stacy knew it was the perfect recipe to get her in trouble.

She watched as Alexis and Jaime talked and figured Jaime had already spotted someone she found attractive by the way they kept looking at a woman across the room. Jaime guzzled her beer, set the bottle down, and got up. Alexis leaned close to Stacy and said, "She's gonna go ask the blonde in the green shirt to dance. I hope she doesn't get rejected, I don't think her ego can take that right now."

They watched as Jaime spoke to the woman for a moment, then the woman stood and took Jaime's hand. "Crisis averted," Stacy said with a smile.

Alexis turned her attention to Stacy. "I'm really sorry for the conversation on the way over here. I did mention to Jaime that you'd also gone through a recent breakup, but I didn't realize she'd bring it up. I hope it hasn't put a damper on your evening."

Stacy smiled. "I'm fine. That chapter of my life ended a long time ago."

Alexis looked around. "You seem to have quite the fan club in here. You're being scoped out from every direction."

"What makes you think they're not looking at you?" Stacy asked with a smile.

"I know you've looked at yourself in a mirror," Alexis deadpanned, then laughed.

"Have you ventured into the dating world since your breakup?" Stacy asked.

113

"I did a while after the split, feeling like I had to get back out there. I dated a few women, but I realized I wasn't ready," Alexis replied with a shrug.

Stacy nodded. "You're not the type of woman to jump into anything."

"Not usually. What about you?" Alexis asked with a smile. "Are you ready to face the dating world again?"

"No, I don't want to shop around." Stacy met Alexis's curious gaze. "I know what I want."

Jaime returned to the table. "Hey, I'm headed to the bar, y'all want anything?"

"I have plenty of ginger ale, thank you," Alexis said and took a drink.

"No, it's my turn," Stacy said as she stood. "You want another beer and a shot?"

Jaime nodded. "Yes, ma'am."

"I'll be right back," Stacy said and walked away.

"You gonna sit here all night nursing your giant sippy cup?" Jaime swatted Alexis on the shoulder. "Ask that woman to dance, or I will."

"I was enjoying my conversation with her, and someone has to guard the table."

"You are so into her," Jaime said as she plopped down into a chair.

Alexis stabbed a finger at Jaime. "You need to slow your ass down. You drink too much too fast, then you get sick."

"Did you hear what I just said to you?"

"Yeah, I heard you, and I move at my own pace." Alexis shrugged. "I haven't decided if I like her that way or not."

"And you said that with a straight face." Jaime shook her head slowly. "Unbelievable."

Chapter Seventeen

Jaime downed her shot when Stacy returned with her drinks, then she grabbed Stacy by the arm and pulled her onto the dance floor. Alexis pretended not to pay them any mind, but she watched out of the corner of her eye as Jaime moved her body against Stacy's backside. Her internal vibrator was rattling the muscles in her stomach so viciously she thought she heard a buzzing in her ears.

When the song ended, Jaime disappeared into the crowd, and Stacy returned to the table. "I apologize for Jaime humping your leg like a dog," Alexis said with a wry smile.

Stacy laughed. "It's a dance floor thing, everybody humps everybody."

"Yeah, but her tongue was hanging out when she did it, and it was kinda gross. The dog obedience classes I sent her to were a total waste of money, she didn't learn anything." Alexis smiled. "She's probably in a corner somewhere chewing a shoe."

"What's your idea of a good time?" Stacy asked before she took a drink of her beer.

"It used to be clubbing, but now I hate to admit that I enjoy playing video games." Alexis held up a hand when Stacy's face went blank. "I know, I'm a total loser geek."

"I have all the *Call of Duty* games, every last one, are you calling me a loser?" Stacy asked seriously.

"Um…no. You've just become the coolest woman on the planet. Do you kill any zombies?"

"Do I?" Stacy exclaimed. "You're looking at a master slayer. I cannot wait to get my hands on *Ghost Dimension*, the new game developed by—"

"I have it! As soon as it was announced, I got on a waiting list." Alexis slapped the table. "It came in the mail yesterday, but I haven't had time to open the box."

"Let's go to your house right now," Stacy said excitedly.

Jaime appeared in front of their table with two more shots, two beers, and the woman she'd danced with earlier. "Hey, y'all, this is Megan, and we want the table, so go dance."

"Nice to meet you, Megan," Alexis yelled over the music as she stood. She didn't need any more prompting from Jaime to dance with Stacy. A woman who loved video games was like the golden goose.

Stacy followed her onto the floor and said, "I can't believe you didn't open the box!"

"I didn't want to rush it," Alexis replied as she moved to the music. "I wanted time to sit back and enjoy it, you know? I don't think I would've been satisfied with a quick play. I know when I put my hands on the controls, I'm not gonna be able to stop for a while, and I don't want to be interrupted when I'm getting into it."

Stacy nodded. "Sometimes, video games are better than sex—sometimes. It's an escape like a book or a movie, but it's adrenaline-filled and you can blow stuff up."

"Exactly. When I've had a stressful day, I take my grenade launcher out for a walk." Alexis grinned when an old song began to play. "Old school, dust off your Cabbage Patch and your Wop. I'm gonna break out the snake."

They danced to several songs that were popular in the eighties, then went back to the table for their drinks. Megan's friends had joined her and Jaime, and the table was covered in empty shot glasses and beer bottles. Jaime waited until Stacy finished off her beer and pressed the last of the shots into Stacy's hand and told her to drink. Then she dragged Stacy back onto the dance floor. Alexis was pissed as she watched them go. Jaime had her own playmate, and Alexis didn't appreciate having to share hers.

When Alexis took a seat, one of Megan's friends scooted her chair close. "Hey, do you mind if I ask if you and that other girl are together?"

Alexis's attraction to Stacy was in full bloom, and the response flew out of her mouth before she had time to really think about it. "Yes, we are—very serious—engaged."

"You make a very nice-looking couple," the woman said.

"Thanks. I'm Alexis."

"Toni—well, it's Tonya, but I don't like that name. Do I look like a Tonya to you?"

Alexis gazed at her. "Um…no?"

"You have beautiful eyes, they're so dark," Toni said with an appreciative smile. "Have you ever heard the song *3* by Britney Spears?"

Stacy was watching the conversation between Alexis and Toni with interest when a couple blocked her line of sight. She grabbed Jaime and moved to get a better view. Jaime laughed and said, "It's so much fun watching two people at this stage. You're both interested in each other, but y'all are still kinda scared of making that first move because just a hint of doubt still lingers in your minds. Does she like me like that? Y'all are watching each other closely for a signal or sign—"

Jaime's head lolled back when Stacy grabbed her and pulled her close. "What do you know? What has she said?" Stacy asked.

"You don't look like it, but you're really fucking strong," Jaime slurred. "Are my feet on the ground?"

"Has she said anything about me?" Stacy persisted.

"She thinks you're very pretty. Alexis is playing it cool, but I can tell she's very interested in you. You are like totally obvious. I'm drunk, and I can tell you're into her big-time." Jaime winced. "Could you loosen your grip on my arm, my humerus feels like it's about to snap…that's a bone."

"Sorry." Stacy released Jaime and smiled. "Yes, I'm interested in Alexis. It's always a tightrope when someone is a friend because signs can be misinterpreted."

117

"Go drag her out of the chair and dance with her again. You want another shot?"

"Yes...no." Stacy shook her head. "I might throw up on her. I don't have much of a tolerance."

"Yeah, that wouldn't go well with your dance of seduction." Jaime took Stacy by the hand. "Come on." They walked over to the table, and Jaime grabbed Alexis by the arm and pulled her up. "Your turn to dance, buddy, I'll guard your ginger ale."

"I'm so glad y'all came when you did," Alexis said against Stacy's ear when they returned to the floor and moved to the music. "I didn't want to give up the table, but the woman next to me asked if we were a couple, and I told her yes because she looked like she was on the prowl. Then she started singing a Britney Spears song about threesomes."

"Yes, that's an oldie but nasty," Stacy said and glanced at Toni, who was staring at them with undisguised interest. Stacy gave Toni her most fierce predatory look. "Let's give her a show." She moved behind Alexis, wrapped one arm around her waist, and began moving rhythmically against her backside.

Stacy's pulse pounded when she felt Alexis's hands on her hips. The booze was doing a number on her brain, which had jumped onto the expressway and was headed south. She sniffed Alexis's hair and found the scent more intoxicating than the liquor robbing her of her sanity. She put her hands on Alexis's shoulders and bent her forward, grinding slowly against her. Stacy flashed a grin at Toni, who to her disappointment was not looking. Jaime was, though, and her jaw was hanging open.

Alexis stood up straight and whirled around laughing. "All right, you've topped me on the dance floor, that's the only chance you're gonna get."

"You went willingly," Stacy shot back with a grin. "Don't act like you didn't like it." She was very pleased with the flush she saw growing on Alexis's neck.

"Prepare yourself, I'm about to put it on you." Alexis popped the kinks out of her neck, stood up straight, and moved in on Stacy. She put her face close to Stacy's cheek and began a slow grind on her hip, then gradually moved in front of her, their mouths inches apart. Alexis moved slowly down Stacy's body and knelt in front of her for a second before she popped back up and spun Stacy around to grind on her backside. Their bodies were pressed tightly together, Alexis's breath was on Stacy's cheek, her hands swept over her, igniting a fire. The flames were dampened by Jaime's voice when she appeared beside them and yelled, "Damn! Y'all need to get a room!"

Alexis pulled away from Stacy abruptly and said, "Did you lose the table?"

"One of Megan's friends was trying to talk me into having a threeway. I had to get outta there because it was starting to sound appealing. I hate to tell y'all this, but I'm ready to go."

Alexis studied Jaime's face. "You're getting sick, aren't you?"

"Megan bought me some shots, and they didn't mix well with everything else I drank," Jaime said and swallowed hard. "I'm sorry, y'all."

"It's okay. Let's just get you out of here before you blow," Stacy said when she noticed that Jaime was growing paler by the second.

They moved quickly through the crowd and out of the building. Once they were outside, Jaime made a dash to where Alexis's truck was parked and went beyond it to the brush. Alexis took Stacy's arm and slowed her stride. "Let's give her a minute or two. If I hear someone retching, I'll do the same. I'm sorry the night was cut short."

"I had a nice time, and I enjoyed the dance."

Alexis gazed at Stacy a moment and gathered her courage. "Would you like to come over tomorrow and play *Ghost Dimension* with me?"

"Yes," Stacy replied enthusiastically. "If you hadn't invited me, I would've gotten your address from Jason and tried to force my way in with pizza."

"Hey, y'all, I'm good now, we can go back in," Jaime said as she rejoined them with watery eyes and a runny nose.

Alexis shook her head. "Jaime, I hate to tell you this, but you look like shit, and your face is as white as a sheet. It's time to take you home."

119

"I forgot to take pictures. I can't even post them and lie about having a good time," Jaime whined.

"Your ex doesn't know me. I'll pose with you if you want," Stacy offered.

"Can I kiss you or pretend like we're kissing?" Jaime asked with a devilish grin until she noticed Alexis's facial expression.

"That was the booze talking, and I have barf breath."

"I will do this." Stacy stood behind Jaime with her arms wrapped around her shoulders. Alexis pulled out her phone and snapped a picture of the pair smiling.

Alexis gazed at it and laughed. "Jaime, you look like a gremlin. Rachel will definitely know you've been partying."

"I've danced, and it's time to pay the piper." Jaime took off running for the bushes again.

They were halfway to Stacy's apartment when Jaime said, "Lex, turn the air up higher, I'm kinda sweating back here."

Alexis gazed at her in the rearview. "You're really pale. Are you gonna—oh, shit!" She whipped her truck into a parking lot, and Jaime threw the door open and jumped out.

"Wow, she's really sick." Stacy watched Jaime from her window. "She looks like a human fountain."

Jaime had left the door open, and Alexis could hear her retching. The sound had an immediate effect, and Alexis threw open her own door and jumped out. Stacy was left alone and stunned by the twin sounds of puking. She leaned over the console and asked Alexis, "Do you want me to hold your hair?"

"No, don't even look at me," Alexis said miserably. "Don't watch."

"Lex, you asshole, why did you let me drink so much?" Jaime cried between gagging.

"I told you to slow down. Look what you made me do!" Alexis yelled. "It splashed on my pants."

"I had a great time. Thank you for inviting me tonight," Stacy said as Alexis walked her to her door.

"Oh, that was a sweet little lie," Alexis said and gazed down at her wet pants and bare feet.

"I thought it was ingenious of you to run through that ditch to wash off your pants and shoes." Stacy unlocked her door and smiled. "Would you like to come in and have something to drink to wash the taste of...well, you know?"

"Thanks, but I should get Jaime to my house before she wakes up and becomes a human hydrant again." Alexis winced. "I really am sorry about how tonight turned out."

Stacy did her best not to laugh. "I had a great time. Do you still want to get together tomorrow?"

"Yes, definitely. I'll call you." Alexis backed away slowly and smiled. "Good night."

"Good night," Stacy replied and watched her go.

Jaime opened her eyes when Alexis climbed into the truck and slammed the door. "Did you kiss her?" she slurred.

"Yeah, I laid one on her with my barf breath." Alexis threw the truck in reverse and backed out of her parking slot. "I can't believe you made me puke in front of her."

"Stacy's cool. She patted my back while I threw up my ribcage. Did you ask her out?"

Alexis shrugged. "Kind of. She's gonna come over to play *Ghost Dimension* with me, she's a gamer."

"Did I eat cotton or hair tonight?"

"Technically, it's not a date." Alexis shrugged. "I mean, I just asked her to come over and play a game. Do you think she thinks it's a date?"

Jaime grimaced. "I feel like I have a sock on my tongue. She likes you, she bruised my arm bone, and she was staring at you."

Alexis glanced from the road. "She did what to your arm?"

"She squeezed it and said she likes you," Jaime mumbled as her head lolled forward.

Alexis was tempted to wake Jaime up and have her elaborate but figured Jaime was smashed and talking out of her ass anyway. She did, however, cut the corner sharply when she turned into her driveway and slung Jaime's limp body against the door just for kicks.

Dear Me,

It's almost one in the morning, but I have to get my thoughts out on paper before I can sleep. I went to a bar tonight with Jaime and Stacy. I danced with Stacy, and I don't think I have ever been that turned on in my life. Here's the really weird thing. I don't know her, but I feel like I've known her all my life. I read what I just wrote, and it makes no sense.

When I met Jaime, I knew we were going to be friends. I didn't really analyze it, I just knew it, and here we are eight years later. I have that same knowing with Stacy, and it's not just about friendship. I know I didn't feel that way about Michelle or any of the other women I've been with. I can't remember if I knew that I'd be with Lily when I first met her, it was so long ago.

I have to be brutally honest with myself and acknowledge when I started writing my thoughts down, I said I wanted to be in love. I went back and read everything before I started writing this, so I have to wonder if I'm feeling this way because I want it. Am I faking myself out? Will I kiss Stacy for the first time and feel that hollow in me opening up and the vibrator dropping off into it?

I know Stacy is interested in me, not because drunk Jaime said it. The way she looks at me is so intense. I don't know what I did to score her interest. She could've had any woman in that bar tonight, but she made me feel like there was nobody in there but us. I almost kissed her on that dance floor, but my best friend, who I love so very much, fucked up my moment. I'm hoping another one will come soon, and when I do kiss Stacy, I have my fingers crossed the hollow won't follow.

Me

122

Chapter Eighteen

Alexis awoke the next morning with coffee on her mind. She made a visit to the bathroom, then opened her bedroom door to find two cats, a mouse toy, and the cardboard insert from a toilet paper roll. Normally, she would've fussed at Sprout for digging in the trash cans, but the smell of food cooking surprised her as she headed to the kitchen flanked by her furry escorts ready for breakfast. When she strode into the kitchen, she found Jaime leaning heavily against the counter staring at the toaster.

"What're you doing awake already?"

Jaime scowled at Ginger and Sprout as they circled Alexis's legs beckoning her to fill their bowls. "Those two furry demons tortured me all night long. Ginger slept on my neck, and it was like wearing a heavy scarf. Sometime before dawn, they demonstrated their feline MMA skills. There was kicking, punching, leaps, and flips. After they got bored with that, I finally fell asleep again, but ten minutes ago, they returned and began to sing a mournful tune."

"I closed your door last night after I dragged you to bed, and they weren't in your room." Alexis opened the pantry and got out the cat food.

Jaime grabbed the toast when it popped out of the toaster and threw it on a plate. "I remember going to the bathroom, and they probably got in then."

"You want me to make some bacon and eggs?" Alexis asked as she fed the cats. "Greasy food is supposed to help with a hangover."

"Oh, God, no. I'm gonna smear some butter on this toast, and that'll be all I need. I'm done with partying now, the after-effects aren't worth it. Time to put my big girl panties back on and handle my life. I'll do this right after a long nap. Hey, did I dream it, or did you tell me you have a date with Stacy today?"

"It's not a date, she's coming over to play *Ghost Dimension.*"

"Oh, shit. Do you mean to tell me that she's like you, an adult fascinated with video games?"

"Yep," Alexis said with a smile.

"Go find a jewelry store right now and buy her a ring. Ask her to marry you when she gets here because you're not gonna find another woman who is pretty, funny, downright sexy, and as big of a dork as you are," Jaime said and completely lost interest in buttering her toast. "Lex, it's like God or the universe dropped your perfect mate into your lap."

Alexis stuffed the cat food bag back into the pantry wondering if Jaime had read her mind or her journal. The latter was tucked between her mattress and box spring, and unless Jaime had sneaked stealthily into her bedroom the night before, there was no chance she'd read it. She wasn't about to admit that she somewhat agreed with Jaime.

"You're a romantic, I'm a realist. Yeah, she's a lot of fun and she likes gaming, but we're from two different worlds. She comes from some serious wealth, and I'm basically a glorified farmer. Even when she's dressed casually, she still manages to look like a million bucks. She probably sees me as someone to have a good time with, but I'm not what she'll want in the long-term category."

"Oh, horse shit. That bar was a grungy hole-in-the-wall with cement floors, and Stacy didn't bat an eye or turn her nose up at it. I get the distinct impression that she's extremely down to earth, and that's not the issue here." Jaime stabbed a finger at Alexis. "You're scared shitless of getting hurt. You're hiding behind excuses. Do you want to be lonely for the rest of your life?"

"I'm not lone—"

"Don't lie to me, and more importantly, don't lie to yourself. Look at Jason and Alana. Jason's wealth hasn't stopped him from wanting to be with her, and she's a hairdresser."

"That's different, he's a man in the provider role, and Alana is perfectly content with that arrangement. I'm a provider too. I take care of things, it's my nature. How do I take care of someone who doesn't need it? What do I have to offer her she doesn't already have?"

Alexis was playing devil's advocate because Jaime's rebuttals were making her feel better about pursuing Stacy, but there was a tiny shred of truth in what she'd just said. Maybe Stacy wasn't wealthy herself, but she'd been raised around the finer things. Alexis wondered if Stacy could be content with her simple lifestyle.

Jaime's jaw sagged. "I've heard you say some dumb things before, like the time you asked why cows didn't wear shoes like horses, but what just came out of your mouth has to be the most idiotic thing you have ever uttered. Are you so insecure that you think you have to give a woman something monetary to make her stay? What about love, acceptance, affection, loyalty?"

"All right. You've made your point. I hear you."

"Listen to me, Lex. There's chemistry between the two of you. I'm begging you to explore it. Please don't let this opportunity pass you by. Yeah, you may find she's not for you, but you can't just cut yourself off like you've been doing. You're gonna hate me for saying this, but you're becoming like your mother."

The last part of Jaime's statement hit Alexis like a punch to the gut. She'd worried about that, but to have Jaime admit she was concerned about it too was a blow. Suddenly, all of Alexis's fears of feeling the hollowness with Stacy filled her with anxiety. She almost didn't want to find out.

"Hey, I'm really sorry. That comment about your mother was out of line. Please forgive me."

"It's okay. You love me enough to tell me the truth. Now I'm gonna be honest with you. While I'm with Stacy, you need to go shopping for new bras. That thing you had on last night— all bad."

Stacy had gotten up that morning and eaten breakfast, and despite drinking a cup of coffee, she went right back to sleep on her sofa. She sat straight up when her phone rang and answered still half asleep. "Hello—hey?"

"I'm sorry, did I wake you?" Alexis asked.

"Oh…no, I was napping."

"Isn't that the same thing as sleeping?" Alexis asked with amusement in her tone.

Stacy laughed. "Well, yeah, but I'm happy you called." She looked at her watch. "I didn't want to sleep the day away."

"Do you still want to get together this afternoon and play?"

"Definitely. A woman I work with has been talking about a pizza place she found, and she says it's absolutely delicious. She gave me a bite of a leftover slice the other day at lunch, and I've been craving it ever since. Do you mind if I bring one?"

"No, of course not, that sounds great. What time do you want to come over?" Alexis asked.

"Now."

Alexis laughed. "Okay, fine with me."

"What do you and Jaime like on your pizza?"

"I like it all. Jaime has just awoken from a long nap, and she's going shopping, so she won't be here. My driveway runs along the west side of the parking lot. I'm not sure if you noticed that the day you came by the garden center."

"Okay, I'll be there soon," Stacy said excitedly.

"Get it together, girl," Stacy said when her pulse picked up as she turned into Alexis's driveway. The asphalt lane ran along the side of the nursery, then curved away from and went behind a massive hedge. A live oak tree dominated the front yard; its long boughs touched the ground in places. There was an outdoor seating area beneath it. Flowering things and broad-leafed plants grew in abundance. Stacy had no idea what they were, but she thought they were beautiful.

She parked next to Alexis's truck and collected the pizza, her ball cap that sat atop the box, and a bag of goodies essential to gaming. She strolled along a flagstone path lined with dark green grass sporting purple flowers to the front porch. Alexis opened the door as Stacy climbed the steps.

"I'm trying to think of the word I want to use to describe your front yard," Stacy said as she turned and gazed at it.

"Snakey, cluttered, scary are the words Alana uses to describe it," Alexis said as she joined Stacy on the porch.

"No." Stacy shook her head slowly. "Ethereal, maybe? If fairies were real, they'd live here. I love it because it's not a typical square plot of grass with a few bushes scattered along the front of the house."

"Let me take this," Alexis said and took the pizza from Stacy. "Come on inside."

Stacy stepped in, and her head lolled back as she gazed up at long tendrils of ivy hanging from the upstairs railing. "Is that the same kind of ivy I have?" she asked in amazement.

"Yep. It really likes the skylights up there. Yours will grow like that if you keep it happy."

"Oh, hey, who are you?" Stacy asked and knelt down to pet the cat buffing her legs.

"That's Sprout, and Ginger is up there on the mantel. Watch Sprout," Alexis warned as she headed to the kitchen with the pizza. "He'll go belly up and make you think you're welcome to pet it, then the claws come out. He's especially mad at me right now because I forgot to dust the coffee table and I'd put my cleaning stuff up when I realized that, so I used him."

Stacy stood slowly and gazed at Sprout. "Did you just say you dusted with a cat?"

"Yeah, and the really great thing is, he cleaned himself up afterward. I need to invent some edible furniture polish, so I can use him more often."

Stacy walked over to the mantel and petted Ginger. "If she ever comes at one of y'all with a long stick and says she's going to clean the ceiling fans, my advice to you is to run," she whispered.

"What would you like to drink? I've got some sodas, ginger ale, iced tea, and wine."

127

"I haven't had ginger ale in a long time, that sounds good."
Stacy walked into the kitchen and was surprised to see there
were no plants in there, but the room had many windows, and
there was plenty of natural light. "Is this a plant-free zone?"

"Yeah," Alexis said with a laugh as she took out a glass and
filled it with ice. "My house used to be full of them, and it was
way too much. Things get damaged, or they're not growing for
one reason or another next door, and I bring them home. I'm like
a vet who takes home all the strays, so if you see anything you
like, I would be more than happy for you to have it."

"Okay, so I can go upstairs and get that ivy growing all over
the place?" Stacy asked as she set a bag and her hat on the bar.

Alexis laughed. "Except for that one, and the only reason is
because the pot is huge, and I don't want to carry it out of here."
She poured the ginger ale and handed it to Stacy. "Let's dig into
this pizza."

Alexis had already set the table and pulled out a chair for
Stacy. "I hope it isn't a disappointment after I played it up as
much as I did," Stacy said as she sat.

"If it is, I won't let you play *Ghost Dimension*." Alexis
laughed when Stacy flipped her off and opened the pizza box
and turned it toward Alexis. "You get first pick. How's Jaime
feeling today?"

After she napped, she showered, took two Excedrin, and was
back to normal," Alexis said before she took a bite of the pizza
and chewed slowly. "It's delicious."

"Okay, I'll stop worrying. I was afraid you weren't going to
let me play *Ghost Dimension*, and I was going to have to knock
you out."

Alexis glanced at the bag Stacy had set on the bar and the
baseball cap sitting atop it. "What's in there?"

"Game snacks. That's my lucky gaming hat, it keeps my
hair out of my eyes. I feel more like a sniper when I wear it
backward." Stacy took a bite of her pizza and looked around.
"This is a cool house."

"Thanks. It was here when I bought the land and was the
original storefront and office for the garden center. After I built
next door, I renovated this place. It took forever. I'd walk over

here every day and bug the shit out of the contractor because I wanted the work done overnight. Alana and I were sharing an apartment then, and she was in her party stage. She'd go out with friends, and they'd all end up back at our place. I woke up one morning, and there was hair dye all over the bathroom and kitchen. Everybody had black hair, it was like being at a goth convention. Poor little Ginger was a baby then, and they'd dyed just her head and tail black. I was so pissed, I shaved off Alana's eyebrows while she slept."

Stacy laughed. "You did not."

"I so did, and the jackass and her friends loved the look. They shaved theirs off too." Alexis shook her head with a smile. "Talk about an ugly bunch of people. Grammy wouldn't even be seen in public with Alana until she returned to her 'human-looking state.'"

"I rocked a buzz cut once. I call it that, but it wasn't a real one. My hair was an inch long all over my head, though, and I made it stand up with gel. That was during my first year of college, and when I came home for a holiday, my mother lost her mind on me. Not only had I cut it, I'd bleached it until it was almost white. I looked like a Q-tip."

Alexis grinned as she grabbed another slice of pizza. "Do you have pictures of that?"

"Yes, but you'll never see them."

"Oh, don't be mean," Alexis said with a laugh.

"You show me an embarrassing picture of you, and I'll show you mine."

Alexis nodded and got up from the table. "I'll take that challenge." She walked over to the counter near the stove and grabbed her phone. "Whenever Alana wants to get on my nerves, she sends me this pic," she said and tapped the screen. "She took this while I was asleep and after I'd let her cut my hair for the first and last time. Hey, I just realized you didn't let Alana cut your hair. I thought she said she was going to that first night we had dinner."

"I chickened out. There was too much change going on in my life then." Stacy wiped her hands on her napkin and took the cellphone. Alexis's dark red hair was short and spiky only on

129

one side of her head, the other side hung down just past her ear. She was also sound asleep, mouth hanging wide open, and what looked like a dental guard was lying on her cheek. Stacy clamped her lips together to keep from laughing. "Yes, that's…a bad one," she squeaked out.

"Do you have one of the Q-tip 'do on your phone?" Alexis asked as she sat back down.

"Oh…no." Stacy averted her gaze.

Alexis stared at her. "Stacy Kirkland, are you lying to me?"

"So you grind your teeth when you sleep?"

"Don't change the subject. Do you have the picture I want to see on your phone?" Alexis pressed.

Stacy sighed and pulled it from her pocket. "I should learn to keep my mouth shut." She tabbed through a few screens and reluctantly handed it to Alexis. She jumped when Alexis cackled loudly. "Be gentle."

Alexis continued to chuckle as she stared at it. "I can say this, you've hardly aged at all. Your face still looks the same, but that hair, wow."

"Give me that." Stacy snatched the phone from Alexis. She stuffed it back into her pocket and grinned as Alexis tried to stop laughing and failed. "I looked like a lightbulb with a face on it."

Chapter Nineteen

"Oh," Stacy said with a breathy sigh when she followed Alexis into the loft and looked around. "Gaming chairs, multiple consoles, big-screen TV. You're very serious."

"Okay, I have to admit that I didn't buy the chairs. A guy I work with got married, and his wife made him get rid of his gear, so he gave me these. That's when I decided to make this a game room. Am I too geeky?"

"No indeed." Stacy sank down into one of the chairs and sighed happily. "Ergonomic, ah." She clapped her hands. "Put the ghost in!"

Alexis opened the packaging and reverently placed the disk in the console. When she turned around, Stacy had her hat on backward, and she was opening a lollipop she'd taken from her snack bag. She looked absolutely adorable as she held it up to Alexis.

"Thanks." Alexis took it and smiled. "These are a requirement for gaming?"

"Uh-huh." Stacy opened her own and popped it into her mouth. She bounced in her seat when ghostly images floated across the screen. "I'm so glad you're into this too. No one ever wants to play with me, and it's more fun when you have someone in the same room."

"I agree." Alexis sat down and handed Stacy a controller. "How much do you know about the game?"

"I've done my homework. Ghosts can drain you and make you sluggish. They can only be sent to the great beyond with the laser. Demons can spit fire, you can shoot them with a regular gun. Oh! They can also morph out of human bystanders." Stacy grinned. "I love spooky stuff. I can't wait until we get to the zombie level because we get katanas in our weapons stash. I'm a badass with a sword, I can...why are you staring at me like that?"

"I'm impressed." Alexis smiled. "Let's kick some ghostly ass."

"Stacy, watch that guy coming up on your left, he may morph."

"I got my eye on him. You've got something coming up on your six, I'm going to take him out. Oops, civilian. I'm sorry about your head, guy."

"Ghost coming up on your—good catch!" Alexis sat back in her chair and breathed a sigh of relief as the game switched to the next level. She gazed at Stacy and laughed at the Tootsie Roll hanging out of the corner of her mouth like a cigar. "You're really good. I'm impressed with your shooting skills."

"Thank you, and may I say you were so stealth when you staked that vampire. Oh! Next phase, graveyard. I can't wait to see what awaits us here."

"Lex?"

"Upstairs in the loft slaying shit, enter if you dare."

Alana climbed the stairs with Jason on her heels. She shook her head slowly when she took in her sister and Stacy feverishly working game controllers. "Oh, my God, Jason, look what my sister has done to your cousin."

"Sweetie, this is the real Stacy you're seeing. She was on her best behavior when she stayed with us. Prepare yourself, she may belch her name next."

"Jason, I haven't revealed that talent to Alexis yet, so thank you very much for outing me," Stacy said distractedly as she stared at the screen.

"We have something important that we need to talk to y'all about." Alana stared at the TV with a look of disgust. "Could y'all stop beheading whatever those things are for a moment?"

Alexis stared at the screen in disbelief. "Stacy! Where'd you find a tank?"

132

"In an alley." She turned the big gun toward Alexis and obliterated her character. "Yes," Stacy cried with an evil laugh.

"You do realize we're on the same team," Alexis said, waving a hand between herself and Stacy.

"What's your point?"

"I've never been up here, this is really nice," Jason said as he walked over to the sofa against the wall and sat down.

Alana rolled her eyes and said, "Well, we know now why neither of you were answering your phones, but I'm glad we have y'all together because we want to talk to you both."

"Well, it better be important if you're gonna barge in on our carnage." Alexis grabbed a Tootsie Roll from the treat bag. "You better be glad we just slew a horde of zombies, and we needed a break."

"I didn't." Stacy jutted her chin. "I'm badass."

Alexis turned and gazed at her. "You know, you really are. You scored so high on the first level you got a flamethrower. I didn't get one until halfway into the second level."

"Yes, but that's only because you let me use your grenade launcher, so I think we're really effective as a team," Stacy said before she chewed up her Tootsie Roll.

"Hey, you two wanna come back to reality for a moment?" Alana asked impatiently. "Jason, tell them what's about to happen."

"Alana and I are going to elope next weekend, and we want you two to come with us to Cape San Blas to stand with us and be our witnesses."

"I don't mean to be a killjoy, but, Jason, your mother is going to kill you, and I don't mean that figuratively," Stacy said with a look of concern.

"You know Mom will be cool with this," Alexis said to Alana. "It's gonna break Grammy's heart, though."

"Well, actually, Allison and Elise are going too," Jason said with a smile. "They're going to be our photographers."

"Are you going to invite your parents?" Alexis asked Jason.

Jason shook his head. "If I do that, Mom will insist that my brothers have to be there with their wives and their kids. If they all come, this will turn into a big fiasco. I want a peaceful

133

ceremony," he said and gazed at Stacy. "This was my idea. I wanted to do this before Alana told me about the anxiety attack she had at the dress shop. What y'all don't know is that Mom has been calling me every day with a new name for the guest list, and she's been pushing me to allow her to take over the invitations. She even picked out some and emailed them to me at work. It's only going to get worse as the wedding date approaches, so I want to elope. She can throw a party later and invite half the state." He smiled at Alana. "We might attend."

"Okay." Stacy nodded rapidly as she absorbed it all. "What about the dress? I doubt it'll be here by next weekend."

"They'll tag us with a cancellation fee. We looked it up on their website," Jason said. "Alana and I will leave here on Tuesday and file for the marriage license, and we'll be able to get married on Saturday. I talked to Garret this morning. He's got a beach house available, and he's going to arrange for the justice of the peace. All we need now is you two, and we're hoping y'all can get off work and spend some time with us at the beach a few days before the ceremony."

Stacy wanted to add "and a suit of armor" for when Jason faced his mother, but she held that comment for when they were alone. Instead she said, "I'll have to talk to Wes first thing in the morning and see what he says. What about your boss?"

"I called Trevor today, and he's much happier with this plan than me taking off in September when we're launching some new campaigns." Jason beamed. "See how this is working out so easily? This is meant to be."

"What about you, Lex?" Alana asked. "Will you take off some time this week?"

"Uh, yeah, of course, whatever y'all want."

"Okay," Jason said as he stood. "Sweetie, let's let them get back to their evening of slaying and beheading ghouls and goblins."

"I'll call you tomorrow and let you know what Wes says," Stacy said as Jason and Alana started down the stairs.

"Okay, have fun, good night," Jason replied.

"Night, Lex."

"Night, Alana."

134

Alexis gazed at Stacy, and when Alana and Jason let themselves out, she said, "You're not happy."

"I want them to have the wedding they want. I don't blame them at all for eloping, it's what I would do." Stacy sighed. "His mother is going to lose her mind on him though. I hope he's prepared for that. The high side to this is we don't have to shop for bridesmaids dresses or wear them."

"Will she resent Alana for this?"

Stacy was slow to answer. "I think she's going to blame everyone but Jason at first because it will be a blow to her emotionally. I imagine it'll be hard for her to accept her own son doesn't want her at his wedding. Audrey isn't the type to sit back and consider her own actions led him to this decision. Don't worry, though, I'll bear the brunt of her wrath instead of Alana because she'll consider me Jason's accomplice." Stacy glanced at her watch and sat up straight. "Oh, my God, it's almost nine o'clock. I've definitely overstayed my welcome."

"No, you haven't. I've really enjoyed the company." Alexis pressed a button on her controller. "I'm gonna save this game, and I promise not to play at all until you come back."

Stacy smiled as she stood. "I'd love to. It's funny, isn't it? At first, we were threatening each other with badminton rackets, and now we're making play dates."

"Yeah, I'm noticing a pattern here. You hit me with a birdie, and tonight, you annihilated me with a tank."

"You'll reanimate." Stacy grinned. "The shuttlecock thing was purely an accident. My aim was off that night, or I would've hit you in the head then too. I'll leave the bag of game snacks here for our next battle."

"I'd ask if you'd like to get together this weekend, but it looks like we'll be in Florida," Alexis said as she followed Stacy downstairs. "You like the beach?"

"Love it. How about you?"

"I feel the same way." Alexis flipped a light switch when they got to the door. "I'll walk you out. Hey, do you wanna ride with me to Florida?"

"Sure," Stacy replied with a smile as they walked outside. "I hate making long trips by myself."

Alexis swatted at a bug. "I've never even heard of Cape San Blas, how far away is it?"

"About seven hours, I think."

"Shit."

Stacy laughed. "That's what I thought when Jason told me that was where he wanted to have the wedding. I look at it like this: seven hours on the road is better than seven in an office."

"Way to find the positive," Alexis said when they arrived at Stacy's car.

Stacy felt as though their evening had gone great. She gave Alexis the look, and Alexis caught the signal. She licked her lips as she gazed at Stacy, then seemed to lose her nerve.

"I had a great time with you this weekend," Alexis said instead.

"I did too." Stacy tried a different approach to get Alexis to respond to her. "Tonight kind of felt like a date."

Alexis nodded. "It did. Would you go to dinner with me sometime?"

"Yes, I will," Stacy answered with a smile and sent her signal again by gazing at Alexis's lips.

Alexis leaned in close to Stacy and gave her a somewhat chaste kiss, until Stacy pulled her closer. Stacy had imagined this moment many times, but fantasy kisses paled in comparison to what Alexis gave her. They parted breathless as Jaime's headlights lit up the entire front yard.

"Jaime, your timing is horrible," Alexis said as they walked inside.

"I'm sorry. I stayed at the mall until it closed."

Alexis sighed. "I'm sorry too. It was a lot to ask you to leave the house for that long."

"It was worth it." Jaime poked Alexis in the shoulder. "You got a kiss, and it looked like a good one."

Alexis opened her eyes wide and raked a hand through her hair. "It was. I have a date too," she said with a smile.

"And I have new bras! It's a good day!"

Dear Me Wooohooo,

I kissed her. No disinterest, no hollowness followed, only an intense desire to see Stacy again. I feel like we go together like peanut butter and jelly. Oh, man, she's an animal with a flamethrower, how sexy is that? And that Tootsie Roll hanging out of her mouth like a cigar, precious! I hope she brushes well tonight, that's a lot of sugar right on the teeth.

Side note: If I should die and someone finds this journal, the flame thrower was in a video game, and Stacy Kirkland is not a homicidal maniac.

I'm craving her like a chocolate peanut butter cup! Do we have any of those here? I don't know, Jaime's doing all the grocery shopping. Anyway, I'm ecstatic about the kiss. It was electric, and my inner vibrator exploded.

Happy Me

Chapter Twenty

"Who is the best cousin in the world?" Jason said as he strode into Stacy's office with a large paper bag the next day. "That would be me because I have your most favorite sensation salad here."

Stacy stared at him for a second, her face blank. "I forgot to call you, I'm sorry."

"You can't get off?" Jason asked with concern.

"No, I can. Wes said I could take off Wednesday, but I have a lot of work to get done in two days, and I've been swamped. That's why I forgot to call."

Jason blew out a breath. "Whew, you scared me there for a second. Everything has worked out. The dress shop is going to sell us the dress Alana tried on, so we don't have to wait for one to come in. They do have to make a couple of alterations, but it'll be ready late tomorrow afternoon. Allison is gonna pick it up for us because we have to leave in the morning. The thing that worried me most was that you might not be able to take off on such short notice."

"I would've driven all Friday night to be there Saturday for the wedding," Stacy said with a smile.

"That's sweet, and I knew you would say that." Jason took a salad from the bag and set it in front of Stacy along with a plastic fork, a bottle of water, and a pile of napkins. "I didn't want you to have to do that because it's a seven-hour drive, and more importantly, I want to be able to spend some time with you."

"What about your honeymoon?" Stacy asked as Jason took out his salad and sat down.

"That'll come later when Alana and I have more time. I'm secretly planning a trip for us in January." Jason smiled. "Besides, every day of our lives right now is a honeymoon."

Stacy opened her salad and picked up her fork. "Jason, I don't want to be the voice of doom—"

"You're not, and I know what you're about to say. Mom is going to be really hurt, and she's going to be furious that all of Alana's family went with us. There's only three of them, though, and like I said last night, Mom would insist on bringing the entire family. They overwhelm Alana when we go over there for lunch or dinner, I don't want her to have a nervous breakdown. Honestly, I was dreading the wedding because everything was a fight with Mom. She was pissed about the locale, she thinks not wearing a suit is bad taste. She was after me to cut my hair again, it was nag, nag, nag. Yes, I know I'll have to put up with years of fury for eloping, but at least I'll have the wedding Alana and I want."

"Okay," Stacy said with a nod before she took a bite of her salad.

"What you're also worried about is being my accomplice because that's how the family will see you after this."

"You're right about that, my friend," Stacy said with a nod. "I told Alexis that would happen."

"I'm about to be a married man, so I need to get used to standing up to my mother, and I'll do that on your behalf. What were you doing at Alexis's house last night?" he asked with a teasing tone.

"We killed some demons and vaporized ghosts together. Why didn't you tell me she was into video games?"

"I didn't know she was until I saw her game room last night. Was that a date?" Jason pressed.

"It wasn't officially until I gave her the look, then I got a kiss that left me dizzy. I got into my car and turned the radio up instead of the AC. I didn't realize this until I was halfway home and sweat was pouring off my face."

"Okay, I hate to ruin your moment, but I have to be really selfish here. You have a pattern, Stacy. Years ago, you broke up with...what's her name...Amanda! After y'all broke up, you went through women like tissues at a funeral. Then you settled down with Carrie, and after y'all broke up, you did the tissue women thing again, and now here you are after Janey. You can't blow your nose on Lex."

"Dear cousin, you have to work on your analogies, but I'm glad you used tissue instead of toilet paper for this one. Let me relieve your concerns. I'm already crazy about Alexis."

Jason released a happy sigh and smiled. He was about to take a bite of his salad and lowered his fork. "How did that happen so quickly?"

"Well, it didn't really. We met a few months ago."

Jason took a bite of his salad and gazed at Stacy as he chewed. She began to squirm because he did have a point. She was already feeling like Alexis was tugging on her heart, and they barely knew each other. It hit her then that she might've been getting wrapped up in her own fantasy.

"You have a strange look on your face. What's going on in your head?"

"I was, um...I was thinking—didn't you say you knew you would marry Alana on your second date?"

"Third," Jason corrected.

"How did you know that?"

Jason shook his head. "I can't explain it so it'll make sense. We were eating ice cream, and she was telling me about something she thought was funny, and it hit me. I won't lie, normally when I go out with a woman, my first priority is sex. Getting to know the real her is somewhere in the back of my mind, but the physical desire is front and center. With Alana..." Jason laughed softly as he tried to put his feelings into words. "It was magical, it's just magic. I wasn't searching for my other half, but I found her in that ice cream shop."

Alexis pulled her phone from her pocket when she felt it vibrate and read Stacy's text. *I'm off Wed, Thur & Fri. I'll call you tonight. Road trip Wed!*

"Hey, Chase, would you like to take off the rest of the day and tomorrow?"

Chase wiped his brow with the back of his forearm and watched as one of the newbies on the forklift unloaded palettes from a truck. "Why would I want to do that?"

"I'm going out of town Wednesday, and I won't be back until late Sunday. I need you to run things, and I thought you might like a day and a half to mentally prepare to be me."

Chase grinned. "You opened the door right there for so many smart-ass comments. I won't make any of them, though, because you'll hose me, and I have my phone in my pocket."

"I would never do anything like that. I have too much respect for you, man."

"Last week, a woman who looked just like you popped up from behind the banana trees and got me in the face. The week before that, she shot me in the crotch."

"Yeah, that was a good one," Alexis said with a maniacal smile.

"Where are you going?"

"Florida. Alana's eloping, and she wants me to tag along."

"She's really gonna do it?" Chase asked, looking stunned. "That Jason guy reeled her in?"

"He did, and she's not even fighting to get off the hook."

"Shit! I bet Elise fifty bucks that Alana would back out," Chase said with disgust.

"You never bet my grandma on anything." Alexis laughed. "I learned that when I was twelve years old. Here she comes, I hope you have a pocket full of cash."

"I need to go check on something," Chase said and quickly walked away.

Elise patted her face with a tissue as she joined Alexis and said, "It's hotter than Satan's balls out here."

"What websites are you visiting, Grammy?"

"All of them. That's how I spend my time when your mother has company and I can't go into the kitchen and paint. Needless to say, I spend a lot of time in my bedroom on my computer." Elise narrowed her eyes. "I heard you had company last night too."

141

Alexis folded her arms. "Oh, I'm sure Alana couldn't wait to share that. Stacy likes video games too, so we got together and played."

"Is that what y'all are calling it these days? According to the sites I've visited, it's referred to as a hookup."

Alexis smiled. "I asked her out last night, and she said yes, so I guess you can call us dating."

"Good for you. I like her. She's a very pretty woman, a real Scooby snack, a stone cold fox, a—" Elise sucked her teeth. "I have to start taking notes. I'm having a retention problem."

"I get the point," Alexis said with a smile.

"What time are we leaving on Wednesday?"

Alexis blinked at the subject change. "We?"

"Well, you don't expect me and your mother to travel alone, do you? Allison can't follow directions and gets lost too easily, and when I drive more than ten miles, I forget I'm behind the wheel."

"I *just* heard from Stacy. How do you already know we were planning on leaving Wednesday?"

"Jason had lunch with her, he told Alana, she texted your mother, who called me and asked that I do the laundry, so we can be ready to leave day after tomorrow." Elise twirled a finger. "See, we all talk, you should learn to get in the loop. You need to get grown on your communication skills."

Alexis's brow furrowed. "Get grown? Is that some of the street chat you've been learning?"

"Yes, get grown means to improve. I used it in a sentence, you should've been able to figure out what it meant. So what time are we leaving?"

Alexis suppressed a sigh and ran a hand through her hair. She was looking forward to seven hours in the car alone with Stacy. "Grammy, Stacy and I haven't even made our plans yet."

"Good, I say we leave at five. If we stop for lunch for an hour, that will put us there at two o'clock with the time change and all. "I Googled that shit. Cape San Blas is in the Eastern time zone."

Alexis snorted. "Did the word 'shit' just cross Elise Holt's lips?"

"Yes, I feel so reckless and wild," Elise replied with a smile. "I'm about to shoplift, or better yet, boost a timer for my sprinkler from your store. I'll need you to come by later and hook it up for me, so my plants will be watered while we're gone."

"Having me install it kinda takes the thrill of the theft away, doesn't it?"

Elise shrugged. "No, not really."

Chapter Twenty-one

"Hey, I'm just now leaving the office," Stacy said when Alexis answered her phone that evening. "I'm going to have to work late tomorrow night too, but I'll be ready to go on Wednesday morning."

Alexis glanced at her watch while she worked on setting up the timer on Elise's sprinkler system. "It's almost eight o'clock. I feel sorry for you."

"What're you doing? You sound like you're struggling with something."

"I'm replacing an old timer on Grammy's sprinkler, which isn't hard at all, but I'm in a gardenia bush that she's allowed to grow all over the place. I have to tell you, Grammy has invited herself and my mom to ride with us."

"They should. It makes no sense to take two cars when we're all going to the same place," Stacy said as she stopped at a light. "I like them both, and I think a road trip with them would be fun."

"Grammy wants to leave at five in the morning. You still like her?" Alexis asked with a laugh.

"Okay, I don't like anybody until at least seven, but I can handle it for one day."

"Allison, will you look at that? The gardenia bush is talking."

"I'm on the phone with Stacy, Grammy, and you need to have your lawn people trim this shrub."

"Tell Stacy I said hello, and I'm looking forward to traveling with her."

144

Alexis relayed the message. "Grammy says to tell you hello, and she looks forward to tormenting you for the seven hours we'll be in the car together."

"I think I'm looking forward to that too," Stacy replied with a smile.

"Tell her to bring a blanket and a pillow for napping."

"Mom, is that you?" Alexis asked.

"Yes, tell Stacy what I said."

"I heard her," Stacy said with a laugh. "It's a good idea. Tell them I have tons of sunscreen, so don't go out and buy any."

"Mom, Grammy, Stacy has sunscreen."

"Tell Stacy—"

"Hey! I'm working in a bush, I'm being eaten by mosquitoes, and this is my phone call. If y'all need to tell Stacy something, give your message to Alana, who will tell Jason, and he will tell Stacy. That's how the information loop works."

"Good night, Stacy," Elise called out.

"Would you tell Elise I said good night?" Stacy asked with a chuckle.

"She says good night." Alexis lowered her voice and said to Stacy, "And you thought I was joking about the seven hours of torment."

"I'm still standing here, Alexis Leigh. I think it's time for me to test the sprinkler," Elise said.

"Grammy, don't you dare. Stacy, I have to go, I'll call you back," Alexis said hurriedly.

"Did Elise make good on her threat?" Stacy asked when Alexis called her back a little later.

"Let's just say I'm thankful I have a waterproof case for my phone," Alexis replied as she took her wet clothes off in her laundry room. "She laughed so hard she stopped breathing for a second. I was afraid I was gonna have to do CPR."

"She really did turn the sprinkler on?"

"No, she opened the kitchen window above the sink and called me over to supposedly ask a question, then she pelted me with the pot sprayer. I can hear you laughing, don't even try to suppress it," Alexis said with a smile. "I assume you had to work late because you're taking off."

"Yes, and I'll have to do the same tomorrow night, but I'll be able to go on this trip stress-free if I have everything taken care of before I go. My car is very fuel-efficient, would you like to take it?"

"Normally, I would say yes," Alexis said as she fed the cats. "But we're probably going to need the truck for Mom and Grammy's luggage. They don't travel light. Plus, I heard Grammy telling Mom there aren't many stores on the cape, so they're planning on going grocery shopping at one of those bulk food stores. I may have to hook a trailer to the truck to haul the load. I was really looking forward to making this trip alone with you."

Stacy smiled as she prepared to eat the leftover salad Jason had brought her at lunch. "That would've been nice, but we'll make up for it once we're there. Have you cheated on me?"

"What?" Alexis asked, completely thrown by the question.

"Have you played *Ghost Dimension*?"

"Oh! No, I'd never be unfaithful to you," Alexis replied with a laugh. "I wouldn't want to face a horde of demons and ghosts without you and your tank by my side."

Stacy smiled. "You say the sweetest things. Are you bringing the game console with you?"

"No, it's bait to keep you coming back to my house," Alexis said as she walked into her kitchen in her underwear and grabbed a bottle of water from the refrigerator.

Stacy sighed. "I wish you and I were walking down a dimly lit street, you with your grenade launcher, me with the flame thrower facing a thong of the undead."

"You have to stop," Alexis said with a groan. "You're making me want things I know I can't have right now."

Stacy continued with a sexy timbre. "I can't wait to take it to the next level. The landscape will be all new, and the battle will be long and fierce."

"You're making me sweat, and my heart is pounding."

Jaime walked into the kitchen at that moment and stopped midstride when she saw that Alexis was in her underwear, the

146

skin of her neck and face flushed. "Are you having phone sex where we eat?"

"We're talking about killing things, thank you very much," Alexis snapped.

"Calvin Klein matching bra and bikini briefs, you must've paid a fortune for that." Jaime shook her head. "I really didn't see you as the designer underwear type, Lex. No wonder you ragged me about my undies."

"What is she saying about your underwear?" Stacy asked with interest.

"It's a long story." Alexis rushed out of the kitchen to her bedroom. "So I'll pick you up at four forty-five Wednesday?"

"I'll come to you, so you don't have to take me home after the long drive on Sunday."

"Okay, I'll be looking forward to seeing you then."

After the conversation, Stacy sat staring at her salad. Her heart was racing, and it had nothing to do with video games. She knew it was irrational to believe Jason's claim that the Holt women were magical. The real Alexis was better than anything she'd ever conjured in her imagination. She was beginning to understand what Jason had felt in the ice cream shop.

Chapter Twenty-two

Preparation for the trip kept Alexis from making new entries in her journal. She tossed it into her bag just in case she felt the need to sort out her innermost thoughts while she was in Florida. She pursed her lips and went over her mental packing list to make sure she had all she intended to take before she closed everything up.

"Coffee's ready," Jaime yelled.

Alexis grabbed her bag and carried it to the front door where she left it. "Not that I don't appreciate the sendoff, but why are you up at this hour?" Alexis asked as she joined Jaime in the kitchen.

"I start getting up early a couple of days before I go back to the rig to prep my body for my shifts." Jaime handed Alexis a cup of coffee. "Now remind me what I need to do about the cats before I leave on Friday morning."

Alexis pointed to a paper held to the refrigerator by a magnet. "I put that there to remind you. Make sure their auto-feeder has food, their water bowls are full, and they are inside before you lock the cat door. Don't stress if you forget a step because Chase will check on them." She smiled sadly. "I wish you were coming with us."

"Me too, but while I'm on this hitch and I have nothing to do but think, I'm gonna decide whether or not I want to keep working there. When I get back here, I'll have a life plan that I'll put in motion."

"Don't worry to be in any hurry to get out of here. I'd be happy if you stayed forever," Alexis said with a smile.

Jaime laughed and gave her a hug. "I know you mean that and I love you for it, but that's one of the items on my life plan. I'm gonna get my own place. I hope I meet someone special and I live happily ever after with her, but if it all goes to shit, she'll be the one who has to go. I'm taking your advice, I haven't spoken to Rachel, and I'm not going to until I get back. I have a feeling that when I do call her, it'll be to say I'm coming to get the rest of my stuff."

"I'll go with you," Alexis promised as she knelt down and petted Ginger and Sprout, who were circling her.

"Yeah, because I'll need your truck." Jaime grinned. "I see headlights in the driveway."

Stacy was getting out of her car by the time Alexis walked outside. Her hair was up in a ponytail, she had on a pair of running shorts and a T-shirt, and she laughed when she noticed that Alexis was dressed the same *sans* ponytail. "I'm certain that not even God is up at this hour," Stacy said with a weary smile.

"Grammy is. She gave me a wakeup call and asked for your number, so she could treat you to the same." Alexis sucked her teeth and stared up at the sky. "I spared you from that. I'm a hero."

"Your sister isn't because when Elise called me, she told me Alana gave her my number."

"Oh, I'm so sorry," Alexis said with a sigh.

"It's okay. She's cooking breakfast and wanted to know how I like my eggs." Stacy held up a finger. "Lightly scrambled, put that in your memory bank."

Alexis smiled, catching the hint that she might one day make breakfast for Stacy. "Are your things in the trunk?"

"Yes." Stacy pressed a button on her key fob, and the lid opened.

Alexis's eyes bugged when she peered inside. "Great googly moogly, you don't pack light either."

"Hey," Stacy said with a laugh. "I brought extra household items because I don't know if the beach house will have everything we need."

149

"Good thinking." Alexis grabbed two bags and moved them to her truck. Stacy pulled out two more and handed them to her.

"Good morning, Stacy," Jaime said as she joined them with Alexis's suitcase.

"Hey you." Stacy gave her a warm hug. "I wish you were going with us."

"I do too. We'll all have to take another beach trip later this summer, and we'll go out dancing again. I promise not to puke, but I will hump you on the dance floor again."

Alexis pointed at Jaime. "Back in the house, Rover."

"The dress cannot go in the back of the truck!" Allison said and held it away from Alexis. "I don't care if you have a bed cover."

"Fine, but that dress will have to hang on your door, and you will ride all day against a plastic sheet."

Allison handed the dress over to Alexis. "Good point. Put it in the back, but place it very carefully."

Alexis walked out to her truck and sighed. The entire bed was full of suitcases, boxes, bags, and two coolers. "Carefully, she says." She laid the dress over two suitcases and pinned it down with Elise's CPAP machine. Next, she placed the cover on the bed and secured it in place. Stacy had helped load the truck, then disappeared. Alexis suspected she was being force-fed in the kitchen and went to rescue her.

"So this is boysenberry?" Alexis heard Stacy say when she walked in the front door.

"Yes, Alexis's favorite, but she won't eat right now because her stomach doesn't wake up until at least nine. One time when she was little, I demanded that she eat breakfast before school, and she forced down some scrambled eggs. I took her out to catch the bus, and she threw up on my shoes," Elise said.

"And she crapped her pants," Allison added.

"I'm sure Stacy is enjoying that story while she eats," Alexis said as she strode into the kitchen. "Are we ready?"

Allison was loading the dishwasher and laughed. "Almost, baby, chill out."

150

"I am." Stacy popped the last bite of a biscuit into her mouth before she got up and took her plate to the sink.

"Stacy, don't you let Alexis rush you. She's like a drill sergeant when she takes a trip." Elise smiled. "We're in no hurry."

Alexis shot her a look. "Then why did you wake me up at four this morning?"

"I'm evil," Elise replied with a shrug.

"Co-pilot, would you turn the air down just a little bit and make it warmer in here?" Elise asked when they'd been on the road for about thirty minutes.

"Yes, ma'am," Stacy replied.

"Are we there yet?" Allison asked and laughed when Alexis glanced at her in the rearview mirror. "Oh, what a pleasant reversal this is. Momma, I think we should fight and whine about how bored we are."

Elise jumped on that bandwagon. "Allison is touching me. I'm hungry. How long—oh, look, it's the sweeping arm of doom!" she cried happily when Alexis reached over the backseat and swatted at them.

"Alexis honey, how fast are you going?" Elise asked.

"Well, let's just say I'm leaving a vapor trail. Stacy, watch for troopers."

"Okay," Stacy said and gripped the side of her seat. She was pretty certain that if she were to spot a cop, Alexis would be on top of them before she could say anything. "You don't play around the pound, do you?"

Alexis stared at the road. "I like being ahead of the pack."

"Don't worry, girls, at this speed, all we'll see is a bright light and the face of God," Elise added. "We won't feel a thing."

Alexis glanced into the rearview. "I intend to cross the Louisiana state line in under an hour to make up for all the restroom breaks."

"You don't have to stop for me. I've already wet the seat in fear," Allison said with a nervous smile.

151

Stacy realized that Elise wasn't kidding when she said Alexis was like a drill sergeant on a trip. When they stopped for bathroom breaks, she gave them five minutes to do their business and get back in the truck. They grabbed food truly on the run. Stacy wasn't sure Alexis even fully stopped at the drive-thru window of a fast-food restaurant. She grabbed the bags and tossed them into the backseat before tearing out of the parking lot.

Allison broke the nervous tension when she began to sing, "Z, Y, X, W, V…is it U? Aw, crap."

"What're you doing?" Elise asked.

"I'm singing the alphabet backward, it's supposed to keep my mind sharp," Allison replied and began to sing the alphabet song correctly. "U! I always mess up on that letter."

Elise patted Allison's arm. "Darling if you only get to U, it means you should give up because half of your brain is already gone."

"Thanks, Mom."

Alexis huffed. "I knew I shouldn't have drunk that bottle of water, now I have to pee. I'm gonna stop at the next exit, and if y'all don't feel like you have to go, try anyway."

"Alexis Leigh! We are grown women, and we will pee when we have to," Allison snapped. "Stop at the next church, so we can have my daddy exorcised from your body. I swear he's possessed you. Your grandmother has blindfolded herself with one of her compression socks and is stuffing pieces of a napkin into her ears. Relax!"

Stacy got a healthy dose of reality in the passenger's seat. Alexis seemed to be perfect in every way, except when it came to driving. She jockeyed in and out of the lanes as though she was in a high-speed chase. She appeared intent on making a seven-hour drive in only three.

Alexis glanced at Stacy and asked, "Am I freaking you out?"

"Uh-huh. Would you like me to drive for a while?"

"Yeah," Alexis said with a sigh. "I may start trying to pee in a coffee can like Grandpa used to when he didn't want to stop, and I don't have the plumbing for that, or a can."

152

At the next exit, Alexis stopped at a gas station and went to the restroom. Stacy got into the driver's seat and adjusted the mirrors. She gazed at Allison in the rearview and asked, "Do you think I offended her when I offered to drive?"

"No, she knows she's being a jackass. Alexis can be intense when she has a goal to meet. Obviously, she thinks she can turn a seven-hour drive into five."

Stacy smiled. "I figured she was shooting for three."

"She may try to get you to drive as aggressively as she does. You'll have to be firm with her," Allison warned.

"Flip her off, dear," Elise added.

"Momma, get that sock off your face."

"I rather like it. I may be able to nap, especially since Stacy's behind the wheel now," Elise said with a sigh. "I need more napkin in my ears."

Alexis returned and climbed into the passenger's seat. "I apologize to everyone for obsessing. While I was hovering over the toilet seat peeing, I was reminded of Grandpa. He made trips pretty miserable. I will do my best—Stacy, pull out of the lot before that semi does, you don't want to merge behind that."

"Since I've never driven your truck, I need to take it at my own pace. I don't want to have an accident."

Alexis nodded. "Good point. I'll sit over here and shut up." She was quiet all of five seconds and asked, "What is your...pace?"

"It's under Mach one."

Chapter Twenty-three

Alexis didn't mind so much that she wasn't behind the wheel as they rode through the town of Port St. Joseph. It was a quaint place right on the water and full of old homes. It didn't look like the other parts of the Florida coast she'd been to. There were no souvenir shops, heavy traffic, or hordes of people. In the distance, she could see the cape, and excitement welled up in her just like it did when she was a kid and her grandparents took her to the beach. The ride to the cape tested her patience, though. It seemed to take forever, and Alexis began to squirm.

"How is my driving?" Stacy asked softly, so as not to wake Allison and Elise.

"You did well. I think you were a little too lenient on the bathroom allowance. I noticed Grammy took eight minutes on the last stop. I think she did it to piss me off. I would've made her chase the truck across the parking lot."

Stacy glanced at Alexis, and she wasn't smiling. "I know you're not serious."

"Maybe," Alexis said with a smirk. "I'm ready to have my toes in the sand."

"Me too, but I'm really looking forward to getting out of this truck. I feel stiff as a board."

Alexis reached over and rubbed the back of Stacy's neck and smiled at the low groan Stacy released. "Better?"

"I'll drive to the Keys if you keep doing that."

Alexis gazed at the screen of the GPS that indicated they had ten more minutes to go. "I'll give you a full-on shoulder rub if you speed up and cut our arrival time in half." She laughed when Stacy flipped her off.

Stacy slowed when the GPS advised her to turn onto the highway that ran the length of the cape. Alexis sat straight up and watched people skate and ride bikes on an asphalt path that ran along the road. Villages of beach houses flanked the other side of the highway.

"Tell me the truth, how many speeding tickets do you have on your record?"

"One…okay three, but two are about to go off my record because I got them on the same day." Alexis folded her arms. "I'm a little…impatient when I make long drives, but I inherited that from my grandfather. I have his eyes and his lead foot, it's genetic. Otherwise, I'm pretty cool. You can ask anybody who works with me. I'm nice, so please don't judge me too harshly."

"Okay, that's a deal, and when you discover my faults, please try to do the same."

"Name one."

"I'm very competitive." Stacy admitted. "I can't accept defeat gracefully. I usually have to tear something up to vent my frustration. That's why I was so glad we were teammates on *Ghost Dimension* because I probably would've shown my ass."

Alexis grinned. "I would've liked to have seen that. I mean not your ass in the flesh…not that I would've minded. What I'm saying—"

"This is where you shut up, baby," Allison said drolly and yawned. "Are we there yet?"

"Almost," Stacy said as she turned off the highway and pulled up to a gate. She looked at a message from Jason saved on her phone and punched in a code on the keypad. The gate swung open, and Stacy followed an asphalt lane until the GPS announced they had reached their destination.

Alexis leaned forward and gazed up at the multistory house with a widow's walk on top. "Wow," she said and threw open her door. "Somebody knock on Grammy's sock and tell her we're here."

Alana came running down the stairs of the house screaming, "Y'all are finally here! I'm so happy."

155

"Me too," Jason cried as he followed. "Allison can cook."

Alana stopped at the bottom of the stairs, and Jason had to grab the railing to keep from running over her. "What did you mean by that?" she asked hotly.

"I mean...I'm hoping she'll make her spaghetti."

The expression on Alana's face said Jason wasn't off the hook, but she returned her attention to her family and threw her arms out. "Mom!"

Allison gave her a robust hug. "You've been in the sun, your cheeks are pink."

"You ought to see the ones in my shorts. Jason and I have been lying out on the roof naked."

Elise hugged Alana next. "Flaunt it while you have it, baby, because I can assure you it's all downhill from here. My breasts have been traveling the southern highway for years."

Jason grimaced and scratched the side of his neck. "I don't know where to file that mental image."

"Hug your cousin," Stacy said and wrapped her arms around him.

Alexis got in on the hugs, as well, and gazed at the beach. "This is nice, and it's right on the water."

"You have to see the inside." Alana grabbed Alexis's arm and pulled her toward the stairs.

"Wait, let me grab an armload of stuff. The back of my truck is full," Alexis said and dug in her heels.

Alana narrowed her eyes and gazed at Jason. "My big strong fiancé will take care of that. The work will make him appreciate my cooking."

Stacy patted Jason on the back as she passed him by and said, "I'd love to help you, but I have to pee and you're being punished. Far be it from me to get in the way of you learning a lesson." She offered her arm to Elise, and they climbed the stairs slowly.

Alana made Alexis and Allison wait with her on the deck until Elise and Stacy arrived, then they all went in together. "As you can see, this is the living room, the kitchen is over there, and there's a bedroom on this floor. I think Grammy should have it, so she doesn't have to climb any more stairs."

156

"Is there a bathroom on this floor?" Stacy asked.

"Two, the guest bath is beneath the staircase. The bedroom has its own bath," Alana explained. "Actually, all the bedrooms have private bathrooms."

Stacy left the group as Alexis craned her head back and gazed up all the way to the skylights in the roof. "There's three floors?"

"Four if you count the garage beneath us. There's an outdoor shower, and the washer and dryer are in a room down there. "There's three bedrooms on both of the upper floors. Jason and I chose one on the top because of the view and the roof access." Alana sighed. "I could live here."

"I could too," Allison agreed as she headed for the kitchen.

Alexis turned in a slow circle and took in the huge TV mounted to the stone wall above the fireplace. The seating area held two sectional couches and one recliner. An archway separated the dining area from the living room.

"There's every appliance and cooking utensil that anyone could ever need in here," Allison exclaimed in the kitchen. "There's a standalone ice maker!"

Elise smiled. "This place has some swag. I can definitely chill with my homies up in here."

Jason arrived with the first load, and it included Alana's dress. "Baby, look what I've got."

"Oh, I'll take that," Alana said excitedly. "Y'all come upstairs with me and pick your rooms."

When Stacy came out of the bathroom, they all headed upstairs with the exception of Elise, who went to have a look at her room. Allison stopped on the second floor. "You really feel your age when you have to climb. I believe I'll choose one of the rooms here. Y'all should probably take the other two since Alana and Jason are on the third floor. Do you get my drift?"

Alexis's mind was on the great views the top floor probably provided. "No."

"They're gonna be making the beast with two backs, taking the hot dog bus to taco town, putting the pecker in the playpen, Alana's gonna take the bologna pony out for a ride." Allison raised her brow. "Do you get it now?"

157

Alana rolled her eyes and continued on to the third floor to put away her dress. Alexis made a face. "Hot dog bus and taco town? Gross, Mom. You and Grammy must be looking at the same websites. You do have a point, though. Maybe we should give the happy couple some space."

"I call this one," Allison said and stepped into the room closest to the stairs.

Stacy shrugged. "I'll take the middle one."

They hadn't even gone out on their first date, so Alexis thought it would be too presumptuous to offer to share. "Cool. I'm gonna go help Jason. I'll bring our things up to this landing, and we can sort them out," Alexis said as she started down the stairs.

"Now this is straight dope," Elise said later while she stood on the deck and gazed at the beach and water beyond.

"You got that right, Grammy." Alexis smiled. "You gonna put on a swimsuit and hit the water?"

Elise laughed. "Later this afternoon when the sun isn't so bright, I will stuff my sagging body into spandex and hope for the best." She eyed Alexis's red board shorts and bikini top. "If you wear those shorts any lower, your personal business will be hanging out."

"Grams, they're made that way. They're snug, my biz is protected."

"You need to make sure all that bare skin is covered in sunscreen. If you burn the first day out here, you'll be miserable for the rest of the time."

Alexis held up a can. "Got it right here. Will you spray my back?"

"I'll be more than happy to paint you," Elise said and took the sunscreen. "This is so convenient. I remember trying to rub two squirming little girls down with lotion. I've never greased a pig before—I don't even know why someone would grease one—but that's what it was like trying to get sunscreen on you and your sister."

The door flew open. Jason came running out first, Alana was second, and Stacy was right behind them. The trio ran across the

158

deck and down the stairs in a race to the water. Stacy was wearing a navy blue bikini, and Alexis was completely mesmerized. She watched Stacy sprint across the sand, heart pounding.

"She has a very nice figure," Elise remarked as she continued to spray and rub the sunscreen into Alexis's back. "Bathing suits these days don't leave a lot to the imagination."

Alexis silently disagreed. She was imagining all sorts of things, and it disturbed her to be thinking lustful thoughts while her grandmother was rubbing her back. "Okay, I think I'm good," she said and stepped away.

"You are not. I haven't even gotten your lower back, come here."

"I'm fine, Grammy. I can get the rest."

Elise didn't listen; she followed Alexis around the deck steadily spraying. "Hold still."

"I can't breathe, you've made a cloud."

"I'm having flashbacks of trying to rub you with lotion. Stand still, Alexis Leigh!"

"Fine. You spray and I'll rub it in," Alexis said as she twirled around in the fog Elise was making.

"Why is your neck and face all flushed? Did I hurt your back when I was rubbing it?" Elise threw a hand on her hip. "You have a back issue, don't you? Baby, how many times have I told you to lift with your legs? I've seen you hefting those bags of soil at the nursery, and you don't use the proper mechanics. Now what is it—a slipped disk?"

"My back is fine, it's the sunscreen in my throat that's causing the problem." Alexis grabbed the can from Elise, and her eyes went wide. "This is almost empty."

"Precisely, because I shellacked your shoulders." Elise pointed at Alexis when Allison walked out the door. "Your daughter has a back problem, and she's been hiding it."

"Ibuprofen, that's what I take when mine gets overworked." Allison winked at Alexis. "Sometimes, you really gotta put your back into it, and I'm not talking about gardening."

"Dear God," Elise said and made a face. "I'm going back inside on that note."

159

"What's wrong with your back?" Allison asked as she took the can from Alexis and sprayed her legs.

"Nothing. I just felt like Grammy was rubbing the sunscreen into my soul." Alexis bit her lip for a second or two and said, "I want to ask you something personal."

Allison glanced at Alexis while she continued to spray on the sunscreen. "So do it, I might answer."

"Is the reason you don't keep a boyfriend because you...don't feel anything for them?" Alexis put up a hand and blew out a breath. "What I mean is, do you think you care for them at first, then you realize you don't, or is it because you're scarred and are afraid to love again?"

"Neither," Allison replied acerbically. "My dear mother can't accept the answer when she asks basically the same thing. I know she's told you I'm wounded. Your father did hurt me, and it took me a little while to get over it. You girls were both pretty small when I began dating again. I met some nice men but never one I thought would be worthy of being in your lives. I enjoy sex, I make no apologies for it. I realized I could have what I wanted in short-term relationships where it was understood there would be no commitments."

Allison set the sunscreen aside and gave Alexis her full attention. "I've never lacked for anything. I have all the love I needed from my family and still do. Why bring in someone I'd have to make many compromises for? When you and Alana were small, you had all my attention. I didn't have to split that with a husband, and I loved it. When y'all grew up and moved out of the house, I was stuck in my ways, and I really don't see any need to change."

"I don't remember you dating at all when I was living at home. It wasn't until Alana moved out that you began to have men at the house."

"Yeah, you believed me when I told you I was in a bowling league." Allison smiled. "That's one ball I have never touched. I wasn't gonna parade a string of men past my girls while they were young and impressionable. I always told y'all that I was incapable of being in love because that was a lot easier than explaining everything I just told you. Well that, and I have an insatiable sexual appetite, and I overwhelm my partners pretty quickly."

Alexis nodded slowly. "Okay."

"You always talk to Momma when you have something on your mind, and sometimes, I'm jealous of that. Then I remind myself that you're a lot like my father, and only Mom could understand him." Allison smiled and brushed Alexis's hair from her face when the wind caught it. "I do know you pretty well, though, and you asked me about this for a reason that pertains to you and your feelings."

"Or lack thereof," Alexis said and gazed at Stacy playing in the surf. "I keep getting involved with women, and it doesn't take me very long to realize that I don't feel as much as I should."

"I knew you weren't in love with Michelle. I asked you if you were once, and you said yes. I didn't know if you were lying to me or yourself. Have you grown uninterested in Stacy already?"

Alexis shook her head. "No. Every minute I'm with her, I find something new to like about her, but I'm afraid that hollow feeling is gonna creep in and ruin everything."

"Baby, that feeling accompanies the wrong one."

"Do you realize how many women I've dated and been involved with? Can there really be that many wrong ones out there?" Alexis asked with a frown.

Allison nodded. "Apparently so, but if I had to bet on anyone, it would be Stacy. Not because of what you just told me about her, but because you let her drive your truck," Allison said with a laugh. "That was very telling because you don't give up control to anyone."

Chapter Twenty-four

"You got a crab, I got a crab, baby," Alexis sang as she stared into the water with a dip net in her hand.

"No." Stacy shook her head. "I have two, and crabs are points, and I'm winning."

"Okay, the second crab you caught was the size of a fifty-cent piece, so I really think that's half a point," Alexis argued.

"No, crabs are points regardless of size, and I have two."

Alexis spotted her prey and lunged. A wave smacked her in the face, but she held her net up, and Stacy's loud wail confirmed to Alexis she had crab gold. "Aha! In your face! Point for me," Alexis yelled as she got to her feet and gazed at her catch. "Look, it's massive."

"Size doesn't matter, we've already gone over that." Stacy pointed her net at Alexis. "Put it in the bucket, you're not allowed to catch the same crab."

Alexis ran up on the beach where Jason and Alana sat with a plastic pail. Jason watched as Alexis carefully untangled the crab from the net. "She's a dick when she's competing," Jason said with a smile.

"It's kinda cute," Alexis said distractedly as she tried to watch Stacy and get the crab into the bucket at the same time.

"Until she clobbers you with her net on a stick. She's not above it. She used to hit me in the ribs and stomp my feet when we played basketball." Jason picked up the plastic bucket and stood. "I'm going to walk down the beach and let these guys go, but don't worry, Alana and I are keeping count."

Alexis raced back in the water and resumed her search for crabs. Stacy was in pounce position and looked as though she was about to get her third point. "You have a nice butt," Alexis said.

"Are you trying to distract me?" Stacy asked without looking away from the crab she was watching.

"Yeah, is it working?"

Stacy swept a crab up in her net in one quick motion. Her smile was triumphant, and she walked over to Alexis and kissed her on the cheek. "No, it didn't work, but I liked what I heard. Three to two, and I'm on top."

"I can't believe they're still at it," Alana said as she and Jason walked down to the water just as Stacy brought up her thirty-third crab to make a tie. Alana waded into the surf, grabbed Stacy's net, and dropped the crab into the water. "Game over. It's time for dinner."

"No, we need a match crab," Alexis yelled as she searched frantically for one.

Alana walked away with Stacy's net before she could snatch it back, but Stacy was determined not to be beaten. After a wave rolled in, she spotted a small crab and went for it. "I win—ow!"

"Are you crazy?" Alexis asked as the crab went flying through the air after Stacy shook it off.

Stacy frowned and gazed at the small cut on her thumb. "No, I'm stupid."

"Let's go wash that out before you contract some sort of aquatic disease." Alexis took Stacy by the arm and led her to shore. "You weren't joking about being competitive."

"You're just as bad," Alana interjected. "We went inside three hours ago. Jason had to grill the cowboy burgers, and they're not gonna be as good as yours."

Jason was steadily nodding until he caught what Alana said and glared at her. "Hey! I didn't burn them."

Alana ignored him and said, "We're ready to eat. Y'all hurry up and rinse off."

"What's a cowboy burger?" Stacy asked as she and Alexis walked toward the house.

163

"Grammy mixes ground sirloin, cheese, bell pepper, onion, and bacon bits. You will have powerful heartburn, but the burger is worth every second of discomfort. I hope she made the sweet potato fries."

"How do y'all eat like this and not weigh five hundred pounds?" Stacy asked as they stepped onto the lower deck.

"I haven't had a cowboy burger since last summer. They're for special occasions, that's why I'm walking so fast. You want to rinse off with me in the shower, or would you prefer to do it alone?"

Stacy opened the outdoor shower enclosure and turned on the water. "We'll both still be in our swimsuits, so I don't imagine we'll get into too much trouble," she answered with a smile. She took Alexis by the arm and pulled her inside.

Alexis was hungry and really wanted a cowboy burger, but thoughts of the coveted meal fled her mind when Stacy's lips brushed against hers. The kiss happened so fast Alexis wasn't sure if she had actually initiated it. Alexis's back hit the rough wood of the shower stall, Stacy's body was pressed firmly against hers, and the warm water cascaded over them as her tongue slipped past Stacy's lips. Alexis tingled from head to toe as her hands roamed.

Stacy pulled away looking dazed. "We need to be clear on something. The crab I caught with my hand still counted. I won."

"After a kiss like that, winning a crab catching game is on your mind?" Alexis asked in amazement.

"If I let my mind go anywhere else, we're going to be even later for dinner, and I really don't want our first time to be in an outdoor shower stall."

"Stacy, breathe," Jason said with a laugh as he watched her eat.

"Most amazing…so good…can't stop."

"I think Stacy likes my burgers," Elise said with a pleased smile.

Alexis nodded. "They get better every time you make them."

"I've honed my skills over the years." Elise chuckled. "I used to pack them too hard, and it was like eating a baseball. Jenny, our neighbor, took a special interest in teaching me the proper way to make a burger, and I noticed that Harmon kept buying her wine. That rascal had asked her behind my back to give me cooking tips. Now Jenny was a marvelous cook, and I can hardly blame Harmon for wanting me to learn from her, but I was a little peeved at him for doing that."

"Harmon," Jason said and repeated the name a few times. "That could actually work for a boy or a girl. We should keep that in mind for our firstborn."

Alana grimaced. "I want kids. It's just the route they take to get here that worries me. Were you a bigheaded baby?"

"Like a bowling ball. He was five before he could hold his head up on his own," Stacy said with a grin.

"Don't listen to her. I had a nice little head in proportion with my body," Jason assured Alana. "I did weigh almost nine pounds, though, and one of my brothers weighed almost ten."

Alana stared at him for a moment. "You know what, let's just get a dog or a cat, or both."

"Sweetie, being pregnant is one of the most wonderful feelings in the world after you get past the morning sickness and just before the baby decides to spend all its time on your bladder." Allison smiled wistfully. "I used to love feeling y'all kick and move around. I didn't know what sex either of you were before you got here. I remember hearing that doctor say, 'It's a girl,' both times, and my heart just melted."

"Tell them what Alexis said the first time she saw me," Alana said with a scowl at Alexis.

"It's ugly and I don't like it," Allison and Elise said in unison and laughed.

"Well, she was the belle of the ball before Alana came along," Elise explained. "We were making a fuss over someone else, and she didn't like it, especially later when she had to share her room, until we got the bunk beds, and that made her happy again."

"But we were small and had little heads, right?" Alana asked. "I need to be clear on that."

Allison nodded. "Yes, you two shot out like darts. I didn't even know I was in labor until the doctor yelled, 'It's a girl.'"

"You screamed like you were dying," Elise said and looked at Allison as though she were crazy.

Allison rolled her eyes. "Work with me, Momma. Do you want a great-grandbaby or not?"

"Oh, yes, I stand corrected. Both girls just hopped out." She smiled at Alana. "As I recall, your mother was reading a book and didn't even notice."

"Then why does she always say 'you ripped my guts out' when she's trying to get us to do something we don't want to?" Alana narrowed her eyes.

"Guilt manipulation," Allison said. "It's a course they give all new mothers at the hospital. You'll enjoy using those skills, and they really don't work all that well on a dog, so you should have a baby instead."

"I'm ready for a baby," Elise said. "I don't even mind changing diapers, just as long as I can snuggle that little thing, I'm happy."

"The baby or the diaper?" Alexis asked.

Elise smiled and narrowed her eyes at Alexis. "Don't make me go medieval on you."

"How long are you gonna do this urban slang thing, Mom?" Allison asked. "Because you're not really good at it."

"You're gonna make me bust a cap up in your ass," Elise said and raised her chin high.

Alana laughed. "Oh, crap, Grammy's talking about shooting people now."

"I thought busting a cap was kicking someone in their butt." Elise looked at Jason. "Am I wrong?"

"Yes, ma'am. You just told your daughter you're going to shoot her."

Elise sighed. "I need to do some more research and get my shit straight."

Allison smiled at Alana and Jason. "Back to babies, when can we expect one?"

"As soon as storks begin delivering them for real. Don't start pressuring us, Mom," Alana warned.

Allison threw up her hands. "Fine, crush my dreams. Alexis, how about you and Stacy?"

"Mom! We just started dating," Alexis exclaimed while Stacy laughed.

"Oh, here's a nice one," Stacy said and picked up a seashell.

Alexis watched Stacy put the shell in the pocket of her shorts. "We passed a dead fish back there. You wanna put that in your pocket?"

"Would you still walk beside me and hold my hand if I did?"

Alexis gazed up at the moon. "Yeah, I probably would."

"You're so sweet...when you're not driving," Stacy said with a laugh and took Alexis's hand again.

"You are too, when you're not competing. Don't think I didn't notice that *accidental* bump you gave me when I was about to get a good crab." Alexis smiled. "That was fun, I wouldn't mind doing that again tomorrow."

"That you enjoy simple silly things makes you all the more appealing."

Alexis gasped and released Stacy's hand as she bent down. She picked up a small starfish and sighed. "It's stiff. I was gonna take it back into the water, but it's dead."

"Aw, poor thing—let's keep it!"

Alexis stood and handed it to Stacy. "You really are determined to stuff a dead fish in your pocket."

"Put it in yours, mine are full of shells."

"Or I'll just hold it," Alexis said with a laugh.

Stacy gazed at Alexis in fascination. She was on a moonlit beach with a woman who made her a quivering mass of sexual tension and at the same time made her feel so relaxed and comfortable. "I really like you."

Alexis smiled. "You say that like you're surprised."

"I am because it stuns me how much...I feel already."

"You're braver than me because I feel the same way, but I was afraid to admit that to you. We haven't even gone out on our first date."

"I know," Stacy said as she continued to gaze at Alexis. "I even liked you when you didn't like me. Alexis, I watched the videos of you on your garden center website before we ever met, and I was totally taken with you. The day I saw you in person for the first time, my brain just shut down, and all I could do was stare at you. I feel like I've known you longer than I actually have."

"You watched my videos?" Alexis asked, unable to believe what she was hearing.

Stacy feared that she'd said too much too soon. "Did I make you uncomfortable?"

"No, I'm floored—flattered. My hair was terrible in those things, I can't even watch them. That's probably the most amazing thing I've ever heard, and that it came from you...I'm speechless."

Stacy smiled and wrapped her arms around Alexis's neck. She hoped her kiss conveyed the growing affection she felt. She dug her toes in the sand as she deepened the kiss and suddenly froze.

Alexis broke the kiss and gazed at her. "What's wrong?"

"Are you rubbing that dead starfish on my back?"

"Oh! I'm so sorry. I got caught up in the moment, and I didn't realize what I was doing." Alexis bit her bottom lip and laughed. "Oops."

"The kisses were great, though, and if I hadn't been wearing a tank top, I probably wouldn't have noticed that you were stroking me with a dead animal that kinda smells."

"I bet no woman has ever done that to you before."

Stacy smiled. "You're definitely the first."

Chapter Twenty-five

By the time Alexis and Stacy arrived at the house, everyone had gone to bed, except for Jason, who was on the couch watching a baseball game. "How was the walk?" he asked behind a yawn.

"It was nice. We didn't realize how far we'd gone until we decided to head back," Stacy said with a smile. "How's the hot water and the pressure? Can we shower at the same time?"

Jason nodded. "Oh, yeah, it's good. Either there's one giant water heater in this place or a dozen regular-sized ones. Alexis, do you mind if I talk to Stacy for a moment?"

"Not at all." Alexis gave Stacy a quick peck on the lips and headed up the stairs.

Stacy walked over to where Jason sat and took a seat on the floor. "If you couldn't talk to me about whatever this is in front of Alexis, it must be bad."

"I lied to my mother today, and I'm feeling kind of guilty. She called and invited me and Alana to dinner on Friday, and I told her we came here to scope everything out before the wedding."

"Oh, man, you're going to be in so much trouble," Stacy said and exhaled loudly.

"I know, but that's not the lie I'm concerned with. She also asked me if Alana had signed the prenup, and I told her yes. The truth is, I never had one drawn up. I know it's sensible, but I'm not going to ask Alana to marry me in one breath, then sign something like that in another. It feels wrong to me."

Stacy's eyes flew open wide. "The importance of the prenuptial agreement has been ground into our heads since we were old enough to date."

"If you decide to get married, are you going to ask your future wife to sign one?"

Stacy was thoughtful for a moment. "If I had been married to Janey, I'd probably be very thankful I did right now. Granted, we're not rich, but when our parents pass on, we're going to inherit a lot. I don't know about you, but I socked away what our grandfather left us. I would hate to have to give half of that to Janey."

"Alana's not anything like Janey." Jason nodded and held up a hand. "I know I'm being naïve, but I can't say to Alana, 'I want to marry you, but if we get divorced, I don't want you having any rights to what I have.' My mind is made up on that, but tonight when Mom called and I lied to her twice, I felt really bad, so what I want you to do is make me feel better."

"Well, if you don't get divorced, your parents will never know you don't have a prenup. However, when you get back to Baton Rouge and your mother sees a wedding band on your finger, she will grow another head, and that one will bite you anytime it sees you. Feel better?"

Jason shook his head. "I'm not quite there yet. Could you try a little harder?"

"Things are going great with Alexis, that's all I've got."

"That does make me happy," Jason said with a big smile.

Alexis showered and lay in her bed with the lamp on, thumbing through a book she found on the bedside table about shells and Florida sea life. She didn't know if Jason and Stacy were still talking and didn't want to disturb them, but she hoped Stacy would see the light and drop by before she turned in for the night. She tossed the book aside when she heard a soft knock on the door. "Come in," she said, keeping her voice low.

Stacy stepped in, her hair still wet from her shower. "I'm sorry about earlier. Jason talked to his mom tonight and felt guilty for lying to her."

170

"He didn't let the eloping cat out of the bag?" Alexis asked as Stacy sat on the bed beside her.

Stacy shook her head. "I feel kind of sorry for my aunt. I know she's going to be hurt when she finds out Jason eloped, but on the other hand, she's so controlling that she forced him to do it. No one likes to be controlled unless it's right here." Stacy patted the bed with her hand.

The comment sent a white-hot bolt of desire shooting through Alexis. "I don't know if I could control you, I think you might be pretty wild," Alexis said as she toyed with a wet lock of Stacy's hair.

Stacy smiled with a look of challenge in her eyes. "Maybe you should try."

Alexis inhaled sharply and gazed at Stacy for a moment. She pulled her close and kissed her. The skin of Stacy's neck felt hot beneath her hand, wet hair fell over the backs of her fingers. Stacy's lips were sweet and soft, she smelled of soap and shampoo. Alexis's brain was cataloging every sensation.

Stacy switched off the lamp and climbed onto Alexis, her pulse pounding. Tender kisses turned almost savage as passion took over. She had imagined this more times than she was willing to count, but when Alexis removed her shirt and took one of her nipples into her mouth, Stacy gasped. It was real, Alexis was sucking and teasing her nipple with her teeth as her hands moved down Stacy's ribcage over her hips and pushed at the waistband of her shorts.

Being on her back was too limiting for Alexis. She rolled Stacy over and quickly removed the rest of her clothes, eager to have Stacy's body beneath her hands and mouth. Her brain steadily imprinted the softness, sounds, and taste, and a loud moan that she knew didn't come from Stacy caught Alexis's attention along with a steady thumping. Stacy's body shook with silent laughter.

"I think Alana and Jason are directly above us," Alexis whispered.

"Either that or a freight train. The high side is, they'll drown us out." Stacy grazed her teeth over the skin of Alexis's neck

171

and whispered against her ear, "Let me take your clothes off. I want to feel all of you against me."

Alexis shuddered and sat up so Stacy could remove her shirt. Then she pulled her shorts off herself and moved on top of Stacy, releasing a moan that rivaled the ones above them. Stacy claimed her mouth quickly.

Every slow thrust of Alexis's hips against her made Stacy hold on tighter, unwilling to allow Alexis to stop. She learned quickly if she pinched one of Alexis's nipples she ground harder against her. Stacy wrapped her legs around Alexis's waist and groaned at the feel of Alexis's wetness against her own. The sounds above them faded as she listened to Alexis's erratic breathing as they kissed. That alone was enough to make Stacy come, but she urged Alexis to grind harder by pinching her nipple.

Alexis was descending into that maddening place where all thought ceased and there was only sensation. She could feel the muscles in Stacy's legs that held her trapped grow harder. Stacy had a serious grip on the back of her neck, the fingers of her other hand dictated Alexis's movements. Stacy suddenly broke from one of Alexis's kisses and gasped as her shoulders rose up from the bed. Alexis basked in the full-body shudder she felt beneath her.

They lay still for a moment or two as they caught their breath. Stacy gently pushed Alexis off of her and quickly descended, pushing Alexis's legs apart. Her tongue grazed the moist heat, and Alexis's hips moved again. Stacy wasted no time; she wanted to feel and hear Alexis come as she slipped a finger inside of her, and her tongue found the spot that made Alexis moan.

Alexis gritted her teeth and tried not to make too much noise. Her eyes were clamped closed, her hands clutched the sheets as Stacy worked her into a state of utter ecstasy with skill that surprised Alexis. The tense muscles in her legs trembled as she teetered on the edge for a moment, then the waves of intense pleasure overtook her.

Alexis gazed wearily at red numbers on the clock beside the bed and stroked Stacy's back while she lay with her head on her shoulder and one leg draped across her stomach. "What time did we come in from the beach?"

"I think it was around ten," Stacy replied behind a yawn.

"It's just after two now, so if you subtract an hour for the time we showered and you talked to Jason, that means we've been driving each other insane for three hours."

Stacy laughed. "We stomped the shit out of their time upstairs."

Alexis laughed too, and winced. She was sore. Stacy had made her use muscles that she hadn't worked in a while. "I'm starving."

"I know, I can hear your stomach growling. How do you feel about a kitchen raid?"

Dear Sore and Happy Me,

Stacy's a lot more athletic than she looks. She maneuvered me into so many positions last night it was like a wrestling match I didn't care at all about losing. Apparently, I'm loud because she pushed my face into the pillow several times. I may have chewed a hole in the pillowcase. I'd go check, but she's sleeping, and I know if I go up there, I'll wake her up on purpose.

The hollow feeling didn't come. Instead, I'm caught up in all kinds of emotions that make me smile. I'm reminded of the lesbian U-Haul joke because I think I'd be thrilled if she moved in with me when we get home. I'm so tempted to ask her. I woke up several times during the night amazed to find she was lying there curled up next to me.

I can't deny I'm paranoid. I keep thinking that hollow uninterested feeling is gonna creep up on me. I'm equally afraid that she might suddenly decide I'm not for her, but I have to say that this crazy, dreamy, blissful feeling keeps my fears way in the back of my mind. Of course, that might be because my brain could be somewhere up there in that bed.

Happy Exhausted Me

Chapter Twenty-six

"Alexis Leigh, do you know who got into the cobbler last night?" Elise asked the second Alexis walked into the kitchen the next morning.

"I saw Alana in here when I came in from the beach," Alexis lied and tried not to laugh.

"I'm gonna wring her neck." Elise checked on her biscuits and slammed the oven door. "I'd planned to serve that cobbler after dinner tonight. There's two huge chunks missing, and she slipped it back into the box to hide her crime. I'm so glad I noticed it this morning, so I can pick up something else while we're out."

"Where're you going?"

"Allison and I want to see Apalachicola and St. George Island. This cape is pretty, but there isn't much to do here if you're not interested in getting into the water. You're welcome to come with us if you'd like."

"I prefer to be a beach bum, but my answer will depend on what Stacy wants to do." Alexis took the bacon out of the skillet and added more slices.

"I got downright tickled at her eating that hamburger last night. She went at it like she was starving." Elise moved close to Alexis as she poured eggs into a skillet. "Are you having a good time?"

Alexis nodded. "I am."

"I didn't even need to ask, I can tell. Yesterday, I stepped out onto the deck and watched you and Stacy chase those crabs. I could hear you laughing, and I was reminded of all the times

175

we went to the beach when you and Alana were girls. Those are some sweet memories and funny too. I remember Alana being scared of something in the water, and she yanked your granddad's shorts to his knees trying to climb up his leg. There was a full moon in Biloxi that day."

"I would've preferred to have seen the moon, but I was in front of him. If I wasn't born gay, that sight turned me." Alexis laughed when Elise swatted her with a spatula. "That was the scariest dolphin I'd ever seen, and it was staring down at me with one eye."

"Coffee, where is it?" Alana said as she walked into the kitchen looking half asleep.

"Let me tell you something, little missy. I don't appreciate you getting into that cobbler. We brought a ton of sweets with us, and if you wanted a snack, you should've gone into the pantry," Elise said, waving the spatula at Alana. "You knew I intended that for a dessert."

"Grammy, I don't even know what you're talking about." Alana shrugged. "I didn't know we had a cobbler. Why would you think I ate it?"

"She said—" Elise narrowed her eyes and stared at Alexis, who was silently laughing so hard she was shaking from head to toe. "Alexis Leigh, I'm gonna bust a cap in your ass."

Stacy awoke when the bed shook. Her eyes flew open, and she didn't recognize where she was for a moment. She rolled over suddenly, and Alexis was standing beside the bed with a tray.

"I didn't mean to scare you, I'm sorry," Alexis said apologetically.

Stacy blinked as she tried to focus on the clock. "It's eight thirty? Why is it so dark in here?"

"There's a storm moving in. I don't think it'll last long," Alexis said as she carefully set the tray on the bed. "I brought breakfast."

"Aw, Alex—my breath is horrible. What did I eat last night?"

"I'm gonna try not to be offended by that remark."

176

"It's garlic. It was in the dip we ate last night in the chips." Stacy got up. "I'm going to brush my teeth because I'm afraid you'll never kiss me again if I breathe on you."

Alexis watched Stacy rush to the bathroom with a smile on her face. Stacy's naked body was lovely. She switched on the bedside lamp, hoping for a better view when Stacy returned.

Stacy closed the door and stayed in the bathroom for almost five minutes. When she returned, her hair was brushed, and she was wearing nothing but a smile. "What time did you get up?" she asked as she picked her shorts up off the floor and slipped them on.

"Since six. My body is programmed to get up at that time." Alexis watched Stacy put on her shirt. "Get back in bed."

"Oh, I am. I can't tell you the last time…I don't think anyone has ever brought me breakfast like this except for my mother when I was sick as a child."

"I noticed these trays in the pantry, and the idea popped in my head." Alexis waited for Stacy to get situated, then she set the tray over her legs. "I griped because Mom and Grammy packed so much, but I'm happy Grammy brought her boysenberry jam. Her muscadine jelly is really good too. I put a dab of it on the plate with the biscuits so you could try it."

"This is really sweet in more ways than one," Stacy said with a smile as she gazed at the tray that held biscuits, bacon, scrambled eggs, juice, and coffee. "Get in here."

Alexis climbed in beside Stacy. "The cobbler theft was discovered by Grammy this morning. I told her Alana ate it, and she believed me until Alana showed up. Oh, do you want to go to some island and some town with a strange name? Mom and Grammy are planning a trip."

"I'll go if you want to," Stacy said as she smeared jelly onto her biscuit and took a bite. "I've never had muscadine, this is delicious."

"I'd rather bum it on the beach."

Stacy nodded as she took another bite. "Good, I'd rather stay here. Do you know if there's peanut butter? This jelly would make an awesome sandwich."

"If there's not, we'll get some. Feed me."

Stacy smiled and gave Alexis a bite of the biscuit. "Was Elise mad about the cobbler?"

"Oh, yeah, she threatened to shoot me. I didn't tell her you were my accomplice or that it was your idea."

"I said it looked good, and you tore into the box. Putting it in that toaster oven was a stroke of genius, though. I don't think the crust would have been as flaky if we had put it in the microwave. "When we get home, I'll have to eat nothing but lettuce to make up for all the calories I consumed. Do you cook?"

"Quite well, if I may say so myself," Alexis replied with a smug smile.

"Will you marry me?"

"You didn't get on one knee, and there's no ring. You'll have to correct that before I consider your proposal." Alexis snagged a slice of bacon. "Now when it comes to jewelry, I'm fairly conservative. I don't like anything that sticks up off my hand since I work with them so much."

"I'll keep that in mind." Stacy handed Alexis a glass of juice and the TV remote. "Since it's stormy outside, find us something to watch. Rainy days call for something spooky."

Alexis turned on the TV. "I like scary movies. Alana and I used to watch them all the time until we saw *The Conjuring*, and she flipped out. The scene where the kid was in bed and—" Alexis nearly spilled the juice when Stacy clamped a hand over her mouth.

"I forgot about that scene, don't remind me of it," Stacy said and slowly released her grip on Alexis's mouth. "If you find that movie is on, keep surfing, it's not Stacy appropriate. What spooky flick scared you the most?"

"None recently, but when I was a kid, *Poltergeist* messed me up. I still don't sleep with the closet door open, and I hate clowns."

"I'll bet you didn't like that movie *It*, either."

Alexis shook her head. "No, I hated that clown, and he was in need of some whitening strips on those sharp nasty teeth of— oh, this is a good movie."

"*Secondhand Lions*," Stacy said with a smile. "It's one of my favorites."

Alexis set the remote aside and said, "Eggs."

Someone knocked on the door as Stacy fed Alexis. "Come in," she said loudly.

Alana poked her head in the door. "I heard the TV, so I figured it was safe to knock."

"It's not," Alexis said after she swallowed, but Alana ignored her and walked on in.

"I hope y'all don't mind, but Jason and I bought what we want y'all to wear in the wedding," Alana said as she sat at the foot of the bed. She smiled at Stacy. "I learned your sizes when you stayed with us and I did laundry. Alexis, don't look at me like that, I didn't pick out anything that would offend you. It's khaki pants and white sleeveless shirts. We wanted y'all to match."

"I can live with that," Alexis said and grabbed a biscuit.

Stacy nodded. "I can too. Are you getting nervous?" she asked with a smile as she steadily fed Alexis.

"I am, and I don't know why. It's gonna be a simple ceremony, it probably won't last but a few minutes. I'm gonna stand in the sand and pledge my life to the man I love and adore. It's a big deal, but at the same time, it's not. Nothing about our lives is gonna change, we already live together," Alana said seemingly more to herself than Alexis and Stacy.

"Nervous excitement maybe," Alexis said before she downed her juice.

"Probably," Alana agreed with a nod. "Yeah, that's probably it."

Alexis and Stacy had fallen back to sleep after their breakfast and slept for a couple of hours. When they awoke and went downstairs, it appeared the house was empty until they found Alana alone outside on the deck. "Where is everybody?" Alexis asked.

"Jason drove Mom and Grammy to Apalachicola. I didn't feel like going, my stomach's kinda cramping," Alana said with obvious tension all over her face. "I needed time alone to decide if I really want to do this…wedding."

"You went from nervous excitement to 'I don't know if I want to do this' in less than a few hours?" Alexis exclaimed.

"Okay, wait, let's not get too excited," Stacy said calmly as she took a seat at the table with Alana. "I think everybody goes through this right before the ceremony. My sisters did, all three of them."

Alana shook her head. "I have no doubts about marrying Jason. It's how we're doing it that's causing the stress. After he talked to his mom yesterday, he got really quiet. I feel so guilty for making him elope with me. I'm honestly to the point of calling this off."

"Alana, he doesn't want a giant wedding, either, you didn't *make* him do anything," Stacy said kindly.

"You know what he's—we're—gonna face when we get back home. Is it fair to expect him to endure what might be years of shit from his mom and family for just a few minutes of my comfort?" Alana shook her head. "No. He'll do anything for my happiness, so I should do the same for him and call off this elopement thing, go home, and marry him in a big scary ceremony like I should've done in the first place."

"What're you gonna tell him, you want the big wedding after all?" Alexis asked. "He's not gonna believe that or agree with it."

"I know. That's why I called his mother after he left this morning," Alana blurted out.

Stacy's eyes grew huge. "You did what?"

"I called to tell her what we were planning and that Jason did it because of my discomfort. I didn't want him to go home to a nightmare. She didn't answer, and the call went to voice mail. I didn't leave a message, but she's probably gonna call back," Alana said miserably as she stared with dread at her phone sitting on the table.

"Don't answer it. Take that phone down to the beach and throw it in the water. Jason will be so upset with you if you tell her about your plans. My aunt will get on a plane, fly into the closest airport, and be here by nightfall." Stacy stabbed the table

180

with her finger. "Then she will throw an epic tantrum, grow two heads, and one of them will bite all our faces off."

"Sounds like me when it's time to pay quarterly taxes," Alexis quipped. "Here's the deal, Alana. You're in a relationship, which means you have to work things like this out with your partner because everything you do affects him too. I know you feel like you're doing him a favor, but it's really not fair."

Alana's phone rang, and everyone stared at it in silence. Alana looked at the ID. "That's her…I should answer and lie about why I called."

"No, that'll make it worse," Stacy snapped. "Don't touch it!"

The phone rang a few more times and stopped. All three women released a collective sigh, then suddenly, it rang again. Stacy grabbed the phone and spiked it on the deck, and it broke into pieces.

Stacy put both hands on top of her head. "I panicked, I'm sorry. I'll get you a new one."

Chapter Twenty-seven

The moment Jason returned to the house, Alana grabbed him by the hand and took him upstairs. "What's going on?" Allison asked with a suspicious look. "Jason got a call from his mother, and she said she'd missed a call from Alana, who didn't leave a message. We all called Alana, and she didn't answer."

"Her phone is broken." Alexis glanced at Stacy and said, "It fell on the deck."

Elise stared at Alexis. "Something's going on, and you know what it is."

"I might." Alexis looked away.

"Well, if you want any of the pizza we brought, you'd better start talking now." When Alexis didn't say anything, Elise turned to Stacy. "It has extra cheese, and it's fully loaded with toppings."

Stacy's mouth flew open, and words started flying out. She told everything and finished with, "I broke Alana's phone when I panicked. I'll go get the plates."

Alexis watched Stacy retreat to the kitchen and smiled. "She doesn't do well under interrogation apparently. I'll go help with the drinks."

"I see no sense in waiting on Alana and Jason," Allison said as they gathered at the table, and she opened one of the pizza boxes. "I hope he's not mad at her."

"After the tongue-lashing he got from his mother, he might be," Elise added as she put a slice of pizza on her plate.

"What was she mad about, did he say?" Stacy asked with concern.

Elise nodded. "She's mad because he came here without telling her first, and he didn't have to tell us anything. We could hear the whole conversation, and she wasn't even on speakerphone. She spoke to him like he was a child. She doesn't seem to realize that he's a thirty-eight-year-old man." Elise smiled apologetically at Stacy. "I mean no offense, it just surprised me."

"Well, her main complaint was she wanted to come here too, so she could see everything. She told Jason she'd planned to do that anyway so she could decide where on the beach they should have the wedding," Allison said. "She had a list of things she wanted to do in preparation that sounded like it was a mile long."

"I think you probably understand now why Jason decided to elope," Stacy said with a sigh. "My aunt is very controlling to begin with, and Jason is her youngest child. She still treats him like a helpless baby. He can argue with her for hours, but she'll still do things exactly as she wants to."

"I, for one, would feel better if Jason did tell her." Elise sighed. "I do understand that they want control over their own wedding, but I feel guilty that we were invited and his parents weren't. I keep putting myself in their shoes, and I know how hurt I'd feel."

"This is yet another reason I'm thrilled I never married—in-laws," Allison said and smiled at Stacy. "I'll be a terrific mother-in-law, though. I'm just saying."

They all quieted when Alana came down the stairs. "All right, stop pretending you're not talking about how stupid I am. I know Lex told y'all what I did," she said when she walked into the room.

"No, it was Stacy who ratted you out, dear," Elise said brightly. "Is everything okay?"

"He was a little upset that I'd tried to call her without talking to him first, but he forgave me when I told him why." Alana shook her head when Allison offered her a slice of pizza. "No, thank you. My stomach is in knots. Jason's on the phone with his mom right now, and I had to leave when he began raising his voice."

"What's he telling her?" Stacy asked.

Alana sat at the table with a sigh. "He's telling her that we're eloping and why."

"Oh, shit." Stacy dropped a half-eaten slice of pizza on her plate. "A dark cloud is about to descend upon us. I have enjoyed this peaceful time with y'all, and I apologize in advance for the boiling cauldron of drama and discontent that is my family."

Allison smiled at Stacy. "We've met them, remember?"

"Oh, no." Stacy shook her head. "You met the public version of the Kirklands. They were wearing the masks they don when they entertain. I can guarantee you they'll show up here, and they'll be all real and raw. It's not a pretty sight. Picture a pack of rabid dogs wearing designer clothes."

"Do you really think they'll come?" Alexis asked Stacy.

Stacy released a derisive snort, but before she could respond to the question, Jason walked out onto the landing and said, "Battle stations, everyone. There's an incoming missile with my mother's face on it. Shit."

Alexis watched as Stacy had the perfect opportunity to grab a crab with her net and let the moment pass her by. "You're really not happy about your aunt coming here, are you?"

"Oh, it won't be just her and my Uncle Howard." Stacy shook her head. "Oh, no. She'll bring an entourage. My mom and dad will probably come too. My sisters won't, they don't do anything on short notice because they have kids and careers. They won't like that I'm seeing you. They prefer that I keep my personal life separate from everything, and with you being Alana's sister, I'm sure they'll view that as complicated."

"I thought they were okay with your sexuality. Audrey practically yelled that you were a lesbian repeatedly at the engagement party."

Stacy flashed a wry smile as the waves lapped at her knees. "She does that to annoy my mother. They have a strange relationship. They're always together, they're like sisters, more than sisters-in-law, but they're also are very competitive. If one

184

gets a new car, then the other rushes out and gets one. It's the same thing with clothes and jewelry, but the most annoying thing is they do it with us too. When Jason's brothers started getting married, my mother hounded my sisters to do the same, then it was a race to see who would have kids first." Stacy swatted at the water with her net. "I turned out to be the bad egg in my mother's eyes because I'm a lesbian, and she's very embarrassed by that. This is why Audrey takes great pleasure throwing it in her face."

"We should talk about some more of my faults before they get here then," Alexis said and watched a crab go by. "I'm protective over those I care about to a fault. If she treats you bad or says something ugly to you, my next fault will show, and that's my temper."

Stacy gazed at Alexis with a warm smile. "I like hearing that you care for me."

"I do. I wouldn't have rubbed a dead starfish on your back last night if I didn't. I don't just do that to anyone, she has to be special." Alexis grinned when Stacy laughed. "I like making you do that."

"I don't consider you being protective as a fault."

"It gets me in trouble sometimes. Grammy and I were in a grocery store one time, and a guy made a lewd remark to her and grabbed his crotch. I punched him in the nuts, and when he doubled over, I hit him in the ear," Alexis admitted and looked away.

"Are you kidding me? You're serious?" Stacy asked, completely taken aback.

Alexis shrugged. "I was eleven, and I thought it was what Grandpa would've done. That was also the day I learned that Grammy can run really fast, or she did that day. She lectured me about hitting all the way home, and I never did it again, even though Grandpa let me eat all the ice cream I wanted that night. So don't worry, I won't pop your mom in the crotch, but I may give her a paw pat."

"I'm almost afraid to ask what that is," Stacy said with a bewildered smile.

"When Sprout gets on Ginger's nerves, she pops him in the head with her paw. It's not hard, but he gets the point and leaves her alone. I tried it once on Alana, and it was very effective."

"Okay, don't paw pat my mother, please. She's the type to press assault charges." Stacy sighed. "I'm having such a great time with you, I don't want that to change when they get here."

"Is there a 'but' that's gonna follow that statement?" Alexis asked when Stacy didn't say anything else.

"No, there will just be a lot of tension. I won't be as relaxed as I am now."

Alexis swept a crab up in her net. "We'll deal with that when they get here, but for now, I'm one crab point ahead of you."

"How did your crab hunt go?" Elise asked when Stacy and Alexis walked into the house later that evening. "I don't see any of your spoils."

"It's catch and release, Grammy. Stacy beat me by three crabs. What're you watching?"

"What is that smell?" Stacy asked.

Elise smiled. "Chicken tortilla casserole, and I'm watching a shopping channel we don't have at home. Stop me before I buy a gadget that makes swirls in hot dog wieners because I don't even eat them. You get three swirlers for the price of one, how could anybody pass that up?"

"Easily." Alexis held out her hand until Elise dropped the remote into it. She flipped through the channels until she landed on one with a movie.

Elise made a face. "What're they doing?"

"Looks like they're having sex." Alexis tilted her head to the side, just as Elise and Stacy did the same.

"So that's what that is. It's been so long I almost didn't recognize it." Elise tilted her head to the other side. "Watching these two makes me wonder if Harmon and I weren't doing it right. She's barking like a dog, I never so much as yipped."

"Arc y'all watching porn?" Allison asked as she joined them.

"It's a sex scene in an action movie," Alexis replied.

186

Elise nodded. "That's definitely action. Look, Allison, this is how the kids are doing it these days."

"I'm fully aware of how it's done." Allison pointed at the screen. "I can get my leg up that high if I stretch first."

Alexis snorted. "You take the time to stretch before you do the dirty fandango, Mom?"

"Depends on the dance partner," Allison replied with a cheeky smile.

"Angels are dancing in my nose holes, when do we eat?" Jason asked as he came bounding down the stairs.

Allison glanced at her watch. "It'll be done as soon as Alexis and Stacy are done with their showers."

"I'll set the table," Stacy said and headed for the kitchen.

"Alexis honey, will you make a pitcher of margaritas when you come back down?" Elise asked. "They'll go good with the casserole, and I'm in the mood for something strong."

Allison flashed a cheeky grin. "I am too, and I'm not talking about anything that goes in a glass."

"There's a guy down on the beach with a cane, so he can't get away fast. Why don't you go down there and tackle him, Mom?"

"What'd he look like?" Allison asked with interest.

Elise shook her head and sighed. "Allison, my dear, I'm beginning to think you're ratchy."

"Ratchet," Alexis corrected.

"What is that?" Allison asked.

"Your momma is telling you you're nasty," Alexis replied with a laugh.

Chapter Twenty-eight

"Stacy honey, are you getting enough to eat between meals?" Allison asked as she watched Stacy basically inhale the casserole.

"It's just so good."

Jason raised his glass. "The margaritas are fantastic. My compliments, Lex."

"Thanks. I mixed three pitchers, so everybody drink up."

"I plan to," Jason said with a sigh. "This is our last night of serenity."

"Did your mom say who was coming with them?" Stacy asked.

Jason shook his head. "She was too busy telling me how selfish I am and how I had ripped out her heart."

"Don't look so glum, you two," Allison said cheerfully. "It won't be all that bad. Let's talk about the bachelor and bachelorette parties. I have a penis hat that shouldn't go to waste."

Elise fanned herself. "Oh, dear God."

Alana shook her head. "We aren't having those kinds of parties. Garret, Jason's friend, is gonna come over tomorrow night, and they're gonna have a few beers, but that's as wild as it's going to get. You might want to save your hat for something else. Besides, I don't think Jason's mother would appreciate something like that."

"We were kind of hoping that you'd make your spaghetti on Saturday, so we can eat it after the wedding," Jason said with a hopeful expression.

Allison beamed. "I'll make my best batch ever."

"Oh, Jason, remind me I have to go to Port St. Joseph on Saturday to pick up the flowers at the florist," Alana said.

"Oh, no, no." Elise shook her head. "You don't run errands on your wedding day. Alexis will do that."

"Normally, I'd make a sarcastic comment right here or refuse, but I'll be sweet on that day and get your flowers," Alexis said with a smile. "But that abruptly ends at midnight."

After dinner, the group watched a movie. Elise was the first to say good night, Allison was next. Jason finished off the margaritas and fell asleep on the couch. Alana and Alexis were left alone when Stacy went in search of a snack.

"You okay?" Alexis asked Alana softly.

"Nervous." Alana gazed at Jason as he slept. "I don't want Audrey to be mad at him or me, but I'm sure she is. And I keep thinking back to what Rene said, about wondering if she would shit her dress before she made it down the aisle. Am I gonna feel that way? Am I gonna shit my dress?"

"Yeah, you probably will. You've done this before, remember?"

"Barely, I was half drunk when I married Ben in a tiny office while a ballgame played on the justice of the peace's TV in the background. I wasn't in love with him, I was just young and stupid." Alana gazed at Jason, who was flat on his back, feet in her lap, with his mouth wide open, bottom jaw sunk in. "But I love this man, isn't he beautiful?"

"Um...yeah."

"Mom says it won't be long before we start gaining weight and fighting over the laundry. She says I'll start bitching at him because I'll ask him to pick up something at the store, and he'll forget. He'll get mad at me because I'll turn down sex when I'm too tired. He'll want me to go somewhere I don't want to go and vice versa. I asked her how she knew those things since she's never been married, and she said she grew up watching and listening to her parents' arguments. She says all successful couples do that, it's normal. She made me feel better because I'd just screamed at Jason for leaving the toilet seat up." Alana's

189

brow furrowed. "I sat right down in the bowl, in the middle of the night. Nothing wakes you up like cold toilet water on your ass. Aren't you glad you'll never have to experience that?"

"Very," Alexis said with a nod and a smile. "When did you realize you were in love with Jason?"

Alana shrugged. "I can't give you a specific time or day. He's always made me feel like I'm something so extraordinary. He pays me sweet compliments, but that's not what does the trick. It's the way he looks at me like he's in awe. Everything I say seems so important to him. It's like all the things we are came together, and we…gelled. I don't know how else to put it." Alana was thoughtful for a moment. "I don't know why they call it 'falling in love.' It's not like I've fallen into anything. I just found someone who's different in many ways, but those differences fill my gaps, and we fit together perfectly."

Alexis tapped her finger against her temple as she absorbed everything Alana had said. "When y'all started going out, did you have any inkling that he might be the one?"

"That was on my mind, yeah. I think it was our third or fourth date, and we were at a really nice restaurant. He went to the bathroom, and when he came back, his fly was open, and I thought this beautiful, charming man is just as goofy as I am. This could work."

Stacy walked into the room and said, "I just discovered the most amazing thing, muscadine jelly on a sugar cookie. It was mind blowing, then I added the boysenberry. It was a complete explosion in my mouth."

Alexis smiled at Alana and pointed at Stacy. "That was kind of like your open fly moment."

"How does the creation of the greatest cookie in the world relate to Jason's open fly?" Stacy asked as she lay in bed with Alexis.

"It was a moment thing. You walked in the room all excited about cookies and jelly, and you were adorkable, a cross of dork and adorable. Your cuteness made me melt."

"Oh," Stacy said, drawing out the word and smiled. "Let me see what else I can do to endear you to me. Turn over."

190

"I don't think that's it."

Stacy cracked up. "Turn. I promise you'll enjoy it."

Alexis turned her back to Stacy, who nibbled and kissed along her spine while her fingers lightly danced along her thigh. "I just need to be clear on one thing," Alexis said with a sigh. "This is because I'm loud, right? You don't have a problem kissing me, do you?"

Stacy moved up, turned Alexis, and kissed her until Alexis tried to take control. She pulled away. "No, I'm calling the shots right now. Go back on your side."

Alexis didn't argue, but she was in the mood to talk. "Not that I don't enjoy this immensely, but I look forward to when we get back home and can be as loud as we want. Do you ever— oh...do you hear your neighbors moving around next door?"

"No, and I don't care what they hear in mine," Stacy replied as she kissed Alexis's shoulder. "Nothing would make me happier than to make you scream."

"I will do it, and I will make you—" Alexis inhaled sharply as Stacy's hand slipped between her legs.

"Did your mind go blank just then?" Stacy teased as she explored Alexis with her fingers.

"Who?"

Stacy cracked up again. "Quit making me laugh, I'm trying to drive you crazy."

"You do," Alexis replied with a shudder when Stacy entered her.

Stacy moaned softly. "You make me crazy too."

Chapter Twenty-nine

Alexis awoke first and looked at the clock. It was nearly three a.m., and someone was downstairs talking loudly. Stacy stirred too, and sat up to listen.

"Is that the TV?" Alexis asked softly.

Stacy listened for a moment longer and said, "Oh, shit," as she scrambled out of bed. "That's Audrey's voice."

Suddenly, the door opened, and the light came on. Stacy grabbed a pair of shorts and tried to cover herself as her eyes adjusted to the light. "Mom!" Alexis rasped. "Why didn't you knock? Why are you in here?"

"Don't you hear the commotion going on downstairs?" Allison asked and winked at Stacy as she frantically pulled on her clothes. "I'm straight as an arrow, but I appreciate what you're working with."

"Mom!"

"They need you to move your truck, so they can back a van in the garage," Allison explained as Stacy headed for the door. "Sweetie, you smell like sex, you might want to wash up before you greet your family. I'm gonna put on a pot of coffee, see y'all downstairs. I came to tell you both it's pretty tense down there so prepare yourselves."

When the door closed behind Allison, Alexis asked, "Why're you even getting dressed? Surely, they don't expect you to visit with them at this time in the morning."

"I don't know, I panicked." Stacy walked into the bathroom and flipped on the light. "I'll go move your truck, you don't have to get up."

Alexis got out of bed and pulled on her clothes. She joined Stacy in the bathroom, and Stacy had a nice foamy beard going as she washed her hands. "You still looked freaked out."

"Your mother just saw me naked."

"I'm really sorry about that," Alexis said and washed her hands and face.

Once they were scrubbed up, Stacy and Alexis walked out onto the landing and peered over the railing. Jason's parents, Audrey and Howard, were down there, along with Theresa, Stacy's mother, and Jason's brother Terrance. There was a man Alexis didn't recognize. "Who's the guy wearing the ball cap?"

"That's Ryan, their chef."

"Are you kidding me?" Alexis said loud enough to draw attention to their presence.

Audrey glared up at Stacy. "I'm as mad at you as I am him," she said, pointing at Jason. "You could've called me."

"Don't drag her into this," Jason said wearily. "You've woken up the whole house, brought your chef—no offense, Ryan—two vehicles, one of which is full of food we have no room for. This was supposed to be a simple occasion."

"I didn't know what to pack since I had no time to prepare. Your father had to cancel a business meeting, and your uncle Malcolm couldn't come because it was too short of a notice, and he really wanted to see you get married." Audrey shook a finger at Jason. "You created this chaos."

Alana gazed up at Alexis. "Hey, Lex, would you move your truck, please?"

"Sure," Alexis replied as she started down the stairs. She spotted Elise sitting at the kitchen table, and the expression on her face was grim. Alexis wondered what she'd missed out on and if Audrey had been rude to Alana. She felt her hackles rise with each step she took.

"This is a major betrayal," Audrey said when Stacy and Alexis reached the bottom of the stairs. "You're older than Jason, I rely on you to look out for him."

"For Pete's sake, Audrey, she's only two months older than he is, and Jason is a grown man, perfectly capable of tearing out your heart on his own," Howard deadpanned. "Where are we sleeping? I need a shower and a bed."

"There's two open rooms on the top floor where Alana and I are staying," Jason said.

"That's all?" Theresa sighed loudly. "Well, this is going to get uncomfortable."

"You can have my room," Stacy offered. "I'll share with Alexis."

Terrance spoke up and said, "I call the other one on the top floor."

"I'll bunk with Mom." Allison smiled at Ryan. "You can have my room."

Alana took Alexis by the arm and led her toward the door. "Let's go move that truck."

When they were outside, Alexis asked, "Was Audrey mean to you?"

"No, just abrupt. They called Jason when they were five minutes out, and I couldn't believe it. They must've gotten on the road not long after he called her. Grammy's pissed, I'm sure she thinks they're rude."

"They are. They barged in here at three o'clock in the morning and brought that chef guy. What, were they afraid they might have to make a sandwich for themselves?"

"Lower your voice." Alana looked around to make sure no one followed them.

"Stacy's mother didn't even hug her, and she let Audrey tear into her. What's wrong with that woman?"

"Stacy didn't make an attempt to hug her, either. Just move your truck, please."

Alexis was about to open her door and turned to gaze at Alana. "I know you love Jason, but are you gonna be able to put up with these people?"

"Are you? What happens if you and Stacy get serious? You'll have to deal with them too."

Alexis smiled sardonically. "Not as kindly as you do."

"Move the truck."

"Where's Stacy?" Alexis asked when she found her mother and Elise alone in the kitchen.

"She went upstairs with her mother." Allison handed Alexis a cup of coffee. "Take this, I know you're not going back to sleep."

"What did I miss?" Alexis asked. "What did Audrey say to Alana?"

"Nothing." Allison sighed. "Anytime Alana tried to speak up, Audrey cut her off and tore into Jason."

Elise put a hand on Alexis's arm. "Now don't let the shit get real, honey. I can tell you're already looking for a fight, and that will just make things worse. Try to understand that Audrey's feelings are hurt, and they've been driving most of the night."

"Excuse me, ladies," Ryan said as he walked into the kitchen with a cooler. "May I put these things in the freezer and refrigerator?"

"Yes, you may, and I'll be happy to assist you. My name is Allison, I don't think we've been properly introduced."

Alexis grabbed Elise's hand and led her from the kitchen. "The woman's hair is a mess, her teeth are probably not brushed, and she's trying to throw the monkey on the chef."

"By monkey, you mean vagina, right?" Elise asked as Alexis led her to her room.

"What, you haven't gotten to that in your slang dictionary?"

"I didn't think I'd have a need to use any of those words, so I skipped that section. Alexis, I know you're very protective, but as a favor to me, please hold that sharp tongue of yours. We only have to spend a few days with them, and I don't want anything else to mess up the wedding."

Alexis hugged Elise. "I'll do my best. I'm gonna go find Stacy and see how she's doing. Are you gonna try to go back to sleep?"

"I'm gonna lie down and see what happens. Keep an eye on your mother. The last thing we need is her schtupping the chef." Elise sighed. "That would compound the drama."

Alexis opened the door to her bedroom and noticed the bathroom light was on. "Are you unpacking your things?"

Stacy peeked out of the door. "I am, is that okay?"

"Yeah," Alexis said with a laugh. "I don't know why you didn't bring your stuff in sooner."

Stacy gazed at the cup in Alexis's hand. "Are you drinking coffee?"

"Yeah, you want me to get you a cup?"

"No, I was hoping we could go back to sleep for a little while."

Alexis shook her head. "I can't. I'm wide awake, but you look like you're about to drop."

"Someone wore me out." Stacy turned off the light in the bathroom and walked over to the bed. "Will you lie down with me?"

"Uh-huh, and I'll even give you head scratches until you fall asleep."

"Oh, I love those." Stacy jumped into bed and threw back the covers.

Alexis set the coffee cup on the nightstand and climbed in next to her. "Did Audrey have anything to say to you after I left?"

"No, they were too busy discussing the sleeping arrangements. I treat her like I do my mother, I let them run their mouths. It's a waste of time arguing with them." Stacy groaned when Alexis began scratching her scalp softly.

"I can't remember Jason's brother's name."

"Terrance, and he does not like to be called Terry. He's quiet like Uncle Howard. The Kirkland men run the businesses, and the women rule the house. Uncle Howard doesn't usually put his two cents in unless Audrey gets on his nerves. Terrance is the same way, and his wife is very sweet. She's one of the few women in my family I get along with. I wish she would've come with them. I guess the kids were involved with something and she couldn't."

Alexis playfully swatted at Stacy's hand when she began to run it up her thigh. "No, you sleep. Your mother is in the room next to ours, remember?"

"That turned me off," Stacy said and laughed. "We might have to put some duct tape over your mouth the next time we have sex."

Alexis grinned. "I think the pillow worked well enough. Hey, is the chef married?"

"I don't think so."

"That's good because Mom was getting flirty with him. She might teach him a few things about cooking, and I'm not talking about in the kitchen."

Stacy yawned and said, "I like your family."

"They like you too."

"Did they like the other women you dated?"

"They were always polite to them," Alexis said thoughtfully. "But they seem to be smitten with you."

"I'm happy...I'm already smitten with you too."

Alexis had curled up next to Stacy and tried to go to sleep, but she couldn't and began to squirm. She worried that she was keeping Stacy awake and got up just before six. The house was quiet as she crept out of her room at the same time Allison left hers.

"I thought the chef was taking your room," Alexis whispered.

"He did."

"Mom." Alexis's eyes grew wide. "Did you schtupp the chef?"

"Twice," Allison replied with a smile.

"Don't judge me, Alexis," Allison said while they sat on the deck with fresh cups of coffee. "You schtupped Stacy last night."

"I'm not judging you. It's your timing I have an issue with. Audrey's underwear is already in a knot, who knows how she'd react if she found out you were defiling her chef."

"How do you think she would react to you doing her niece?"

"You make a good point." Alexis blew out a breath and watched the rising sun. "Why should we care?"

"Exactly."

"I guess the only reason we should worry about it is the wedding. We shouldn't add to the strife," Alexis said before she took a sip of her coffee.

"I will secretly defile her chef." Allison cleared her throat and smiled. "So you and Stacy make a cute couple."

Alexis smiled. "She is adorable, isn't she?"

"I'm glad to see you getting back into the world of romance. You finally found one who made you want to take that step, so she must be very special." Allison smiled. "I saw a lot of her attributes this morning. I wish I still had a body like that. It's a damn shame what happens to you as you age. Gravity is a hateful bitch. Sometimes, I will stare down at my hand mirror and I look just like a bulldog, jowls hanging, it's scary. My boobs still look okay, but when I lie down, they hide in my armpits. I hate that."

"I had a warm fuzzy feeling for a second when we were talking about Stacy, and you smothered it with hiding breasts," Alexis said and took a sip of her coffee.

"Then I don't suppose you want to hear about what happened to my vagina during menopause," Allison said with a grin.

Alexis snorted and choked on her coffee. She laughed every time she caught her breath and continued to cough. "You're killing me," she rasped.

"This is so nice. We haven't had a lot of alone time lately. You're busy with work, so am I, then there's my cougar training that keeps me humping night and day."

Alexis continue to cough. "Stop making me laugh. I have coffee in my lungs."

"You need to laugh. I saw the look on your face when you came downstairs this morning. You were prepared to get somebody's ass in your teeth. Stacy doesn't like her family, but she still loves them. If you fight with them, it's gonna put her in a tough spot, Alana and Jason too."

"It was rude for them to show up the way they did and cause a commotion at that hour," Alexis said and cleared her throat. "They changed the atmosphere just like Stacy said they would. Everybody is tense, and we're all flapping around trying to accommodate their wants. You had to give up your room, Stacy had to give up hers, although she wasn't sleeping in it anyway."

Allison smiled. "I got a bonus too, and I wore him out."

Alexis studied her mother's face intently. "Are you really happy?"

"Sometimes yes, sometimes no. There are times when I've had a bad day and I'd just like to be held, but you pay a price for that, and it's called compromise. I'm not willing to do that. I'm selfish in that way. I know that about myself. I'm sure that sounds bad, but there are plenty of people like me in relationships making their partners miserable." Allison gazed at Alexis. "You're not like me in that way."

"Are you sure?"

Allison nodded. "Positive. I know my children."

"You were never selfish with us."

Allison gently squeezed Alexis's arm. "Because there's nothing else on this earth I love more."

"I love you too, Mom," Alexis said with a smile.

Chapter Thirty

"Why is the wedding scheduled for seven in the evening?" Audrey asked as everyone sat around the table for brunch served by Chef Ryan, who had a perpetual smile on his face that grew brighter when he looked at Allison.

"The sun is setting then, and we want it in the background," Jason replied patiently.

Audrey tried to keep her tone light as she asked, "Did you hire a photographer?"

"I'm her." Allison raised her hand and smiled.

"Mom has a very expensive camera, the kind professionals use, and she's really good with it," Alana added meekly.

Audrey didn't appear to be impressed and simply nodded. Alexis had been asked to play nice and she was doing her best, but she didn't like the way everyone seemed to cower in Audrey's presence. She focused on her omelet, which was tasty, but it wasn't nearly as good as her grandma's breakfasts.

"Did I understand correctly that Stacy and Alexis will be standing in the wedding?" Audrey asked with her gaze set on Jason.

He nodded. "Yes."

Audrey turned her focus to Stacy. "What will you be wearing?"

Jason didn't allow Stacy a chance to respond and said, "Khaki pants and white shirts that Alana and I picked out. It's a beach wedding after all. I'll be wearing khaki trousers, a shirt, and tie."

"I'm jealous of you, man," Terrance said, speaking up for the first time. "I had to stand in front of a church wearing a tux for what seemed like hours waiting on Emily to finally come down the aisle. I was soaked in sweat because the photographer had a spotlight on me. I was dehydrated by the time the ceremony actually started, and that's why I passed out."

Jason laughed. "It had nothing to do with what you drank at the bachelor party, and I seem to recall you passed out then too."

"Your brother had a proper wedding," Audrey interjected.

"Yes, he did," Howard agreed, "and he fainted and fell into the quartet playing beside him. Jason will only fall into the sand, and I won't have to replace a violin."

"What about music?" Theresa asked.

"The waves and gulls will provide that for us," Jason said and smiled at Alana.

Alexis caught Audrey's eye roll and bit her tongue as her anger mounted. She thought it was ridiculous that Audrey wouldn't let it drop and go with the flow. It amazed her that the woman was so intent to have her way that she didn't bother to consider her son's feelings.

"I think it's great that Jason and Alana are not following the traditional standard. They're doing their own thing, and most importantly, they're happy about it," Stacy said, her tone light.

"The rebel speaks." Theresa gazed at Stacy with a smile that was anything but warm. "You certainly aren't a fan of convention."

Commotion began under the table. Elise nudged Alexis with her foot when Alexis's eyes narrowed, and she sat up straight. Alana, who was seated beside Alexis, patted her knee.

"Oh, goodness, a rat!" Allison said suddenly. "I-I saw it running along the wall toward the kitchen."

Everyone at the table jumped to their feet with the exception of Alexis, Stacy, and Howard, who didn't slack up on eating his breakfast. Ryan ran out of the kitchen and took refuge in the living room, while everyone else stared at the floor. Alexis gazed at her mother, who glanced at her and winked before making a show of kneeling in her chair.

"Ryan, do something about that rat," Audrey ordered.

"Mrs. Kirkland, with all due respect, I'm a chef, not an exterminator."

No one made a move, as though they expected the rat to come walking out of the kitchen on two feet swinging a skillet. Audrey released an exasperated sigh. "It's in there with our food."

"This is exactly why I don't care for rental properties, there's always vermin." Theresa wrapped her arms around herself. "I need to go upstairs and take something for my nerves. Terrance, escort me, please."

Terrance looked as though he was about to be attacked by a rabid dog. He took two tentative steps, then raced across the room to the stairs. "Okay, it's clear," he said and waved Theresa along.

Theresa moved as fast as her high heels would allow. Audrey was next to head for higher ground and pranced across the floor with a whimper until she reached the stairs. Jason patted Alana on the back. "I'll go look for the rat, sweetie. You stay here where it's safe."

Alana grinned at everyone and said, "He's so manly."

Jason wasn't able to find the rat, and Ryan eventually returned to the kitchen. When Howard finally went upstairs, Elise gazed at Allison with a smirk and asked, "Did you really see a rat?"

"Nope, but if we continue to say we do, we'll have this floor to ourselves."

Jason's eyes went wide. "You lied?"

"Yeah, well, as Momma says, 'shit was about to get real,' and I'm all about keeping the peace," Allison replied glibly.

Jason smiled. "Do you mind if I hug you?"

Allison opened her arms wide. "Bring it on in, son." She embraced him with a smile, then began to rub her hands over his back. "This is nice."

"Move those hands any lower, Momma, and I will stomp all over your peace," Alana said with a hand on her hip.

202

"You should let me rub sunscreen into your shoulders and back before we go," Stacy said as she and Alexis went into their room to get dressed for the beach.

Alexis smiled. "If you start touching me, we won't go anywhere."

"I don't see that as a problem."

"Your mother's in the room next door," Alexis said as Stacy took a step toward her.

"Aw, shit." Stacy thought for a moment. "You go out into the hall and yell that you saw a rat go under her door."

"A rat isn't gonna fit in that small space. Maybe we should go to Port St. Joe and see if they have a pet store that sells ferrets. I've always heard they can get into anything. We'll get a half dozen, turn them loose in here, and see what happens."

Stacy grinned. "It would be easier to find a roll of duct tape and cover your mouth."

"But I wanna use it." Alexis pulled Stacy close and nibbled her neck.

"Let's go take a very long shower," Stacy said with a sigh.

They were on their way to the bathroom when someone knocked on the door. "It's me, let me in," Allison whispered.

"Sorry," Alexis said with disappointment and gave Stacy a quick kiss. She walked over to the door and opened it. "I hope you're not planning on hiding in here."

"No," Allison said as she stepped in. "Jason's friend Garret is downstairs, and he and Terrance are trying to convince Jason to let them take him out tonight for a bachelor thing. If he goes with them, I think we should take Alana somewhere or have a little party on the beach. I really want to see her in the penis hat."

"Momma, where did you find a hat like that?" Alexis asked with a laugh.

"I got it with my rewards points from the online store where I buy my lingerie and sex toys."

Alexis grinned at the mental image of Alana wearing a pecker on her head. "We have to invite Audrey and Theresa, and Alana has already said the hat is a no-go in front of them."

"You don't have to worry about what my mother and aunt think about it. They won't attend the party, it's not their sort of fun," Stacy said.

"Would you invite them anyway, so it won't be awkward?" Allison asked.

Stacy nodded. "Sure."

"Where's your phone?" Allison asked Alexis when they heard a bell chime.

Alexis looked around. "Um...I don't exactly know."

"Well, find it because Mom has mine, and she's eavesdropping on Jason's conversation downstairs. That's her texting us what the plans are."

Alexis grabbed the phone beneath a shirt lying next to her suitcase. "I didn't know Grammy knew how to text."

Allison grabbed the phone and looked at it. "She says...Q."

"What does that mean?" Stacy asked.

Alexis shrugged, and Allison began speaking as she typed, "What does that mean?"

Elise's response to the question was "Yes."

"Yes, what?" Allison said and typed the question. When the phone dinged announcing a new text, Allison groaned. "She sent the number seven. Maybe that means they're leaving at seven. Will you two get online and search for places to take Alana? A male stripper bar would be preferable."

Alexis recoiled at the idea. "Why don't we just have a party on the beach like you mentioned earlier? That way, all of us can get a little silly."

"Well," Allison began with a sigh, "that's probably the safest option, and she can wear the penis on her head. I'll whip up some finger foods. I'll put you two in charge of getting the booze. We used all we had for the margaritas. Remember, Mom and I don't like beer."

When Allison left the room, Stacy and Alexis gazed at each other. "We're gonna have to go to the store, and we need to be clean to do that," Alexis said with a grin and locked the bedroom door. "We're gonna need a long shower."

Chapter Thirty-one

Stacy found her mother and Audrey setting on the deck. She took a seat and listened to them complain about the heat, bugs, and the men gathered around the TV watching a baseball game and waited for them to acknowledge her presence. Theresa finally gazed at her and said, "You look like you have something on your mind."

"I do. Since Jason is going to go out with the boys, we've decided to throw Alana a bachelorette party on the beach tonight. There will be drinking and snacking, and Alana will be wearing a penis hat. I've come to invite you both."

"I think not," Theresa said with a derisive tone.

"What time will you be having this party?" Audrey asked.

"At eight, but Alana doesn't know anything about it, so please don't say anything," Stacy said.

"Why are y'all having the party on the beach?" Audrey asked.

"I don't think Uncle Howard is going with the guys, so we don't want to disturb anyone."

"This is Alana's last night as an unmarried woman, and the best y'all can do is get drunk on the beach?" Audrey asked with a frown.

"She didn't want a party," Stacy explained patiently. "When we found out that Jason was going with the guys, we threw this together."

Audrey shook her head. "Unacceptable. Howard can go out with the boys. There's no reason to have that party out on the beach where everyone will be eaten by mosquitoes and gnats besides, you can't decorate out there. We'll have it in the house, and Ryan will prepare hors d'oeuvres. What kind of theme are we going with?"

"I think it's going to be penis," Stacy said, unable to believe Audrey wanted to participate.

Theresa couldn't believe it, either, and said, "We?"

"What else are we going to do—hide in our rooms?" Audrey asked Theresa.

"Yes! Have you forgotten there's a rat somewhere in the kitchen? Audrey, any party where someone is wearing a male member on her head is not for us."

"I was robbed of the opportunity to plan my son's wedding." Audrey fanned a hand at Stacy. "Find me something to write on and a pen."

"Wait," Stacy said nervously. "Allison is planning this, and since she's the mother of the bride, we should let her."

Audrey stood. "Where is she?"

"In the kitchen with Ryan," Stacy said, feeling deflated.

There was a private meeting in Elise's room. Stacy scrubbed her face with both hands and said miserably, "I am so sorry! Never in my wildest dreams did I think they'd want anything to do with this party. They never went to any of my sisters'."

"It's okay, sweetie." Elise patted Stacy on the back. "We had to invite them, otherwise we would've been rude."

Allison held up a sheet of paper. "Audrey made a list of what she felt we should have for the party. It includes twenty different colored nail polishes and a smooth jazz CD. I couldn't get through the rest of it without yawning. She developed a nervous tic when I told her I planned to cut the cocktail sausages into tiny penises." She pulled another piece of paper from her pocket. "This is what you're going to the store with. I think you'll have to go into Port St. Joe to find everything. Ryan says he can make a punch so smooth no one will know what hit them. If you can't find the liquor on this list, call me because Ryan will have to decide on the substitutions. Don't let your sister see any of this stuff when you get back. I think she's on to us, but Mom

206

and I will lock her in her room if we have to. Do you think you can find a strap-on and do a strip tease?"

"I am not humping my sister with a rubber dick!" Alexis spat out.

"I was thinking if we dressed Stacy like a guy and drew a mustache—"

"No!" Alexis shook her head vehemently.

Allison looked genuinely disappointed. "I thought about asking Ryan to do it, but I think that would fall under sexual harassment since he's working for the Kirklands. I just really feel like we should have a stripper."

"She's hysterical, Grammy, slap her."

"I'm still..." Elise frowned. "What is a strap-on?"

Alexis stuck a finger in her mother's face when she looked like she was about to answer. "No. Stacy and I are leaving now."

"Wait, if you find a really nice-looking guy in the store, ask him if he'd be interested in making some quick cash," Allison said as she followed Stacy and Alexis to the door.

"I didn't hear that." Alexis grabbed Stacy by the arm and fled from the room.

Stacy and Alexis returned a few hours later with a truckload of food and as many party favors as they could find. Allison was disappointed to learn that they were unable to locate a penis-shaped cake pan, but Ryan assured her he would do his best to create obscene cupcakes. She was happy, however, that they were able to find everything on the liquor list.

Alana had pretty much figured out what was going on after she was forbidden from going into the kitchen. She didn't argue when she was sent to her room after the guys left. Stacy, Alexis, and Elise decorated with streamers while everyone else helped with the food. Once everything was done, they gathered in the living room.

Allison held up a video camera. "Tonight, I want everyone to take this and record a message. I'll put them on a CD, and they'll be a nice memento for her."

"That's a great idea—music," Alexis said suddenly. "We need that too."

Stacy pointed to a table by one of the windows. "There's a docking station over there. I saw an iPod in your truck. What kind of music does it have on it?"

"It's a mixture, I think it'll work," Alexis said and headed for the door.

"What will we do when she comes down?" Theresa asked. "Do we sing or yell surprise? I've never been to a bachelorette party, I don't know the procedure."

Stacy gazed at her in amazement. "You didn't have one before you got married?"

Theresa shook her head. "I had dinner with my parents."

"So did I," Audrey added.

"I spent the evening in the bathroom," Elise said with a smile. "I was very nervous, and my mother had to give me a nerve tonic."

Audrey pointed at Stacy. "We're looking to you, give us direction."

"Well...at Christine's, everybody had a few drinks first, then she opened gifts. Some male strippers dressed like firemen sneaked into the room, turned the music up loud, and danced around with their hoses."

"I love firemen," Allison said with a goofy grin. "The ones on those calendars start fires, not put them out, know what I mean?"

"I did happen to see one of those calendar photos." Audrey clasped her hands together and shrugged slightly. "The men were...very handsome."

"Okay, I have the iPod," Alexis said as she rushed into the room and put it in the docking station.

"I think we should all call to her now," Allison said, waving her hands around as though she were directing a chorus.

Everyone began singing Alana's name except for Alexis who barked out, "Alana! Get down here."

Alana appeared on the landing above them. "Did someone call me? Am I allowed to leave my room now?"

"Yes, get down here." Allison pranced around excitedly and grabbed the hat she'd hidden behind a chair. When Alana timidly joined them, Allison placed it on her head and said, "Bachelorette, I now crown you."

Audrey took one look at the erect plastic penis standing atop Alana's head and the two balls resting on her brow and bellowed, "Ryan, we need the drinks."

The passion punch started to flow, and dance music played softly from Alexis's iPod, but the party was low-key as Alana opened her gifts. Alexis gave her a set of cookbooks and a certificate for free landscaping. Stacy gave her two champagne flutes with their names etched into the glass and a beautiful frame for a wedding photo.

"These are actually wedding gifts, but we wanted you to have something to open tonight," Elise said and placed a box on Alana's lap. "I started making this when you first introduced us to Jason, and I saw that twinkle in your eye and his too."

Alana opened the box and gazed at a quilt. "Oh, Grammy, it's beautiful."

"Wait," Elise said as Alana began to pull it out of the box. "Don't take it out just yet, I'm not finished with it. There's only enough there to cover your legs up to the knees."

Alexis stiffened when Allison placed a box in Alana's lap and said, "Now mine." Knowing her mother as she did, Alexis was certain that whatever was in that box was sure to offend just about everybody in the room.

Alana looked a tad nervous as she opened it too. She laughed and pulled out a plastic pair of handcuffs. "Mom!"

"Those are for when you fight," Allison said seriously. "You lock your wrist to his, and you stay together until you work it out." She went on to explain every item in the box. "The caffeine pills are for when one of you is sick, and the other needs energy to stay awake and pamper. The jar that has your names engraved on it is for your wishes. Each night, you write one down together on the little pad included and drop it into the jar. When rough times come, you open it and remind yourselves of what you've hoped for, then you work together to make your dreams come true. I started it for you. That paper inside says, 'Live happily ever after.' The flavored lubricants, well, you know what to do with that."

"Mom," Alana said tearfully, "that's so sweet."

"Theresa and I didn't have time to get wedding gifts before we came here," Audrey said as she handed Alana two envelopes. "Cash in my opinion is a very impersonal gift, but as I said, we had no time to do any shopping."

Alana's brow arched when she opened Audrey's card and saw five crisp one hundred-dollar bills. "Oh, Audrey, thank you so much."

Theresa's card held the same thing, and Alana had to drink an entire glass of punch before she could say, "Thank you so much, but this is really too much." She thanked Audrey and Theresa with air kisses.

The passion punch flowed, and the room was filled with music, voices, and laughter. Alexis joined Theresa at the table where she was contemplating a cupcake with a penis drawn in icing. "I have spent so much time avoiding one of these, and now I'm actually considering eating one."

"Maybe you should chomp it angrily. More punch?" Alexis asked as she held the ladle over the punchbowl.

"Yes, please." Theresa took the cup and downed the drink. "That is delicious."

Alexis smiled and poured a refill as Theresa contemplated the cupcake on her plate. Suddenly, she thumped the carefully drawn penis off of it, and what icing didn't stick to her finger landed on the table. "I always wanted to do that. I wonder if it's as easy to get rid of a real one that way," Theresa said with a triumphant smile, then snorted with laughter.

"I'll whip my Nae, show me how," Elise said and joined Alana in the middle of the living room. "Alexis, turn the music up."

Ryan, Alexis, and Stacy hid in the kitchen doorway and watched the show in the living room. The song *Watch Me (Whip Nae Nae)* was on repeat, and a group of older women were trying to master the moves Alana was teaching them. Elise seemed to be the only one catching on; she even had the stanky leg down.

210

Stacy shook her head as she held the video camera capturing the whole event. "My mother has no rhythm."

"Allison sure does," Ryan said, then cleared his throat and looked away when Alexis glared at him.

Alexis bumped him with her shoulder. "That passion punch is magical stuff, thank you for whipping that up. I doubt we'd be witnessing this dance revolution if we were all sipping wine."

"I have created life," Ryan said happily.

Stacy turned the camera to video herself and Alexis. "Alana, I read this on a card once, and I hope I can repeat it correctly. 'If you love your mate for who they are and not…for what you think they should be, you'll always be happy.'" Stacy grinned. "I hope you love Jason's feet because they're hideous."

Alexis nodded. "He's got some ugly-ass toes. They look like hairy sausages. He's sweet, though, and I hope you'll always be happy together and that your kids don't get those toes. Then again, your feet are ugly too. Don't let your kids go barefooted."

Stacy turned the camera to Ryan and said, "Say something."

"Alana, your family is beautiful, especially your mother," Ryan said and glanced at Alexis. "Anyway, I hope you and Jason have wonderful days together all of your lives. I do some catering work on the side, so if you ever have a need, be sure to remember me."

Audrey dropped onto the couch and fanned herself. "I think I whipped my Nae right out the window," she said and cackled with laughter.

"I think we're ready for a new song, Lex," Alana called out as she and Elise did some more of the stanky leg.

Alexis went over to her iPod and chose one of her mother's favorite songs. When Tina Turner's *Proud Mary* started to play, Audrey jumped up with renewed vigor. The song began slow, and all the women moved to the tempo.

"Oh, this brings me back," Theresa cried as she swayed back and forth. "Tell me, ladies, do you remember?"

"Oh, God, she's morphing into James Brown," Stacy said, afraid of what she was about to see.

Everyone sang along, even Ryan, who'd left the safety of the kitchen. When the song sped up, Theresa started belting out

211

the lyrics with grit. Stacy grabbed the camera and caught Audrey slinging her hair around and shimmying. Alexis got into the mix and tried to keep up with her mother's footwork. Elise did something that was a cross between the shimmy and the twist. Stacy laughed hysterically and set the camera down with the lens trained on the group and joined in.

A little while later, the camera was picked up again, and Audrey's and Theresa's faces filled the screen. Their hair was a mess, their makeup ruined. "I have had the best time of my life," Theresa said, eyes wide and glassy.

"Rollin'!" Audrey shouted. "Proud Mary's rollin' on the Gulf."

They took turns holding the camera close to their faces and yelling, "Rollin'!"

The camera turned to Allison, who looked a little frightened. "We drank all the punch."

It went to Elise next, and she whispered, "Don't judge us harshly when you see this, dear. We love you, and I'm so happy to gain Jason as a grandson." The camera panned over to where Alexis and Stacy were feeding each other a cupcake and returned to Elise's face. "I think I'm about to add another granddaughter to our happy family too."

The camera moved back to Allison, who said, "Baby, remember, a happy marriage is made in the bedroom," she slurred. "Even when you don't feel like it, you grab that thing and—"

Elise's face filled the camera screen again, and she shook her head. "This is one time you shouldn't listen to your momma."

Whitney Houston's *I Wanna Dance with Somebody* began to play, and the camera dropped to the couch and recorded the doorway. Moments later, the door opened, and Howard was first to walk in. His mouth opened slightly as his brow furrowed. The music came to an abrupt end.

"What the hell?" Jason said as he walked in holding a to-go bag from a Mexican restaurant.

Audrey staggered over to Howard. "I whipped my Nae Nae." Her laugh that followed sounded like the gasp someone would make after nearly drowning.

Jason gazed at Alana wrapped in a streamer shawl. "Baby, are you drunk?" he asked as Terrance and Garret stepped through the door behind him.

"No," she replied and shook her head. The movement made her dizzy, and she took two steps to the left before she sank to her knees.

Jason looked at all the food on the table, the empty punch bowl, and his mother who looked as though she'd been in a tornado. "I should've stayed here with y'all. All I got was two margaritas and a chimichanga plate."

After Alexis and Stacy helped Ryan clean up, they went upstairs, turned the bed down, and fell into it. "I don't want to shower." Stacy groaned into the pillow.

"We'll change the sheets in the morning." Alexis lay with an arm draped over her eyes. "I don't even have the energy to take off my clothes. I feel like we were in constant movement all day and night."

"Would you do that dance you did to the Tina Turner song one more time? Whip your hair back and forth and shake your ass."

Alexis raised her arm and squinted at Stacy. "Was it sexy?"

"No, but it was hilarious, and I caught it on video."

"I'm gonna have to do a lot of editing before Mom gets a hold of it," Alexis said wearily. "Where is the video camera?"

"I saw Elise with it. I think she took it to her room along with a plate full of cupcakes." Stacy took Alexis's hand and kissed it. "I can't talk...any...more."

Alexis gazed at Stacy as her eyes closed, and she drifted into deep sleep. "I really, really, really like you, Stacy," she whispered.

213

Chapter Thirty-two

The following day was complete chaos. Ryan and Elise prepared breakfast for everyone as they woke up. Allison was in the middle of everything making her sauce, so it could slow cook throughout the day. Howard and Terrance took Jason golfing to keep the bride and groom separated. Alana was a nervous hungover wreck. Audrey and Theresa had unfortunately awoken the same old snooty grumps they were before they drank the passion punch. When Alexis and Stacy went to Port St. Joseph to get the flowers, they bought more ingredients for the magical elixir in hopes that Audrey and Theresa would drink again.

"I'm surprised Alana didn't want to come out here with us and escape the madness in the house," Stacy said while she and Alexis sat at the water's edge with the waves lapping at their legs and feet.

"She wouldn't relax. She probably won't take a deep breath until the ceremony is over and we're all on the way home."

Stacy gazed at Alexis in wonder, amazed at her luck. She no longer worried about the lines of fantasy and reality being blurred, Alexis was her fantasy come to life. Her mouth went dry when a question she wanted to ask was on the tip of her tongue.

"Lex, would you make a wish jar with me?"

Alexis turned to her and smiled. "You called me Lex, and yes, I would love to fill that jar with wishes with you."

"It's a commitment. We have to stay together to fill it, and I'm not talking about the sweet little thing your mom gave Alana. I want to find a giant pickle jar and fill it with you."

Alexis grinned. "I know where we can get one of those big plastic drums. We might be too old to actually see what we wrote on those slips of paper, but I'm willing to find out."

Stacy leaned over and kissed Alexis. "Let's get the drum."

"You two look...nice," Theresa said as Alexis and Stacy came downstairs after a very long shower. Her gaze swept over the matching khaki pants and sleeveless white button-down shirts they wore. "Will you two be standing with Jason when Alana comes walking down the...sand, or, Alexis, will you walk with your sister?"

"We really don't know the answers to those questions," Alexis replied distractedly as she looked around for Jason.

"You four didn't rehearse this, you don't have a plan?" Theresa asked, aghast.

Before they could reply, Audrey came rushing into the house clutching her brow. "The justice of the peace looks like a sumo wrestler, and he's wearing a Hawaiian shirt and shorts, and his hair—" She blinked rapidly at Alexis's and Stacy's attire. "Is that what you're wearing?"

"This is what Alana and Jason picked out, yes," Stacy replied. "Try to remember they want a very plain and simple service."

"Well, they got it. You're not even wearing shoes!" Audrey began rubbing her brow again. "Breathe deep, let it out slow."

Jason walked in from the deck and scrubbed his hands together. "In thirty minutes or so, I'll be Mr. Holt."

"What?" Audrey exclaimed.

"Joking, Mom. Hey, Lex and Stacy, you need to roll the bottom of your pants up like mine." He kissed them both on the forehead. "Y'all look so cute."

"What's the plan? Do I walk with Alana or stand with you, Stacy, and the sumo wrestler?" Alexis asked as she knelt and rolled up Stacy's pants legs.

Jason rubbed the back of his neck. "Um...it's whatever Alana wants."

"Okay, I'm gonna go up and ask her. If I don't come back down, you'll know she wants me to walk with her," Alexis said and turned to go.

Stacy caught her by the arm and gave her a quick kiss. "Don't trip," she said with a smile.

Theresa pulled Stacy close. "What was that? Are you seeing her?"

Stacy smiled. "Yes, I am and plan to do it forever."

"Couldn't that be construed as something incestuous?" Audrey asked.

"Of course not!" Theresa snapped. "I can't believe you would ask such a dumb question, yet have the sense to use the word construed in it."

"Don't try to belittle me, Theresa," Audrey shot back.

"You did it yourself, you didn't need my help."

"Ryan whipped up some more of that punch, and I strongly suggest you go have a few glasses of it before we begin, or I will lock you both in the pantry," Jason said with a smile. He gazed at Stacy as the bickering two stormed off. "We have a lot to talk about, don't we?"

Stacy nodded. "It took you three dates, and it took me less than one. I win."

"Incoming," Alexis said as she walked into Alana's room. Elise had a flat iron and was working on Alana's hair while Allison painted something on her eyelids. "Hey, sis, you want me to walk with you, or do I go stand with Jason and Stacy?"

Alana was silent for a moment as she thought. "Walk with me. Lex, do you have Jason's ring?"

"Right here in my pocket. Stacy hocked yours and replaced it with a plastic ring she got out of a gumball machine. After the ceremony, we're taking the money and going to the Bahamas. I'll get a job as a coconut farmer, and she's gonna strip at an old lesbians' home. We're gonna build a thatched hut that will look really small on the outside, but it'll have thirteen bedrooms and a gourmet kitchen."

"Baby, did you get into the punch?" Allison asked as she continued to work on Alana's makeup.

"I'm just trying to distract my sister because I know she's worried about shitting her dress."

"That and what if Jason changes his mind? What if I go down there, and he's not there?" Alana's voice rose. "His mother might talk him out of marrying me."

Alexis walked over to the vanity where Alana sat and placed a hand on her shoulder. "He's downstairs all excited because he's about to become your husband. He's hyper, and he can't stop smiling."

"Don't cry." Allison blew into Alana's face. "Dry it up, you're gonna mess up what I'm doing."

Alexis moved into Alana's line of sight in the mirror and said, "You look like a hooker." She grinned when Alana chuckled.

Allison admired her artwork, then stepped out of the way so Alana could get a good look at herself in the mirror. "Thank you, Mom," she said with a happy sigh.

"I think we're ready for hairspray," Elise said, and everyone stepped back as she sprayed enough of the stuff to make a cloud. She grew misty-eyed as Alana stood and walked into the center of the room.

Alana released a shaky breath. "This is it."

Alexis gazed at the off-shoulder white dress that hugged Alana's form and ended at her calves. "You're beautiful."

"You are," Allison agreed and gave Alana a light hug so she wouldn't muss the dress.

Elise glanced at her watch. "Allison, we have to go downstairs now. You need to be able to take pictures as Alana walks out, and I need to video. Alana, we'll text you when everything is set up and you can come on down."

Allison nodded as she backed toward the door. "We'll see you girls downstairs in just a bit."

When the door closed behind Allison and Elise, Alexis knelt, rolled her pants legs, and said, "I'm glad you wanted me to walk down with you. I'm the only woman in this family strong enough to tackle you if you try to run away."

217

Alana laughed and released a heavy breath. "I have no desire to run. I want to live the rest of my life with Jason, arguing over stupid things, making up, debating what to eat for dinner, stealing the remote and changing the TV channels when he isn't looking. I want to go to sleep with him every night and wake up to his dog shit-smelling sleep breath."

Alexis stood up straight and laughed. "You must really love him to submit yourself to all this crap just to say a few minutes of vows."

"I do, and one day, you might want to do the same."

Alexis shook her head. "No, the day Stacy and I get married, we will really elope."

"Do you realize what you just said?"

"I do. I haven't known her for very long, but I know she's that one that's gonna fill my gaps." Alexis shrugged. "I can't tell you how I know, I just do."

Alana beamed. "You may end up taking your vows on this same beach."

"Maybe so," Alexis replied when Alana's phone chimed. She took it from the dresser and gazed at the message to make sure it was from Elise. "It's just the letter C."

"What does that mean? Do we go?"

The phone chimed again. "New letter, O," Alexis said with a laugh. M followed and eventually the E. "We have got to teach Grammy to text." Alexis tossed the phone aside, walked over to Alana, and held out her arm.

"You're swaying, are you okay?" Stacy asked Jason.

"I'm good…okay…good. Oh, my God," Jason breathed out as Alana appeared on the deck with Alexis and started down the stairs. "She's beautiful. Oh, God, I'm going to cry. Punch me in the kidney."

Stacy's heart pounded as she watched Alexis walk alongside Alana. She felt as though she was the one getting married and couldn't take her eyes off her bride-to-be. She had a lot of wishes in mind for the wish barrel, but the biggest had already been fulfilled.

After the ceremony and a seemingly endless photo session, everyone returned to the house but Alexis and Stacy. They strolled down to the water's edge hand in hand. Alexis inhaled deeply and said, "Is to too early to admit that I'm falling for you?"

"You'd better be," Stacy said with a laugh. "You committed to filling a wish barrel with me." She leaned close and pecked Alexis on the lips. "I've been falling for you for a while, so that puts me ahead. I'm winning."

Alexis smiled. "Are we making this into a competition too?"

"No, but I still feel like I'm winning," Stacy answered with a laugh. "I have it all—a sexy, gorgeous girlfriend, and she's falling for me."

"Well, in that case, we're tied," Alexis said and punctuated the statement with a kiss.

Dear Me,

I haven't written in a while because I've been very busy. Stacy stayed with me the night we returned from Cape San Blas, and she never left. Over the course of five months, she gradually moved her things to my place, and it became ours. I guess we had our U-Haul moment. We're as loud as we wanna be, and we're loud a lot.

Instead of a wish barrel, we got a really big pickle jar since it fits better on the mantel. We drop wishes into it daily. Her ivy is up there too, and I'm proud to say it's growing up the brick.

We share household chores like any other couple. I cook and do the laundry since Stacy is either allergic to it or she's afraid to go near the washer. She keeps the kitchen clean, and I have to say she makes sure there's not a speck of dust in the house, and she doesn't even use a cat.

Speaking of cats, Stacy and I employ the paw pat on a regular basis, though I feel I'm patted more often than she is. Her pats are gentle, but they always seem to come when I mention that her dirty laundry has to go into the hamper before I will wash it. I don't know what it is with this woman and dirty clothes. The hamper is two feet away, and she throws her shirt on the floor. I don't know if it's bad aim or absolute refusal to comply with the proper order of things. I suspect the latter.

Jaime rented a house not long after she returned from the rig, which she quit, by the way. She went to work for a local ambulance service where she met a really nice woman. Stacy and I approve, especially since she loves video games.

220

Stacy and I conquered Ghost Dimension. *It took us nearly every weekend for a few months. We are now playing a game as opponents, and it's probably not a good idea for our relationship. The gleam in Stacy's eyes when she takes me out with various weapons is disconcerting. I'm not allowed any Tootsie Rolls or suckers when I obliterate her.*

Alana and Jason come by often for dinner, and we go to their place and play badminton. Stacy and I still argue over birdie versus shuttlecock, but it's cute now. Oh, and Alana's pregnant. Instead of morning sickness, she got uncontrollable bitch syndrome. Jason says he likes to take her over to his parents' place and release her like a Tasmanian devil. Audrey has had her ass verbally whipped many times. To date, Alana is the only person who can shut her up.

Mom is still schtupping the chef. Grammy is still painting naked fruit. Our kitchen wall is sporting the latest Elise Holt, which is a lot of pears that look like breasts.

The hollow that I feared never came, and I know it never will again. I'm finally one hundred percent deeply in love. Stacy fills my gaps, and I fill hers. I think it's time to get loud.

Blissfully Happy Me

About the Author

Robin Alexander is the author of the Goldie Award-winning *Gloria's Secret* and other novels for Intaglio Publications, including *Gloria's Inn, Gift of Time, The Taking of Eden, Love's Someday, Pitifully Ugly, Undeniable, A Devil in Disguise, Half to Death, Gloria's Legacy, A Kiss Doesn't Lie, The Secret of St. Claire, Magnetic, The Lure of White Oak Lake, The Summer of Our Discontent, Just Jorie, Scaredy Cat, The Magic of White Oak Lake, Always Alex, The Fall, Ticket 1207, Next Time, The Trip* and *Rusty Logic.*

She was also a 2013 winner of the Alice B Readers Appreciation Award, which she considers a true feather in her cap.

Robin spends her days working with the staff of Intaglio and her nights with her own writings. She still manages to find time to spend with her partner, Becky, and their three dogs and four cats.

You can reach her at robinalex65@yahoo.com. You can visit her website at www.robinalexanderbooks.com and find her on Facebook.

Made in the USA
Middletown, DE
19 February 2017